Hugh C Peacock, Allan Mackenzie

Robert Burns

Poet-Laureate of Lodge Canongate Kilwinning

Hugh C Peacock, Allan Mackenzie

Robert Burns
Poet-Laureate of Lodge Canongate Kilwinning

ISBN/EAN: 9783337398774

Printed in Europe, USA, Canada, Australia, Japan

Cover: Foto ©Raphael Reischuk / pixelio.de

More available books at **www.hansebooks.com**

ROBERT BURNS

POET-LAUREATE

OF

LODGE CANONGATE KILWINNING

FACTS

Substantiating his Election and Inauguration

ON 1ST MARCH 1787

Gleaned from the Lodge Records and other Authentic Sources

BY

HUGH C. PEACOCK

PAST DEPUTE MASTER LODGE CANONGATE KILWINNING; SECRETARY TO THE LODGE 1872-73
AND MANY YEARS SUBSEQUENTLY;
PAST PRINCIPAL H AND PAST SCRIBE E ROYAL ARCH CHAPTER CANONGATE KILWINNING
ETC., ETC.

AND ASSISTED BY

ALLAN MACKENZIE

HISTORIAN AND P.M. CAN. KIL., NO. 2, ETC.

PUBLISHED BY AUTHORITY OF THE LODGE

PRINTED BY

CHRISTIE & SON, 10 NORTH ST. ANDREW STREET, EDINBURGH

MDCCCXCIV.

PREFACE.

I HAVE been asked by some of the principal Office-bearers, past and present, of Lodge Canongate Kilwinning, No. 2, to write a few words by way of Preface to the statement of the evidence, compiled mainly by Brother Allan Mackenzie, as to the formerly undoubted, but recently controverted fact that Robert Burns held the Honorary Office of Poet Laureate of that Lodge. I have accordingly gone carefully through that evidence, which is so well arranged, so exhaustive, and I may add so conclusive, that it might well be left to speak for itself. I propose, therefore, to confine my remarks to the most salient points in the evidence, and to the nature of the case sought to be made against the hitherto received tradition. And first, as to the positive evidence of the fact. Not, certainly, the oldest, but certainly the principal document in its support, is the Resolution passed on the 8th June 1815, and duly recorded in the Minutes of the Lodge, authorising a Subscription for a Mausoleum to Robert Burns, who is therein described as one "*who had been Poet Laureate of the Lodge.*" This resolution was seconded by Charles More, who was a prominent official of the Royal Bank of Scotland, who had been Depute Master of the Canongate Kilwinning Lodge, No. 2, both before and in the year 1787, (in which year Robert Burns joined the Lodge as an Honorary affiliated member, and is traditionally alleged to have been also appointed Poet Laureate of the Lodge), and who had continued in unbroken connection with the Lodge from that time to the signing of the Minute of 8th June 1815. Surely, if any man must have known whether this statement of the resolution was accurate or not, that man must have been the seconder, Brother Charles More. But it does not stop there. At the time when this resolution was passed, the Lodge included amongst its members about one hundred persons, who had been members before and during the events of 1787, many of whom had continued members down to 1815. A number of those must in the nature of things have been present at the Meeting at which the resolution was passed. Moreover, this resolution was sent round with a subscription list to all the members, so that it must have come to the knowledge of those members who were not present. Amongst the one hundred members referred to were many who knew Robert Burns intimately, including Louis Cauvin, Burns's French Teacher; Alexander Nasmyth, who painted his portrait; Lord Balcarres, Dugald Stewart, Sir John Sinclair of Ulbster; Sir Ilay Campbell, President of the Court of Session; Dr. Andrew Duncan; Sir Henry Jardine, R. W. Master, 1790; Sir Charles Hope of Granton, President of the Court of Session, who survived till 1851; and many others. A Committee was appointed to carry out the object of this resolution, and on the 2nd January 1817, George Simson, Esq., Past Master of the Lodge, who appears to have acted as the Secretary, wrote to George Burnet, Esq., Advocate, R. W. Master of Canongate Kilwinning Lodge, as follows:—" I beg leave to report to you that having been furnished by your Secretary with the sum of Twenty Guineas voted by the Lodge as a contri-bution towards the erection of a Mausoleum *to the memory of our late Poet Laureate, Burns,* I, in obedience to the instructions of the Committee, remitted that sum to the Rev. Dr. Duncan, Dumfries." From this it is evident that after eighteen months' publicity amongst all those most likely, nay certain to know whether the statement which constituted the express ground and plea on which their subscriptions were solicited was true or false, not only had none denied it, but the Lodge itself had formally ratified and adopted it on a second occasion by voting twenty guineas to the fund on this very ground and title. A goodly number of these hundred members must have been still alive in 1835, when Hogg, the Ettrick Shepherd, was elected to succeed Robert Burns as Poet Laureate, and when at his initiation or on the occasion of his being made a Mason, he expressly acknowledged the compliment of being asked to succeed Robert Burns, and the Lodge toasted the memory of

Burns as "*the last Poet Laureate of the Lodge.*" Nay, some of them,—*e.g.*
Sir Charles Hope—were alive in 1845, when the Lodge resolved to commemorate
the event by a Picture. All this is on record, nor is it contested that the
tradition has been handed down continuously to the present time.

There is, however, one piece of documentary evidence older than any of
the above entries, though not, of course, as old as the memory and knowledge
of the persons above-mentioned, who were all members and contemporaries
of Burns in 1787. This is the engraved portrait of Burns still hanging in
the Lodge, and which appears to have been placed there in the beginning
of this century, within a few years of his death. That portrait bears a
contemporary Inscription, describing him as *Poet Laureate of the Lodge.*
This carries the documentary evidence of the tradition back to the very
beginning of the century; but the evidence does not stop there. It appears
that Brother William Petrie, who was connected with several Lodges, and
down to a date shortly before his death in 1845, was one of the Tylers
of the Lodge, bore testimony to the fact of having been present at the
inauguration of Burns as Poet Laureate of Lodge No. 2. It is true
that Brother William Officer rejects this direct and specific evidence, on
the ground that as Petrie is not recorded in Grand Lodge Books as a
member of No. 2, he cannot have been a member of No. 2. But in
another place (see his letter of 12th January 1889) he himself demolishes
his own argument by frankly admitting that "The registration of the
members of the Lodge (No. 2) in the Register of Grand Lodge in the
beginning of the present century was irregular." The same applies to the
Minutes of No. 2 in the year 1787, and all the neighbouring years—as
Brother Mackenzie has conclusively shewn.

Neither Brother Officer nor any other person has adduced a single
fact to lead one to suppose that Brother Petrie was not a truthful person,
or that he had any motive to give false evidence. His evidence is in
entire accordance with all the current of tradition and of authority above
referred to; and in the absence of any positive evidence to the contrary
is worthy of confidence and respect.

One remark falls to be made with regard to the whole of the above evidence. It is of a *positive* character, and is such as reasonable men are in the habit of accepting as sufficient in the absence of any *positive* evidence to the contrary. *Is* there any positive evidence to the contrary? ·None whatever. Those who, in recent times, have attacked the long received tradition, and in particular, Brothers Officer and Murray Lyon, rely wholly, not on the *presence* of any, even the smallest *contrary* evidence, but only on the *absence* of certain records, which, if they existed, would give contemporary corroboration to the positive evidence adduced. That this is no exaggeration will be seen at a glance, if we consider the principal arguments put forward by them by way of "disproof" of the received tradition. These are :—

1. No contemporary entry of the appointment in the Minutes of No. 2.
2. Before such appointment the office must have been created ; and this could not be done without the consent of Grand Lodge. There is no entry of the creation, or of such consent.
3. If created, it must be annual, and re-election must be annual ; whereas there is no entry of any further election till 1835, when (as they allege) the office was created.
4. Burns himself does not mention it.
5. The testimony adduced to prove it is not contemporaneous.

It is obvious that all this amounts to no more than pointing out what additional evidence would in their judgment place the tradition beyond all possible doubt. Not one of the five points, nor all of them together, is logically inconsistent with the truth of the positive evidence adduced.

But let us look more closely at the five points *seriatim*.

1. "No contemporary Minute of the appointment."

This is plainly their principal, one may say their only material point.

If such a Minute existed, where would be their case? And yet, so far is such an entry from being necessary to satisfactory evidence of the transaction it professes to record, that in English Common Law such an entry is not admissible as any evidence at all of the transaction. The only use that could be made of it would be to refresh the memory of the person who had made the entry, as to his own recollection of the transaction which he recorded, and then only if he had been present at the transaction.

Brother Petrie's evidence, on the contrary, though given many years after, would have been admissible primary evidence of an eye-witness. No doubt, however, apart from legal rules of evidence, the absence of any entry is a suspicious circumstance, provided it appears that the books have been regularly and carefully kept. If it appears they have been irregularly and carelessly kept, such omission would carry no weight. Which, then, is the case here? Brother Mackenzie has conclusively shewn by many instances that the Books of No. 2 were at this time most carelessly and irregularly kept. I refer for brevity to his statement, and will quote only one instance.

The Hon. Henry Erskine is entered as elected to the chair on 24th June 1780, but no previous Minute exists to show that he ever joined the Lodge. This is the exact converse of Burns' case, where his admission as Honorary member is recorded, but not his appointment as Poet-Laureate. It is worthy of note that the omission to record the act of making a man a Mason, or of admitting him member of a Lodge, is a much more serious omission than the omission to record a merely honorary appointment within the Lodge, which is in no way essential to the practical working of the Lodge, and might fall into desuetude without affecting that working. In point of fact, not only after Burns's death was this office left unfilled, but twice or thrice after 1835, when Brothers Officer and Murray Lyon admit it was in existence, the Lodge omitted to fill it up, though careful to fill up those offices which are essential to the practical working and constitutional completeness of the Lodge. These omissions are duly shewn in a table of appointments inserted in Brother Mackenzie's statement. May I here be permitted to suggest that the admirable and scrupulously exact manner in which Brother Murray Lyon keeps the Books of Grand Lodge, tends perhaps to make him too exacting in his demands upon the past.

    2. "Before Burns could have been appointed, the office must have been created, and this required the consent of Grand Lodge, which has no record of such consent."

This is merely an erroneous and very pedantic objection. Where is the rule of Grand Lodge forbidding any Lodge to appoint an Honorary Poet Laureate without previous solemn *creation* of the *office* with the *consent of Grand*

Lodge? Moreover, it proves a great deal too much, and is in fact contradicted by Brothers Officer and Murray Lyon themselves. They both assert that the office was created in 1835, and has existed since then to the present time. They deny that it existed before the appointment of Hogg. Was the appointment of Hogg preceded by any "creation of the office?" Is there any record in Grand Lodge of any previous application to Grand Lodge for its consent to "create the office?" Or do our incredulous Brethren suggest that such application and consent was doubtless made and given, though the officials of Grand Lodge omitted to record it? If they don't, they give up this objection as untenable. If they do, why are they so ready to believe an unrecorded transaction which has *no* tradition and *no* vestige of evidence to support it, whilst they find it so impossible to believe an unrecorded transaction which has both evidence and tradition in its favour? If they answer "no such consent was asked or granted, because both Canongate Kilwinning, No. 2, and Grand Lodge supposed it had been obtained in 1787," this would still be fatal to the actual existence of the office; moreover, they must admit that Grand Lodge assented to the truth of the tradition, and either thought its consent unnecessary, or that it had been given in 1787, though unrecorded, thus regarding the record as not essential nor conclusive. Moreover, Grand Lodge must have considered that such office did not cease to exist, though unfilled for more than 35 years, in other words, that it need not be filled up annually.

    3. "If created, it must be annually vacated and filled, whereas no further election till 1835."

This is sufficiently answered by the remarks just made. No one took that view in 1835, nor since. The office had then been vacant at least since Burns's death. The refilling of it then by Hogg was public and notorious, and the power of the Lodge to refill it was unquestioned, and, I may add unquestionable. The Lodge has, since then, several times omitted to fill it, when vacant, and have afterwards filled it, as of right, and without question. The truth is, this objection also is both erroneous and pedantic. It loses sight of the distinction between a mere honorary and non-essential office, and those which are essential to the proper constitution and working of a Lodge.

4. "Burns himself does not mention it."

This objection is so trivial that it seems hardly worth answering, but as it is much insisted on, I may point out that they have not the least right to say Burns never mentioned it. All they can say is that in the very limited number of letters of his which have been preserved and published, such mention does not happen to occur. What sort of argument is that? They suggest that Canongate Kilwinning, No. 2, was so distinguished a Lodge, it was impossible he should not have mentioned it at the time. Well, perhaps he did. How can they prove he did not? But let me ask them this: In February 1787, they themselves admit that this distinguished Lodge did Burns the distinguished honour of electing him an honorary member. Where does Burns mention this fact? And if Burns does not mention this honour, why should he mention the other? Perhaps, on second thoughts, they may suggest that the entry of February 1st 1787 cannot be true, because, if true, Burns must have mentioned it! That would at least make their argument consistent.

5. "The testimony adduced is not *contemporaneous.*"

That depends upon what "contemporaneous" evidence means. If it means what it means in ordinary usage, in Courts of Law, or in historical evidence, then it *is* contemporaneous—*i.e.* it is evidence derived from the assertions, or the acts of *contemporaries* who were in a position to know, or who claim to have such knowledge. Brother Charles More and Brother Petrie are both of this class, and so are all those who were continuously members of the Lodge during 1787, and thence to 1815,—nay, some of them to 1835, when Hogg was elected expressly as *his successor*, and even to 1845, when the picture commemorative of it was sanctioned. The meaning which our objecting brethren put on the word is singular. They say that Brother Petrie's testimony that he was present and saw the fact is not contemporary, because it (the testimony) was not given at the time of the occurrence itself! That the witness was there at the time is nothing! The question is, *did he give his evidence on the spot where and when the occurrence took place!* This sense of "contemporaneous testimony," is unique, and the laws of time and space and common sense are likely to keep it so.

To sum up, there is a large body of evidence, direct and indirect, including the assertions, acts and conduct of those most likely to know and most entitled to speak and to be believed. There is a continuous, and, till recent times, unchallenged tradition resting on that evidence. On the other side there is no evidence to the contrary, but only an eager insistence upon the *absence* of certain *additional* evidence, mainly inadmissible in Law, even if it existed, and all of it such as not to present any logical contradiction of any part of the positive evidence in favour of the fact. It is not too much to say that nothing could ever be proved, if the absence of additional proof were admitted to countervail positive evidence of the fact.

R. W. MACLEOD FULLARTON,
Q.C.
M.M., No. 2, P.J.W., No. 770,
and Grand Bard, Grand Lodge of Scotland.

ILLUSTRATIONS.

CONTENTS.

PART I.

PART II.

APPENDIX.

ERRATA.

INTRODUCTION.

THE CELEBRATED PAINTING which depicts the Inauguration of Robert Burns as Poet Laureate of Lodge Canongate Kilwinning, No. 2, Edinburgh, was presented to the Grand Lodge of Scotland thirty-one years ago, by the late much-respected Brother James Ballantine, Grand Bard, on behalf of the family of the late Brother SIR JAMES BURNES, M.D., LL.D., D.C.L., F.R.S.L., F.R.C.P.E., Knight of Hanover, etc., and Physician-General of the Bombay Army, who was related to the Poet.

Brother Sir James Burnes [otherwise designated the Chevalier Burnes] had long been a highly esteemed and active member of Lodge Canongate Kilwinning. He was the first Provincial Grand Master of Western India—appointed on occasion of the celebration of the first centenary of Grand Lodge, 30th November 1836—and was ultimately appointed Grand Master of Scottish Freemasonry in India, which eminent position he held till nearly the end of his life. He died at Manchester on the 19th September 1862.

Shortly before his death the late Brother Sir James Burnes expressed a wish to personally present the Inauguration Picture to Grand Lodge. Unfortunately, he did not live to carry out that wish, but his family lost no time after his decease in giving effect to the generous donor's purpose regarding the Picture, and, accordingly, presentation of it was made to Grand Lodge in due form at the Quarterly Communication, held 2nd February 1863.

The Inauguration Picture, received at that time by Grand Lodge, was at once placed on view in the Board-room, and there it has remained ever since. Appended to it then was, and still is, the following inscription :—

"THE INAUGURATION

OF

ROBERT BURNS

AS POET LAUREATE OF

THE LODGE CANONGATE KILWINNING,

EDINBURGH, 1st MARCH, 1787.

Presented by JAMES BURNES, K.H., F.R.S., &c.
To the Grand Lodge of Scotland, 1862."

This valuable gift was then made to Grand Lodge in the full view of a numerous company, embracing many worthy, learned, and distinguished brethren, presided over by His Grace the Duke of Athole, K.T., &c., M.W. Grand Master; and NOW, Brother David Murray Lyon, Grand Secretary, asserts that no such inauguration ever took place, and submits, "in the interests of truth, " as set against a fable, it is necessary that steps should be taken by Grand " Committee to have the inscription on the picture *amended*" !

He also submitted and appealed to the "Printed Copy of Correspondence " between " Brothers A. Mackenzie, the historian and Past Master of No. 2, and William Officer," Past Master of No. 1, as "clearly" establishing his (Grand Secretary's) contention. Brother Lyon himself contributed two letters to that correspondence, in which he charges the Canongate Kilwinning Office-bearers of 1873 with having furnished him with "unfounded" statements, etc., and which letters, with those of the Past Master of No. 1, as is now shown, contain much apocryphical writing.

It was pointed out to Grand Committee that no *official* information on the subject was vouchsafed to them, consequently Brother Mackenzie councilled delay, and undertook to produce whatever documentary evidence existed in the archives of Canongate Kilwinning Lodge on the subject of the Election and Inauguration. This was cordially acquiesced in, and the result will be seen in the following pages.

In the first place, it was deemed proper to ask Brother Hugh C. Peacock, the Canongate Kilwinning Secretary of 1873, to substantiate "the statements," which Grand Secretary now so emphatically stigmatises as "unfounded ;" and, in the second place, to publish certified copies of the Minutes and other authentic documents of the Burns and Hogg periods, so that every Brother can judge of the matter for himself.

Whatever the object of questioning the truth of the Inscription at this distant date may be, assuredly Grand Lodge, on learning full particulars, will impartially judge; and it is earnestly hoped that this Inscription, hallowed by time—rendered doubly valuable for the interesting circumstances connected with the record of such an historical event, as well as for the eminent and worthy names and memories associated therewith—will be ordered to remain in its original state, so that no future historian, or any other writer, will think of mutilating such a precious heirloom to the Masonic Brotherhood as that Picture descriptive of "The Inauguration of Robert Burns as Poet-Laureate of The "Lodge Canongate Kilwinning, Edinburgh, 1st March 1787," which now hangs on view in the board-room of the Grand Lodge of Scotland.

A. MACKENZIE,
P.M. Can. Kil., No. 2.

July 1894.

PART I.

LETTER

FROM

Brother ALLAN MACKENZIE,

Past Master of Lodge Canongate Kilwinning, and Member of the Special Committee appointed by the Grand Committee to Consider and Report to Grand Lodge upon the whole question of the Inauguration of Robert Burns as Poet Laureate of Lodge Canongate Kilwinning,

TO

Brother HUGH C. PEACOCK,

Past Secretary, Past Substitute-Master, and Past Depute-Master, Lodge Canongate Kilwinning.

———————————

17 St. Andrew Square,
Edinburgh, *20th March* 1893.

H. C. Peacock, Esq.,
    8 York Buildings.
        Dear Sir and Brother,

Robt. Burns,
Poet Laureate of Can. Kil. No. 2.

In Grand Lodge Proceedings you have no doubt observed that on 29th Dec. last, Bro. D. Murray Lyon, Grand Secretary, submitted a statement to Grand Committee, in the course of which he asserts that, in 1873, the office-bearers of Can. Kil. Lodge communicated through you, as Secretary, certain "*alleged facts which he unfortunately accepted as true, and in his History modified the opinion which he had originally formed,*" and that steps should be taken to have the inscription on the Inauguration Picture in the Board Room amended.

In my reply to this extraordinary assertion, I undertook to produce whatever documentary evidence exists in the Lodge on the subject; and, in order to bring up a full and complete report on the whole question, I shall be obliged by your furnishing me with the evidence upon which you made "the statements" contained in your letter to Bro. D. Murray Lyon of 7th Feby. 1873, and which he complains of as being "*unfounded.*"—Yours faithfully and fraternally,

A. Mackenzie,
P. M. Can. Kil., No. 2,
and "Member of the Special Committee
"appointed to Consider and Report
"upon the Whole Question."

b

II.

REPLY

FROM

Brother HUGH C. PEACOCK

TO

Past Master ALLAN MACKENZIE.

ARGYLE CRESCENT,
PORTOBELLO, 16th November 1893.

ALLAN MACKENZIE, Esq.,
    Past Master Lodge Canongate Kilwinning,
        Etc., etc.

    WORSHIPFUL AND DEAR SIR,

        Thanks for your letter inviting my attention to Grand Lodge Proceedings of 29th December 1892, and requesting evidence from me in substantiation of "the statements" contained in my letter to Brother David Murray Lyon, dated so far back as 7th February 1873, which he now complains of as being "unfounded."

    With respect to "the printed copy of the correspondence" between you and another member of the craft, which is referred to in said Proceedings of 29th December 1892 as having been submitted to the meeting held that date, I may remark that it is not altogether new. Much of it was contained in cuttings from *The Freemason*, which, about four years ago, you enclosed to me with an invitation to take part in the discussion. You will remember that I at once called upon you and returned the cuttings, declining to add one word to what had been said. My reasons were, that, as you had entered on the correspondence in *The Freemason* on your own responsibility, in defence of what you had said in the History of Lodge Canongate Kilwinning regarding Burns, quite independently of, and unknown to me or any of the other office-bearers, therefore, such correspondence—so far at least as I was concerned—should remain wholly your own. Further, I remarked, it was evident to me that no good result to the one side or the other could accrue from discussing in any such desultory manner, throughout several years, a subject of the kind in a public journal :—irregularly and at long intervals discussed —quite as irregularly read by the average reader—and the whole question never at any one period before him in a complete form, it seemed to me a sheer waste of time to follow up the discussion—in *The Freemason*.

    Brother Lyon professed himself satisfied with the information communicated to him in my letter of 7th February 1873,* and gave effect to a portion of it in his History,

---

* Brother Lyon's reply, dated Feby. 11, 1873, is reproduced in Part II., page 61.

which was published shortly afterwards—in the year 1873—and *then* I fully believed that the question raised by the correspondence was settled. I did not expect that NOW I would now have occasion to defend anything said in that 1873 letter, *after so many old brethren who helped me with it are dead*, and that Grand Secretary, in his recently acquired anxiety "to have the inscription on the picture" (of the inauguration) "amended," would complain to Grand Lodge in those Proceedings of 29th December 1892 (*vide* Part II., page 1), that, so far back as twenty years ago, in that letter I had "laid *a statement* before him embodying alleged facts, which he unfortunately accepted as true, and in his History modified the opinion which he had originally formed "—and, that in said Proceedings [still with respect to same letter] he "asserts that *the statements* made to him were unfounded."

Fortunately, I am in a position to prove my case, independently of those old members now dead ; and, agreeably with your request, I have much pleasure in now furnishing, by the matter which follows this reply, abundant evidence to establish beyond any reasonable doubt or cavil the essential facts set forth in my letter to which you refer.

It is my duty to add, that, with the very utmost respect and esteem for Bro. D. Murray Lyon, Grand Secretary ; for his attainments as a Masonic author—as shown forth in his excellent "History of the Lodge of Edinburgh (Mary's Chapel), No. 1"— and for his well-known great knowledge of Masonic matters generally, I nevertheless claim to have a more intimate knowledge than he of the many books and documents, and other valuable memorabilia belonging to Lodge Canongate Kilwinning, and of its very interesting history—apart from so much of it as has been published :—such knowledge of mine being derived mainly from a continuous active membership of twenty-one years, during much of which time I have served the Lodge as Secretary.

Therefore, while I very much regret having to express an opinion different from that of Grand Secretary regarding the question under notice, I feel it my bounden duty to the Lodge Committee of 1873, the Canongate Kilwinning Lodge of to-day, and the Craft in general, to distinctly deny, as I hereby do, Grand Secretary's belated assertions against "*the statements made to him*" in that letter of mine, written so very long ago as in the beginning of 1873,—those assertions being utterly unwarrantable.

Finally, I respectfully request that you will invite Grand Secretary to put his finger on any one statement in said letter of mine, *essential to the question*, which he claims to be unfounded—AND PROVE IT.

The evidence you ask for follows this letter.—I am, Worshipful and Dear Sir, yours truly and fraternally,

HUGH C. PEACOCK,
Past Secretary and Past Depute-Master, Can. Kil.
Proxy Master, No. 476.

III.

COMMENTARY

GRAND SECRETARY'S Assertions impugning "the Statements"
contained in the LETTER written by the SECRETARY of LODGE
CANONGATE KILWINNING, 7th February 1873.*

My letter, dated 7th February 1873, containing "the statements," of which
·evidence is now requested from me, was written in the course of a correspondence which,
as Secretary of Lodge Canongate Kilwinning, I had been instructed by the Committee
of that Lodge to have with Brother David Murray Lyon, who was then resident in Ayr.
I had been so instructed by reason of a report having reached Lodge Committee to
the effect that, in the "History of the Lodge of Edinburgh (Mary's Chapel) No. 1,
embracing an Account of the Rise and Progress of Freemasonry in Scotland," which
Brother Lyon was at that time compiling, the commonly accepted association of Robert
Burns to Lodge Canongate Kilwinning was discredited.

Before entering fully on such evidence, I feel privileged to make a few
comments on the assertions so freely advanced by Grand·Secretary to Grand Committee
on 29th December 1892 impugning the statements contained in my letter.†

Bro. Mackenzie calls my .attention to the fact "that, on 29th December last,
Bro. D. Murray Lyon, Grand Secretary, submitted a statement to Grand Committee,
in the course of which he asserts that in 1873 the Office-bearers of Can. Kil. Lodge
communicated through you, as Secretary, certain 'alleged facts which he unfortunately
accepted as true, and in his History modified the opinion which he had originally
formed,' and that steps should be taken to have the inscription on the Inauguration
Picture in the Board-room amended."

In the "Extract from Grand Lodge Proceedings, 29th December 1892," Grand
Secretary also asserted that, in the year 1873 [*before* my letter dated 7th February 1873
was written, and *before* his History of the Lodge of Edinburgh (Mary's Chapel), No. 1,
was printed]—he made "A MINUTE EXAMINATION OF CANONGATE KILWINNING'S
RECORDS." In making such "minute examination" he would certainly, as an eminent
historian, carefully examine the record dated 1st February 1787, containing mention

---

* A copy of that letter will be found in Part II., page 57.
† The "Extract from Grand Lodge Proceedings, 29th December 1892," is given in Part II., page 1.

of the affiliation of Robert Burns. Brother D. Murray Lyon would also, quite as carefully, examine the record of 1st March 1787—the date which he knew was inscribed on the Inauguration Picture as being that on which the Inauguration ceremony was claimed to have taken place—but in the latter record he would find that the name of Robert Burns is not mentioned. Nevertheless, Brother Lyon, in his response acknowledging receipt of my letter concerning Burns' inauguration, made no reference whatever to such omission.*

Further, in the "Extract from Grand Lodge Proceedings, 29th December 1892," Grand Secretary announced that, "in all statements and discussions in support of the story, the minute of the meeting at which the event is alleged to have happened has been kept out of sight. It is as follows"†—[and the quotation of minute followed accordingly].

Grand Secretary apparently forgets, in casting such an unworthy taunt at brethren whose opinions happen to differ from his on such a matter, that, *if* the minute of 1st March 1787 had ever been "kept out of sight" in the sense implied, which I deny, he has himself for twenty years contributed to the doing so. *Bro. Lyon certainly noted that special minute when he made "a minute examination of Canongate Kilwinning's records,"* BEFORE *publishing his History of No. 1.* Nevertheless, throughout all his reference to Canongate Kilwinning and Burns in his History, Bro. Lyon *studiously refrained from quoting that minute* which he so prominently exhibits NOW, as if it were quite a recent and important discovery in Burns' literature.

There is another aspect of this part of the subject which Grand Secretary appears to have quite overlooked when making the inapplicable taunt about the minute of 1st March 1787 having been "kept out of sight," but which must be perfectly obvious to any one perusing these pages,—to wit, that, if the minute of 1st March 1787 had contained any account of the election and inauguration of Robert Burns, I had no need whatever to write that letter of 7th February 1873, which consisted of several pages of duly verified statements and quotations from minutes, and argument well founded upon them, in evidence of such election and inauguration. Had these events been recorded when they occurred, I would only have needed to quote the one minute of 1st March 1787—a few lines;—[the minutes were brief in those days.] Bro. Lyon was quite well aware of all that. Yet, in his comparatively recent change of front, he ostentatiously produced to Grand Lodge, 29th December 1892, a copy of said minute of 1st March 1787, as if that settled the question!

On same occasion [29th December 1892], Grand Secretary submitted to Grand Lodge "the printed copy of correspondence," asserting that it "clearly established" his contention. That little work concludes with a letter from himself, dated 18th August 1891, containing a copy of the minute of 1st March 1787, which he states, in said

---

* Copy of that response will be found in Part II., page 61.

† The minute of 1st March 1787 need not be reproduced here, because it appears twice elsewhere in these papers—to wit, firstly, in the "Extract from Grand Lodge Proceedings, 29th December 1892," Part II., pages 1 and 2; and, secondly, in its proper order and place, along with other minutes of the Burns period, in Part II., page 14.

letter, "has been *studiously kept out of sight.*" He continues the subject with the following assertion :—

"The concluding sentence of the foregoing minute *proves* beyond question that no such event as the inauguration of Burns as Poet Laureate of Canongate Kilwinning took place at the meeting of 1st March 1787."

Not so: such self-imposed task of attempting to *prove a negative* remains unaccomplished.

I comment more fully upon the minute of 1st March 1787 in Part II., pages 7 and 8, where it appears in its proper place, along with its companion records of the years 1786-7-8.

The editor of "the printed correspondence," in letter VI. at page 44 of that work, with reference to the minute-book containing the record of 1st March 1787, makes the bold assertion : "*It is well and continuously kept.*"

In absolute proof of the very reverse of that assertion being true, I respectfully crave a careful perusal and scrutiny of the series of minutes comprised within the period June 1786 to December 1788. They are faithfully reproduced in Part II., pages 12 to 19. At a glance those minutes afford clear evidence of my statement, and by reference to Part II., pages 4 to 11, wherein those minutes are carefully reviewed, it will be seen in detail that *the minute-book referred to has been very carelessly and irregularly kept.*

Those Canongate Kilwinning records of the years 1786, 1787, and 1788 stand forth very observably in the old minute-book as a melancholy memorial of neglected duties on the part of the Lodge Secretary during the eventful period of the Scottish Bard's frequent sojourns in Edinburgh. And yet, Brother Mackenzie's correspondent in *The Freemason* had the boldness to assert that those minutes were "*kept with care !*" Indeed, more than that, he asserted that "the minutes of the Canongate Lodge, at the period in question, were kept by a practising solicitor," as if, *per se*, that were a guarantee for carefulness, and as if such announcement should awe us into acceptance of the minutes at his (the correspondent's) valuation; also, that "*they appear to have been kept with care and ample fulness of detail !!!*" The correspondent had the temerity to continue his undue praising of the "practising solicitor" who acted as Canongate Kilwinning's Secretary in 1787, by saying in support of the extraordinary assertion in the words now quoted, "*The very minute, assuming Burns a member of the Lodge, illustrates this fact, for it bears evidence of careful revision, being partially erased in at least two places.*"

The real fact of the matter is, that the "careful revision"—the erasement—has evidently *not* been done by the same bungling hand that laboriously composed the minute in its primitive phraseology; but by some clever, neat-handed, supervising brother who had been ashamed of the Secretary's work. More upon this point will be found in Part II., page 5, also page 6, continued into page 7.

Apart from various other irregularities—which may or may not be less faulty—I need only mention at this stage of the evidence one instance, namely, that in the minute-book professedly containing Lodge records of the years 1787 and 1788, there are *blank pages left for many minutes of meetings of the Lodge and of Committee that never have been recorded,* and, by such extraordinary instances of neglect, there has been lost all knowledge of events which occurred in the Lodge Canongate Kilwinning during *eleven months* of perhaps the most eventful and most interesting period of her history. Notwithstanding all that, Grand Secretary now, following up such unmerited bepraising of the 1787 Secretary of Lodge Canongate Kilwinning as has been quoted, produces copy of one of those precious minutes, dated 1st March 1787—just as precious and more imperfect than the minute of 1st February 1787—from such a grossly defective record-book, as a proof that the election and inauguration of Robert Burns as Poet Laureate DID NOT take place!

Quite on same grounds Grand Secretary might assert that Robert Burns DID NOT appear in the Lodge St. Andrew, Edinburgh, No. 48, on 12th January, 1787, when Grand Master Charteris gave the toast, "Caledonia and Caledonia's Bard—Robert Burns," because the Lodge Secretary omitted to engross a minute of that important meeting, and because even the minute entered of that date in the St. Andrew's Lodge minute-book on behalf of Grand Lodge [which is framed quite in the "stick to the form" manner commented on by Brother James Marshall in his "Winter with Robert Burns," page 67], contains no reference whatever to "Caledonia's Bard." There is proof of the event notwithstanding.

Quite on same grounds Grand Secretary might assert that the Lodge St. David, Edinburgh, No. 36, DID NOT elect Gavin Wilson to the office of Poet Laureate of that Lodge, simply because the Secretary had not recorded such event, and there is no statement in any of the minutes of that Lodge during all its history showing that Gavin Wilson had been Poet Laureate. Yet there is absolute proof that Brother Gavin Wilson was Poet Laureate of the Lodge St. David, Edinburgh.

Quite on same grounds Grand Secretary might assert that the Town Council of the Royal Burgh of Linlithgow DID NOT admit Burns as a Burgess and Guild Brother on 16th November, 1787, simply because the Town Clerk of that ancient Burgh omitted to record such important event in his minute of that date, and because *Burns never mentioned the circumstance in any of his writings.* Nevertheless, it was proved on 4th January, 1859, that the Poet had such honour conferred on him, and that he duly received his burgess ticket, which was produced on the latter date.

Reverting to my comments on the "Extract from Grand Lodge Proceedings 29th "December 1892," I quote the following passage from that document :—

"As will be seen in the printed copy of the correspondence between Brothers Allan "Mackenzie, the Historian of No. 2, and William Officer, now submitted, Grand Secretary "asserts that the statements made to him were unfounded, and that it is clearly estab-"lished that the story of the Installation of Burns as Poet Laureate is a myth."

These are utterly gratuitous and unfounded assertions by Grand Secretary.

In the course of this evidence I shall expose many of the very gross errors contained throughout the fifty-three pages of adverse criticism of the Burns' Laureateship, occurring in "the printed copy of the correspondence," which Grand Secretary appears to consider a supreme authority on this question.

Brother Mackenzie's correspondent concludes all he had to say by the letter dated 15th October, 1889, in which he made the following extraordinary assertion respecting one of the statements which had special reference to the testimony of Bro. William Petrie, contained in my letter to Brother D. Murray Lyon, dated 7th February, 1873.

"Coming from such a source it was accepted without enquiry as correct, *and* "*misled our eminent historian.*"*

I may here point out that the author of the History of the Lodge of Edinburgh [Mary's Chapel] does not appear to have discovered any occasion to change his belief in Robert Burns having been Poet Laureate of Lodge Canongate Kilwinning from such belief as expressed in his History, *until* the correspondence regarding the Laureateship had been continued some time in the columns of *The Freemason*,—that is, until any date from November 1888 to January 1889.

That correspondence was begun shortly after the publication in 1888 of Brother Allan Mackenzie's History of the Lodge Canongate Kilwinning,—*which contained a reproduction of my letter on the Laureateship, dated 7th February*, 1873. It was begun by a letter appearing in *The Freemason*, dated 14th November, 1888 [pages 9 to 21 of "the printed correspondence"], calling in question what had been stated in my said letter as it had appeared in Brother Mackenzie's history relative to Robert Burns having been Poet Laureate of Lodge Canongate Kilwinning.

Ere long Brother D. Murray Lyon, Grand Secretary, contributed to the discussion, in *The Freemason*, a letter, dated February 12th, 1889 [*vide* page 36 of "the printed correspondence"], in which he professed to discredit the fact of Burns having been Poet Laureate, and asserted that he, Grand Secretary, "made a serious mistake" in accepting the statements made in my letter to him of 7th February, 1873. Grand Secretary concluded his letter by ominously saying, "I shall take the first opportunity in my power of correcting the statement I then too readily adopted."

In proof of those statements of mine relative to his comparatively recent change of opinion, I quote portion of a letter from Brother D. Murray Lyon, Grand Secretary, which appeared in the *Scotsman* newspaper towards the close of the year 1886. The letter was dated 14th December, 1886, and was printed under the headline— "Was the Ettrick Shepherd a Freemason?" Grand Secretary answered the question in a very erroneous manner. In the meantime I need only quote one part of his answer, which is so far correct;—I shall give an account of the remaining part further on:—

"Hogg did become a Freemason, and his association with the Lodge Canongate "Kilwinning is at once peculiar and interesting. In treating of Burns' connection with "a distinguished Lodge in my History of Freemasonry in Scotland (1873), I wrote— "'The Laureateship is again referred to in the minute of 16th January 1835, which "'records the restoration in the person of James Hogg, the Ettrick Shepherd, of the "'honorary office of Poet Laureate of the Lodge, which had been in abeyance since the "'death of the immortal brother Robert Burns.'"

From this it is perfectly obvious that towards the close of the year 1886 Grand Secretary had a thorough belief in the fact that Burns had been Poet Laureate of Lodge

---

* Quoted from page 66 of "the printed correspondence."

Canongate Kilwinning, and there is no reason to doubt that he had continued "steadfast in the faith" from the time of our correspondence in 1873, *until certainly* the date of said letter from him of 14th December, 1886, and *very probably* until he resolved to contribute his letter, dated 12th February, 1889, to the correspondence of *The Freemason* in support of the adverse views regarding the Laureateship contended for by the Past Master of the Lodge of Edinburgh [Mary's Chapel].

The story about the Secretary of Lodge Canongate Kilwinning having "MISLED OUR EMINENT HISTORIAN" was published last year in two varieties at widely different times, and from two very different sources.

The following reproductions exhibit a singular resemblance between them :—

As Narrated by THE AUTHOR *of* "PREFATORY NOTE" *to* "THE PRINTED COPY OF THE CORRESPONDENCE."	*As Narrated by* GRAND SECRETARY *in the* "EXTRACT FROM GRAND LODGE PROCEEDINGS."
June 1892.	*29th December,* 1892.
"About twenty years ago Brother David Murray Lyon, then a well-known and active masonic student, agreed to write a HISTORY OF THE LODGE OF EDINBURGH (MARY'S CHAPEL), No. 1, which undertaking ultimately resulted in his admirable 'History of Freemasonry in Scotland.' At that time the writer was Master of that Lodge, and rendered some help to Bro. Lyon in the production of his History, and, while examining the minute-books and other writings of the Lodge Canongate Kilwinning, found that the Office of Poet Laureate had no existence in the Lodge during the Poet's lifetime, nor until many years after his lamented death, and that the Lodge's minutes were absolutely silent on the subject.	"The story of the inauguration was never challenged until 1873, when the present Grand Secretary, while preparing his 'History of Freemasonry in Scotland,' and after a minute examination of Canongate Kilwinning's records,
"Bro. Murray Lyon having considered the matter, formed the opinion that Burns never was elected to, and never held the office of, Poet Laureate of the Lodge, and never was installed into such an office. His views becoming known to its Office-bearers, by their instructions the Secretary of the Lodge questioned the soundness of his opinion, and laid a statement before him embodying alleged facts, which he unfortunately accepted as true, and in his History modified the opinion which he had originally formed. As will be seen in this correspondence,	formed the opinion that Burns never was elected to, and never held the Office of, Poet-Laureate of the Lodge, and never was installed into such an Office. His views having become known to its Office-bearers, by their instructions the Secretary of the Lodge questioned the soundness of his opinion, and laid a statement before him embodying alleged facts, which he unfortunately accepted as true, and in his History modified the opinion which he had originally formed. As will be seen in the printed copy of the correspondence between Brothers Allan Mackenzie, the historian of No. 2, and William Officer, now submitted, Grand Secretary asserts that the statements made to him
he now states that the statements submitted to him were unfounded, and that it is clearly established that Burns never was elected or held the office of Poet Laureate of the Lodge Canongate Kilwinning, and that his "installation" never took place."	were unfounded, and that it is clearly established that the story of the installation of
[NOTE.—The Editor of "the printed copy of the correspondence," which was submitted by Grand Secretary to Grand Committee, December 29th, 1892, prepared his readers for error by the extraordinary heading to his title-page,—to wit,—	
"BURNS, "POET-LAUREATE OF CANONGATE KILWINNING, "A MYTH."]	Burns, as Poet Laureate, is a myth.

IV

FACTS WORTH KNOWING

About the LETTER Written to BROTHER D. MURRAY LYON by the SECRETARY
OF LODGE CANONGATE KILWINNING, 7th February 1873.*

At the time that my correspondence with Brother David Murray Lyon was
begun, I had not been half-a-year Secretary of Lodge Canongate Kilwinning.

Nevertheless, I have every reason to be gratified by the fact that, within two
weeks after receiving Bro. Lyon's brief reply to me, dated 24th Jany., 1873, containing the
imperative injunction, "COMMUNICATE AT ONCE," I had so thoroughly mastered the
subject as to write him, on 7th February 1873, that letter which was cordially approved
of by the Lodge Committee, and has been approved of by every impartial reader since
then, and which is allowed to contain—*so far as it goes*—[in the absence, through gross
neglect by the Lodge Secretary of 1787, of any record of the inauguration of Robert
Burns as Poet Laureate], a well-reasoned and conclusive chain of evidence in support of
the time-honoured belief that such event took place on the 1st March 1787. The
opportunity of contributing more information by letter was denied me.

New as the matter was to me in the year 1873, I was careful not to be hurried
into making any assertions on the subject without having obtained most satisfactory evidence regarding them ; hence it is, that in the whole argument throughout my
letter, in its main lines, and wherein I make distinct and emphatic statements, that letter
stands to this day—and will stand in all time coming—irrefutable.

That letter was well founded—mainly upon various records of the Lodge
Canongate Kilwinning, also upon the earnest and assured personal statements
made to me by prominent old members hereinafter named, who formed the Lodge
Committee, concerning facts communicated to them by brethren who had shared in the
Lodge events of 1787, and further [by recognition and approval of said committee], upon
Brother James Marshall's narrative in "*A Winter with Robert Burns*," the testimony
contained in which valuable little work has not been in any degree affected by all the
strong assertions and weak arguments advanced by Brother Mackenzie's disputant in
The Freemason, and reproduced in "the printed copy of the correspondence" submitted
by Grand Secretary, 29th December 1892.

Long as that letter of mine is, any reader may easily observe that the subject of
it was not exhausted. It will be seen that I offered to communicate further, but Bro.
Lyon did not give me the opportunity. In his response, dated 11th Feb., 1873 (*vide*

* A copy of that letter will be found in Part II., page 57.
† Copy of the Correspondence occurs in Part II., pages 55 to 61.

Part II., page 61), he said he recognised "the satisfactory nature of the evidence" which I had submitted, and would "have pleasure in giving effect to it" in his forthcoming work; and, in answer to a request of mine [made with a view to further correspondence] for a copy or proof of what he intended saying as to Burns and the Lodge Canongate Kilwinning, he wrote—"The delay which has occurred on your part prevents my being able to submit a slip of my remarks, the printers being close up to that particular part of my MS." Of course that closed the correspondence. I had no wish to press my attentions upon Bro. Lyon with a word more on the subject.

Had not Brother David Murray Lyon in that very effective way cut short our 1873 correspondence, I would gladly have supplemented the testimony given in my letter with a few interesting items which I had in reserve for his information. Certainly, the very first reference I was prepared to give would have been to the engraving of Burns as it appeared then, and as it appears now on the east wall of the Lodge-room, having the date 29th October 1798 upon it, with the prominent inscription on its old-fashioned glass mount, in large Roman characters:—

"ROBERT BURNS, THE SCOTTISH BARD,

"POET LAUREAT,

"LODGE No. 2, CANNONGATE

"KILWINNING." *

In the year 1873 that manifestly antique engraving of our "Poet Laureat" was prized very highly by old members of the Lodge and by many interested new ones, although I, for one, was not *then* aware of the reference to it in the minute of 24th June 1802, which I afterwards discovered, and which I quote in Part II., page 20, of this evidence.

Although the matter is dealt with conclusively in that part of the evidence, it is well to mention in passing, that I took some trouble during 1873, in communicating with old members of that time, with the view to acquire all available information regarding the engraving above described, and the answer from each brother was, that the engraving had been exhibited in the Lodge room as long as *he* had been attending meetings of the Lodge Canongate Kilwinning.

Among those brethren whom I refer to as old members in 1873 were Past Master Dr Sam. Somerville of Ampherlaw, Past Master W. N. Fraser of Tornaveen, Past Master Thomas Drybrough, Past Depute-Master David Crawford, also Bro. Thos. Elder MacRitchie, whose recollections of the Lodge reached back to the year 1818, and others referred to elsewhere in these papers. During *their* early experiences of Lodge Canongate Kilwinning, they had learnt from brethren whose membership in the Lodge, and whose recollections pertaining to it, extended to the latter years of last century, that that treasured engraving of Robert Burns as "Poet Laureat" of Canongate Kilwinning, had been in possession of the Lodge since those old days, and such fact is obviously proved by the verbal testimony communicated from brother to brother in the manner thus narrated, independently of the proof given in Part II., page 20.

---

* *Vide* Frontispiece.

V.

"THE STATEMENTS" SUBSTANTIATED

WHICH WERE CONTAINED

IN LETTER written to BROTHER D. MURRAY LYON,

By the SECRETARY of LODGE CANONGATE KILWINNING, 7th February 1873;[*]

AND WHICH

GRAND SECRETARY NOW asserts are "unfounded."

In the "Extract from Grand Lodge Proceedings, 29th December 1892" [*vide* page 1 of Part II.], the following assertions have been made with reference to the letter which, as Secretary to Canongate Kilwinning, I wrote to Brother David Murray Lyon, 7th February 1873 :—

GRAND SECRETARY'S ASSERTIONS.

" The story of the inauguration was never challenged until 1873, when the present Grand Secretary, while preparing his 'History of Freemasonry in Scotland,' and after a minute examination of Canongate Kilwinning's records, formed the opinion that Burns never was elected to, and never held the office of, Poet Laureate of the Lodge, and never was installed into such an office. His views having become known to its office-bearers, by their instructions the Secretary of the Lodge questioned the soundness of his opinion, and laid a statement before him embodying alleged facts which he unfortunately accepted as true, and in his History modified the opinion which he had originally formed. As will be seen in the printed copy of the correspondence between Brothers Allan Mackenzie, the historian of No. 2, and William Officer, now submitted, Grand Secretary asserts that the statements made to him were unfounded, and that it is clearly established that the story of the Installation of Burns as Poet Laureate is a myth."

In illustration of the thorough accuracy of the statements made in my letter of 7th February 1873, and the erroneousness of Grand Secretary's tardy assertions against them, I will now indicate the chief statements contained in that letter, accompanied by references to the various productions in proof of same.

"THE STATEMENTS."
1. *In re* BROTHER CHARLES MORE.
1769-1818.

One of the principal statements in my letter is with reference to Brother Charles More of the Royal Bank. It will be found in page 59 of Part II., lines 13 to 26.

Proofs of the truth of my statement can be seen in pages 12 to 35 of Part II., more particularly in pages 12 to 15, pages 22, 29, 31, 32, and 33, also in the Appendix, comprising the Chart of Office-bearers, and its Supplement showing Members of Committee.

---

* For copy of that letter *vide* Part II. page 57 :—Copy of Brother Lyon's reply to it occurs in Part II. page 61, showing that he recognised "the satisfactory nature of the evidence" which I had then submitted.

Brother Charles More was Depute Master of Canongate Kilwinning from June 1784 till June 1787. He was constant in his attendance at meetings of the Lodge during the Burns' period, and he signed, as Depute Master, every one of the minutes of that time to which any signature has been appended, as is proved by the minutes at pages 12 to 15 of Part II.; he was constantly a member of the Lodge Committee from 1784 to 1817, as is proved by authenticated particulars contained in the Supplement to Chart in Appendix; and he was closely associated with Brother William Campbell, Writer to the Signet, and other eminent men, while this century was young, as may be seen at pages 21, 22, and pages 25 to 29 of Part II.

He was the same Brother Charles More who, while still a Member of Committee in the year 1815, seconded a resolution relative to a subscription of twenty guineas towards a mausoleum to the memory of "*the lamented Bard* ROBERT BURNS," *because* ROBERT BURNS "HAD BEEN POET LAUREAT TO THE LODGE."

Proof of the fact that Brother Charles More seconded such resolution will be seen in the minute of "Meeting of the General Committee of this Lodge," held upon the 8th June 1815, which is quoted in pages 31 and 32 of Part II.

Grand Secretary has not ventured to impugn *directly* the clear testimony of Brother Charles More which connects and binds indissolubly the Lodge events of 1815— referring to the memory of Burns—with those of 1787, when the brethren had Burns present with them. Nevertheless, Grand Secretary does impugn by *implication* all such testimony in making his bald, unfounded assertions against "the statements" in my letter of 7th February 1873.

But, it is undeniable, that, unless Grand Secretary can prove that Brother Charles More—whom the brethren delighted to honour throughout so very many years —had ever uttered an untruth, or deceived any person, or conducted himself in any other manner dishonourably, unbecoming a gentleman and a mason, *the testimony given by said Brother* CHARLES MORE on 8th June 1815 above referred to MUST BE ACCEPTED AS TRUE."

Brother Charles More's testimony is of considerable value to Lodge Canongate Kilwinning, and Brother D. Murray Lyon evidently thought so too when he wrote me 11th February 1873, acknowledging receipt of my letter, *vide* Part II., page 61. In that reply of his (which closed the correspondence), he thanked me for "the very full statement" I had made, but asserted that he would "not require to *alter* a single sentence of what" he "had previously written," and pointedly added, "the *report* to which you have twice alluded must certainly have been exaggerated." Nevertheless, on the publication of his History of the Lodge of Edinburgh (Mary's Chapel), No. 1, I found that Brother D. Murray Lyon had embodied *minor items* of information *verbatim et literatim* within the text matter of his book which were supplied to him in my letter of 7th February 1873, while he carefully relegated the *special information* contained in said letter relative to Brother Charles More's important testimony [which had evidently escaped Brother Lyon's notice when making his "minute examination of Canongate Kilwinning's records"], to a laconic footnote in page 334 of his history.

Brother Charles More's testimony to Robert Burns having been Poet Laureate of the Lodge, as above indicated, is conclusive.

2. *In re* BROTHER WILLIAM CAMPBELL.

1787–1801–1849.

Another of the chief statements in my letter of 7th February 1873 is with reference to "Brother William Campbell, Writer to her Majesty's Signet—*that is, an Edinburgh solicitor*"—as is carefully but very inaccurately defined in page 47 of "the printed correspondence," by the Editor of that compilation.

I need not recapitulate the statement here; it will be found in the copy of my letter at page 60 of Part II., lines 4 to 22. Much of my evidence in support of it is given in Part II., page 21, pages 25 to 29, and pages 41 and 21, also in page 49.

Brother Mackenzie's Correspondent of *The Freemason*, in his undated letter reproduced at page 48 of "the printed correspondence," says, regarding Brother William Campbell:—" We are told that he was a travelling companion of the Poet's in 1787, when he was in his *eleventh year!* and that at Auchtertyre, in 1787, he 'spent two of the most happy days!' Is it credible that Burns associated himself with, and made a companion and friend of, a child, and took that child as a companion on the long journey, which, by the way, was made on horseback?"

" But Brother Campbell's statement is contradicted by all the biographers of Burns, who state that he made this journey in company with Dr Adair only; and Brother Mackenzie himself, in his History (page 115), says the same thing. In Dr Adair's own account of it, he states—' Burns *and I* left Edinburgh *together in August 1787.*[*] *We* rode by Linlithgow and Carron to Stirling. *We* visited the ironworks at Carron, with which the Poet was forcibly struck,' and so on. Brother Campbell's name is never mentioned as having accompanied them, nor is his presence at Auchtertyre referred to. The statement that Brother Campbell 'spent two of the most happy days with him' (Burns), shows an intimacy between the two which would have led to some notice having been taken of Campbell by the Poet and Dr Adair in their writings, had such existed; and the expression is not such as would have been used by one who was but a child when the intercourse to which it refers occurred."

The author of that quotation concludes his extraordinary flight of imagination thus :—" If, then, it be untrue that Brother Campbell travelled with the Poet, as the minute of the Lodge states, no reliance can be placed otherwise on his testimony."

What transparent sophistry is that of Brother Allan Mackenzie's Correspondent of The Freemason, *in view of the incontrovertible fact that Brother William Campbell never said* HOW, *or* WHERE, *or* WHEN, *he travelled with Burns!* *Brother Campbell never said that he* TRAVELLED FROM EDINBURGH TO AUCHTERTYRE *with Burns. He never spoke of any journey* ON HORSEBACK *with Burns.*!!

In corroboration of my words, I refer to the minute of meeting held 12th November 1845, page 42 of Part II., wherein it is reported that Brother William Campbell, in seconding the motion with reference to the Inauguration Picture, said of Robert Burns that he (Bro. Campbell) "*had travelled in his company, and spent two of the most happy days with him at Auchtertyre Castle,* the seat of Sir William Murray." That is all that is recorded in the minutes of Canongate Kilwinning, or has been alleged by me, as to Brother William Campbell having travelled with Burns.

---

[*] Such journey of Burns and Dr Adair was not undertaken till October 1787.

Hence we find that the airy argument, and the illusory data upon which it was professedly founded—as quoted from page 48 of "the printed correspondence"—have originated solely from the fertile fancy of Brother Mackenzie's correspondent.

In the endeavour made by Brother Mackenzie's correspondent of *The Freemason* to minimise the obviously valuable testimony of Brother William Campbell, much capital is sought to be made out of the circumstance of him having been in the year 1787 a boy, or, as is said by the correspondent, "a child," of only eleven years of age. He is referred to three times in the above brief quotation as " a child," of course, in order to impress the reader with a due sense of the extreme juvenility of the boy William Campbell, who was one of the company at Auchtertyre during the visit of Robert Burns.

There was about that time another mere boy, called WALTER SCOTT [who cannot be spoken of as a child, although *he was then barely four years older than William Campbell*]. He once met Robert Burns, and, after an interval of forty-three years, wrote thus of him :—*

"I was a lad of fifteen in 1786-7, when he came first to Edinburgh, but had sense and feeling enough to be much interested in his poetry, and would have given the world to know him; but I had very little acquaintance with any literary people, and still less with the gentry of the west country—the two sets that he most frequented. Mr Thomas Grierson was at that time a clerk of my father's. He knew Burns, and promised to ask him to his lodgings to dinner, but had no opportunity to keep his word, otherwise I might have seen more of this distinguished man. As it was, I saw him one day at the late venerable Professor Fergusson's, where there were several gentlemen of literary reputation, among whom I remember the celebrated Mr Dugald Stewart. Of course, we youngsters sat silent, looked, and listened. The only thing I remember which was remarkable in Burns' manner, was the effect produced upon him by a print of Bunbury's representing a soldier lying dead on the snow, his dog sitting in misery on the one side, on the other, his widow, with a child in her arms. These lines were written beneath :—

> " ' Cold on Canadian hills, or Minden's plains,
> Perhaps that parent wept her soldier slain ;
> Bent o'er her babe, her eye dissolved in dew,
> The big drops mingling with the milk he drew,
> Gave the sad presage of his future years,
> The child of misery baptized in tears.'

"Burns seemed much affected by the print, or rather, the ideas which it suggested to his mind. He actually shed tears. He asked whose the lines were, and it chanced that nobody but myself remembered that they occur in a half-forgotten poem of Langhorne's, called by the unpromising title of 'The Justice of the Peace.' I whispered my information to a friend present, who mentioned it to Burns, who rewarded me with a look and a word, which, though of mere civility, I then received, and still recollect, with very great pleasure."

* What is now quoted was written for Lockhart's "Life of Sir Walter Scott."

Part of the above extract appeared in " Life and Works of Robert Burns," by Mr Robert Chambers, second vol., page 57, along with additional matter; from the latter I quote as follows :—

" Sir Adam Ferguson favours me with some particulars of the visit of Burns to his father's house on this occasion. It was the custom of Dr Ferguson to have a conversazione at his house in the Sheens* once a week for his principal literary friends. Professor Stewart on this occasion offered to bring Burns, a proposal to which Dr Ferguson readily assented. The poet found himself amongst the most brilliant literary society which Edinburgh then afforded. Sir Adam thinks that Black, Hutton, and John Home were amongst those present. He had himself brought his young friend WALTER SCOTT, as yet unnoticed by his seniors. Burns seemed at first little inclined to mingle easily in the company; he went about the room, looking at the pictures on the walls. The print described by Scott arrested his attention; he read aloud the lines underneath, but before getting to the end of them his voice faltered and his big black eye filled with tears. A little after, he turned with much interest to the company, pointed to the picture, and with some eagerness asked if any one could tell him who had written those affecting lines. The philosophers were silent; no one knew : but after a decent interval, *the pale lame boy* near by said, in a negligent manner : ' They're written by one Langhorne.' An explanation of the place where they occur followed, and Burns fixed a look of half serious interest on the youth, while he said : ' You'll be a man yet, sir.' Scott may be said to have derived literary ordination from Burns."

'· Somewhere about the very day on which the interview above referred to happened, Francis Jeffrey, then a lad of thirteen, was going up the High Street of Edinburgh, and staring diligently about him, was attracted by the appearance of a man whom he saw standing on the pavement. He was taking a good and attentive view of the object of his curiosity, when some one idling at a shop-door tapped him on the shoulder, and said, ' Ay, laddie, ye may weel look at that man ! That's Robert Burns.'"†

Reverting to the Auchtertyre episode, it is worthy of note that Brother Mackenzie's correspondent,—in his vain efforts to make out Brother William Campbell to have been untruthful,—says in his letter of 12th January 1889—copy of which is in "the printed copy of the correspondence," page 30 :—

" We are told that Brother William Campbell, at a meeting of the Lodge on the 12th November 1845,‡ stated that he had ' had many opportunities of giving testimony in favour of the particulars referred to, that *he had travelled in company with Burns,* and spent two of the most happy days with him at Auchtertyre Castle.'"

" Whether Brother Campbell met Burns as here stated *I have no means of knowing.* Certainly, he did not travel with Burns to Auchtertyre, and Burns, in his letters written from that place and elsewhere, makes no mention of this Brother."

Brother Mackenzie's correspondent, according to the latter paragraph, professes that he had " no means of knowing whether Brother Campbell met Burns :" he ought not to forget that the " means of knowing " were contained in the paragraph which he had just

---

* Sciennes.   † Ex. *The Scottish Nation,* Div. iii. p. 511.   ‡ *Vide* Part II. pp. 42 and 60.

quoted, containing words from the minute of 12th November 1845, setting forth that Brother William Campbell "*had travelled in company with Burns*, and spent two of the most happy days with him at Auchtertyre Castle." The correspondent asserts that Campbell "did not travel with Burns to Auchtertyre." Brother Campbell never said he travelled with Burns to Auchtertyre. He *may* have done so nevertheless, but not necessarily from Edinburgh; and, as to the assertion that "Burns in his letters written from that place, and elsewhere, makes no mention of this Brother"—it goes for absolutely nothing, as is proved by the well-known fact that Robert Burns never mentioned in any of his letters, or other writings, the very memorable and noteworthy incident narrated in the quotations given at pages 15 and 16 *ante*, of his having met "the pale, lame BOY," WALTER SCOTT.

Relative to the bright times of Lodge Canongate Kilwinning comprised within the years 1801, 1802, and 1803, when Brother William Campbell was a prominent office-bearer, it is well to mention a few of the distinguished brethren frequenting the Lodge who were his associates. Among them all he was welcomed and honoured—proved by the fact that, on the first annual election, 24th June 1801, after he became a member he was elected Senior Warden, and, on 24th June 1802, he was further honoured by being again elected to that office.

I shall here only refer to the following brethren as his associates at that period :—*

> HENRY BROUGHAM, Advocate, admitted to the Scottish Bar in the year 1800 ; joined the Lodge a few months before William Campbell was initiated ; practised several years in Edinburgh; removed to London, 1807 ; in 1808 became a barrister in London, and ultimately Lord High Chancellor. Lord Brougham was the second member of Canongate Kilwinning who attained such eminence.
>
> JAMES BROUGHAM, Writer, who had been initiated in 1797, a brother of Henry Brougham.
>
> DR ALEXANDER ADAM, Rector of the High School; author of Roman Antiquities," etc. ; initiated 1771.
>
> DUGALD STEWART, Professor of Mathematics ; initiated 1775, an intimate friend of Burns.
>
> HONOURABLE HENRY ERSKINE, Advocate ; R.W.M., 1780, who introduced Robert Burns to the Lodge, and to the *élite* of Edinburgh Society.
>
> JAMES GREGORY, M.D., Professor of the Practice of Physic in the University of Edinburgh.
>
> JOHN LEYDEN, Poet and Orientalist.
>
> JOHN HORNER, junior, York Place ; E.P.R., April 1802.
>
> AND
>
> LEONARD HORNER, F.R.S., son of Mr John Horner, an Edinburgh merchant, and brother to above-named John Horner, junior, was initiated in Canongate Kilwinning while Brother William Campbell was still Senior

---

* For office-bearers and a few other brethren who were Brother Campbell's associates, *vide* Part II. pages 20 to 29.

Warden. He was at this time an intimate and valued friend of Lord Brougham, as also of all the other brethren above named.

In Cockburn's "Life of Lord Jeffrey" much is said about his friend Leonard Horner, who is therein referred to as "the most enlightened and active of our citizens."

In evidence that Brother Leonard Horner's masonic sympathies were not confined solely to the Canongate Kilwinning, it will be deemed of interest to mention that the Lodge Kirknewton and Ratho, No. 85, have a very handsome Bible in use at the present time, bearing the following inscription:—

To the Lodge
of
KIRKNEWTON AND RATHO,
As a testimony of the regard
Of their loving Brother
LEONARD HORNER,
Elected an Honorary Member
Of their Lodge,
30th September 1803.

As illustrating Leonard Horner's other associations with the above mentioned brethren and other eminent men at this time, it is mentioned in Cockburn's "Life of Jeffrey," that in 1803 a club was started, called "The Friday Club," of literary and social men. "The idea was Walter Scott's," and consisted of Sir Walter Scott, DUGALD STEWART, Sidney Smith, Francis Jeffrey, HENRY BROUGHAM, Francis Horner, M.P. for St. Ives, and his brother LEONARD HORNER.

In Laurie's "History of Freemasonry," page 193, it is recorded that, "At the Quarterly Communication on 4th February 1822, a letter was read from LEONARD HORNER, Esq., Secretary to the Edinburgh School of Arts, thanking the Grand Lodge for the very liberal manner in which they had granted the use of the Hall for the accommodation of that institution."

The work entitled "Cockburn's Memorials" contains statements with regard to the School of Arts, and to LEONARD HORNER having originated or opened that institution in the year 1821, thus—"If not the first, it was certainly the second establishment of the kind in Britain. The whole merit, both of its conception, and of its first three or four years' management, was due to Leonard Horner. His good sense, mildness, and purity made it a favourite with the reasonable of all parties and classes."

"Leonard Horner was Fellow of the Royal Society, President of the Geological Society, London, and for some time Warden of the London University."

Of his literary compositions, the work for which he has been most esteemed is entitled, "Memoirs and Correspondence of Francis Horner, M.P., edited by his brother Leonard Horner, Esq., F.R.S."

One day, in course of a walk that Lord Cockburn had with Leonard Horner on the Pentland Hills, between the two the idea was projected of the Edinburgh Academy. Thereafter they enlisted Sir Walter Scott, Henry Mackenzie, and others into the scheme, and within a few days the sum of £10,000 was subscribed for it. The Academy was opened on 1st October 1824.

The School of Arts, in the year 1851, adopted the title of The Watt Institution and School of Arts, which ultimately developed into the Heriot-Watt College, situate in Chambers' Street. One of the pieces of statuary on the portico of that building is a memorial of George Heriot, the other commemorates LEONARD HORNER.

I have named only a few of the very distinguished men who were associates of Brother WILLIAM CAMPBELL during the eventful and brilliant period of the Lodge's history included in the first three or four years of this century. His companion office-bearers, who were all worthy brethren likewise, are chronicled in pages 28 and 29 of Part II., and still more fully in Appendix.

Brother William Campbell was second son of Sir James Campbell of Aberuchil,* Baronet, whom Robert Burns visited when on one of his Highland tours; was born 1776; admitted a Writer to His Majesty's Signet, 1800; became a full member of Canongate Kilwinning, April 1, 1801; had made such progress in masonry, that the brethren elected him Senior Warden on 24th June same year; re-elected, 1802. Married (1), 5th January 1804, Eliza, daughter of William Hunter, Esq., of Glenormiston; and (2), 25th October 1820, Jane, second daughter of Hugh Cleghorn, Esq., of Stravithie, Fifeshire. He had an honourable career in his profession of almost half a century. He died 28th April 1849.

The foregoing paragraph will doubtless prove interesting and instructive. From it and the previous matter it is seen that Brother William Campbell occupied a prominent position amongst men of the highest honour and integrity, and was much esteemed by them; therefore, unless Grand Secretary can prove that this respected brother ever uttered an untruth, or ever misconducted himself, or behaved otherwise than as a gentleman and a mason, the testimony borne by Brother William Campbell, in 1845, to Robert Burns having been elected and inaugurated Poet Laureate of Lodge Canongate Kilwinning, MUST BE ACCEPTED AS TRUE.

---

3. *In re* BROTHER WILLIAM PETRIE.
1787-1845.

The statement made in my letter to Brother D. Murray Lyon in 1873, relative to Brother William Petrie, appears in copy of the letter, at page 60 of Part II.; it is brief, and had better be quoted here :—

"I have had conversation on this matter" (the Laureateship) "with a distinguished member of the Canongate Kilwinning, who has been connected with it for more than five-and-thirty years, and who stands high in the craft" [this brother, as explained in a footnote, was Past Master Dr Samuel Somerville of Ampherlaw.] "He knew *Brother William Petrie* of our Lodge, who had been *present* at the inauguration of Burns as Poet Laureate, and has heard from his lips many very interesting reminiscences of the Poet, and of events which had occurred in the Lodge when there in company with him."

Past Master Samuel Somerville of Ampherlaw, M.D., who, in 1873 and onwards,

---

* Aberuchil, in Strathearn, Perthshire, is distant only a few miles west from Auchtertyre, where Burns stayed two days.

communicated such information on repeated occasions to me regarding Brother William Petrie, was a highly esteemed and influential member of the craft. Not only had he a long-continued and loyal association with Lodge Canongate Kilwinning, through several of the chief offices to that of Right Worshipful Master, but, for years he was First Principal of the Canongate Kilwinning Royal Arch Chapter, for years held prominent offices in the Supreme R.A. Chapter, and took much interest in the Temple Priory of the Lothians, of which he was a distinguished member, as well as of other masonic Orders. He began his masonic career, October 14, 1840, in the Lodge Canongate Kilwinning, and very many brethren of this and other Lodges and Orders have to this day pleasant recollections of him. Past Master Somerville had been an intimate friend of Brother William Campbell, W.S., who had spent two days with Burns at Auchtertyre. Past Master Somerville was present at the Canongate Kilwinning Lodge meeting along with all the other chief office-bearers, on 12th November 1845, when Brother William Campbell seconded the motion for having the Inauguration Picture painted.

It was this worthy Past Master Somerville who communicated to me, in the year 1873, the information which I gave regarding William Petrie, in my letter of 7th February that year. No person *at that time* would have thought of doubting Dr Somerville's word. *He is now dead;* and the bald, unsupported assertion, to the effect that the "statement" concerning Brother William Petrie is "unfounded," does not come at this late period with a very good grace.

I distinctly and emphatically re-affirm the statement made in my letter, dated 7th February 1873, regarding brother William Petrie, which was acknowledged, along with the other matter communicated, in the following words of Brother D. Murray Lyon's letter to me, dated 11th February 1873:—"I recognise the satisfactory nature of the evidence you have submitted, and shall have pleasure in giving effect to it in my forthcoming work."

Why did Brother D. Murray Lyon not object to Past Master Somerville's testimony while that worthy brother was alive?

The testimony given on this subject by the late Past Master Samuel Somerville, which I reported to Brother D. Murray Lyon in 1873, and now re-affirm, was, in its main features, set forth very clearly by Brother James Marshall in his "Winter with Robert Burns." At page 91 of that valuable memorial of the Inauguration, we are informed that the compiler visited Brother William Petrie in November 1845, accompanied by Brother Stewart Watson, the artist of the Inauguration Picture. Brother Watson remarked that "he" (Brother Petrie) "would remember Robert Burns? The name operated like electricity;" . . . "and he reiterated—Rabbie Burns! mind Rabbie! I'll no forget him, puir fallow! Eh, but he *was* the life o' the Lodge."

More details of this interesting interview will be found in Part II., page 50.

Brother Mackenzie's correspondent of *The Freemason* made a great mistake in attempting to disparage, or in affecting to discredit, the matter he found at page 121 of Brother Mackenzie's History of Lodge Canongate Kilwinning, containing a special reference to Brother William Petrie, as it had appeared in my letter of 7th February 1873. The correspondent would have done wisely had he left the matter alone, but, in his letter dated 15th October 1889, as may be seen at page 65 of "the printed correspondence," he quotes the statement of Brother Samuel Somerville of Ampherlaw from my letter, and goes on to argue from it as follows:—

"This statement, if true, would be conclusive of the question, for it expressly states that Petrie witnessed the act of inauguration! But, like every other statement made in support of this contention, it does not bear the test of investigation. The statement was originally made in 1873, in a letter to Brother David Murray Lyon, by Brother H. C. Peacock, who was then, and for several years subsequently, Secretary of the Lodge Canongate Kilwinning, and custodian of its records. Coming from such a source, it was accepted without inquiry as correct, and MISLED OUR EMINENT HISTORIAN."

"Brother Peacock appears to have made the statement without the slightest inquiry, for Brother William Petrie was not, as he stated, a member of the Lodge Canongate Kilwinning in 1787. He is neither recorded as such in the books of the Lodge nor in the register of its members in Grand Lodge."

At this point in the quotation from the letter of Brother Mackenzie's correspondent I must protest against such loose assertions. I never alleged that Brother William Petrie was a member of the Lodge Canongate Kilwinning in 1787. The words of that portion of my letter can be seen at page 60 of Part II. I refer therein to "*Brother William Petrie* of our Lodge, who had been *present* at the Inauguration of "Burns as Poet Laureate." Brother William Petrie was most assuredly "*of our Lodge,*" because,—without taking into consideration Brother James Marshall's statement in 1845, at page 91 of "A Winter with Burns," regarding "William Petrie, who was initiated during 1787, and had acted as *serving brother* and as *tiler* to this and other Lodges during the greater part of the intervening period," he had most certainly been "*of our Lodge,*" for the reason which I prove—that William Petrie and Robert Stewart were tylers to Lodge Canongate Kilwinning from the year 1835 to 1845. The evidence of this is beyond all possibility of truthful contradiction. I refer to the chart of office-bearers in Appendix for abundant proof of it with details. Any one who desires further satisfaction will find it in the Lodge records. It is possible that Petrie may have been only a "visiting brother" when he attended the various meetings in 1786-87 at which Robert Burns was present; but it is quite probable that he may have been even then a member of the Lodge—I cannot say. Some quidnunc might tell me that James Marshall did not state distinctly that Petrie was "initiated during 1787" in the Lodge Canongate Kilwinning. I have nothing to do with that. On this question it is clear that the historian of the Lodge of Edinburgh (Mary's Chapel), and the indefatigable Past Master of that Lodge, who claims to have helped him in the history, have signally failed to prove that this statement of mine relative to William Petrie is "unfounded."

The bold assertion made by Brother Mackenzie's correspondent, to the effect that Brother William Petrie is neither recorded as a member of Canongate Kilwinning "in "the books of the Lodge nor in the register of its members in Grand Lodge," is worthy of no consideration. Everybody knows the laxity with which entries were made in the minute books of Lodges during last century. Most of us in Canongate Kilwinning know that fifteen of our Right Worshipful Masters do not appear at all in the records as to when they were admitted members of the Lodge. Yet, there can be no doubt that they must have been duly E.P. and R., or duly affiliated from some other Lodge, otherwise they could never have been promoted to the chair of Canongate Kilwinning. What, then, may we not assume as the fact regarding Brother William Petrie, seeing we have only in the minute-books the bare record of him as Tyler during the years 1835 to 1845, while we have reliable independent testimony from two sources that he was present in the Lodge at meetings during the year 1787? Brother James Marshall, who was personally well acquainted with William Petrie in the year 1845, vouched for him as having been "initiated during 1787." I leave that evidence as I find it in the "Winter with Robert Burns," and, despite the correspondent's over-confident assertions to the contrary, claim Brother William Petrie as having been a member of Lodge Canongate Kilwinning, simply from the fact just stated, that in the records he appears year by year, from 1835 to 1845, appointed one of the Tylers of Canongate Kilwinning. Evidence of his election as one of the Tylers on 24th June 1835 will be seen at page 40 of Part II. Before me, while I write, are the accounts of the Lodge Treasurer for the period ·19th July 1839 to 15th June 1840; and, under the heads of "Discharge, Branch IX," "Tyler's Salaries," I find the following items, proving, *independently of the minutes*, Petrie's connection with the Lodge:—

"1839.
"Dec. 27. Paid Wm. Petrie half-year's salary to Christmas . £1 10 0
"1840.
"Jany. 31. Paid R. Stewart half-year's salary to do. . 4 4 0
"June 12. Paid do half-year's do. to 24th inst. . . 4 4 0
" ,, Paid Wm. Petrie do. do. to do. . . 1 10 0
"Sum . ————£11 8 c."

As already stated, the earliest record in the minutes of William Petrie having been one of the Tylers of the Lodge is 24th June 1835, but there is every reason for believing that he must have been admitted a member of the Lodge long before that period in regular form, and was frequent at Canongate Kilwinning meetings.

Nevertheless, William Petrie does not appear recorded as a member, which circumstance leads me to conclude that Brother James Marshall may be quite correct in the statement occurring at page 91 of the "Winter with Robert Burns," to the effect that "he, after the remit in November 1845, visited *William Petrie, who was initiated during* "1787, and had acted as serving brother and *tiler* to this *and other lodges* during the "greater part of the intervening period." Although William Petrie does not appear on record as one of the entrants or affiliates of the year 1787, that is not surprising after what is learned in these papers of the lamentable neglect of Canongate Kilwinning records during the years 1786, 1787, and 1788.

Incidentally, in looking over one of the Lodge accounts of the year 1835, I find the following interesting items:—

"1835. Feb. 6. Paid *Wm. Petrie* to get a white neckcloth, . 0 1 0
" ,,   ,, Paid for pair of Shoes and Buckles for Tyler, . 0 9 6."

This extract from the records shows that William Petrie was connected with the Lodge *prior* to the date when he was first recorded as being appointed Tyler.

Doubtless, if I could devote the time and attention required to exhume more items such as these from old accounts, old letters, and other material among the archives of the Lodge, much valuable information could be derived on this matter, which no amount of careful scrutiny poring over the *minute books*, upon which our two controversialists affect to rely so much, would ever reveal.

Past Master Sam. Somerville of Ampherlaw, M.D., who frequently in the year 1873 informed me of William Petrie's reminiscences of Lodge events which occurred last century, and especially of his having been present on occasion of the Inauguration in 1787,—was very regular in attendance at meetings of Canongate Kilwinning for several years before Brother William Petrie died (1845), and therefore had many special opportunities of acquiring information from him about old times in the Lodge.

At page 66 of "the printed correspondence," Brother Mackenzie's disputant goes on to say, with reference to Brother William Petrie in 1787, as follows :—

" He was then a mere youth in humble circumstances. He was *a* TAILOR *by trade*, and he never rose in it, *in so far as I have been able to discover*, above the rank of *a journeyman or operative.* *His social circumstances were very different from those* (sic) *who formed the membership of the Lodge Canongate Kilwinning.* They were all (?) men of high social and professional position, and most unlikely to identify their associations and surroundings with a youth of Petrie's stamp."

The above much exaggerated affirmation—so very confidently made—as to the "high social and professional position " of *all* the brethren of 1787, is not likely to be favourably appreciated by the brethren of "*professional position*," or even by any brethren who may perchance have *patrician* sympathies in the Lodge Canongate Kilwinning of the present day.

Such a style of composition as I have now quoted was very different from that of Robert Burns! His style, when descanting on such a theme, was this :—

"The honest man, though e'er so poor,
Is king o' men for a' that."

Past Master Somerville, of Ampherlaw, Past Master Thomas Drybrough, and other old members of the Lodge, who had known William Petrie well, placed implicit reliance in his statements relative to Robert Burns and old times in the Canongate Kilwinning ; also, Brother Stewart Watson, who painted the inauguration picture, and Brother James Marshall, who wrote " A Winter with Robert Burns," had likewise implicit faith in the words of William Petrie, as uttered by him in course of their interview, described at page 20 *ante*, otherwise the narrative of that interview would not have appeared in the " Winter with Robert Burns."

Therefore, until it can be proved that William Petrie was not a truthful or not an honest man, I claim that his statements,—as reported by Brother James Marshall and Past Master Somerville,—must be accepted as true in every particular.

I have proved throughout these pages that the strictures indulged in by Brother

Mackenzie's correspondent regarding William Petrie are absolutely "unfounded," so far, at least, as the reference to his association with Canongate Kilwinning is concerned.

In contrast to the correspondent's vain and unworthy attempt to undervalue Bro. William Petrie, and to disparage the obvious worth of his testimony—merely because it so happened that he was "A TAILOR by trade, and he never rose in it,—in so far as *I* [Bro. Mackenzie's correspondent] have been able to discover—above the rank of a journeyman or operative," the following quotation from a valuable address which was delivered in Lodge "Quatuor Coronati," 2076 E. C., 4th March 1892, by Brother Sir Benjamin Ward Richardson, M.D., etc., etc., on "The Masonic Genius of Robert Burns," deserves special notice :—

"Robert Burns was in the twenty-third year of his age, and living with his father at the farm of Lochlea, in the parish of Tarbolton, when, on the 4th July 1781, he was entered an apprentice in the Lodge St. David, Tarbolton."

*   *   *   *   *   *   *

"The brother who had the honour of thus ushering into the light of masonry our illustrious brother was one Alexander Wood, a TAILOR, of Tarbolton, and, on the 1st of October of the same year, Burns was passed and raised." *

It may be safely averred that Robert Burns never was, and never aspired to be, one of the "men of high social and professional position," "most unlikely to identify their associations and surroundings with a youth of Petrie's stamp."

Reverting to page 66 of "the printed correspondence," I continue the quotation thus :—

"Brother Murray Lyon has very kindly, at my request, been at pains to examine the registers of Grand Lodge from 1736, the date of the institution of Grand Lodge, for many years downwards, and he has failed to find that Petrie was a member of any Lodge within the Edinburgh district within the period of his search."

That laborious task, said to have been performed by Brother Murray Lyon, seems to have been quite an extravagant work of supererogation, because Brother Mackenzie's correspondent asserts that Petrie's age is "ascertained as having been twenty-one in 1787, the date of Burns' alleged inauguration." Why then should Brother Murray Lyon have " been at pains to examine the registers of Grand Lodge *from* 1736"—*thirty years before William Petrie was born?*

The reference in "the printed correspondence," p. 67, to William Petrie's age, is as follows :—

"Petrie's age is thus ascertained as having been twenty-one in 1787, the date of Burns' alleged inauguration, at which he is said to have been present. Now, although so young a man, it was perfectly possible, but I think unlikely, that he was then a member of the craft. The History of the Lodge, however, sets forth that he was 'of *our* Lodge,' and 'had been *present* at the inauguration of Burns as Poet Laureate,'— *that is, that he was a member of the Lodge Canongate Kilwinning in* 1787. This vital statement is shown by the Lodge's records, and other circumstances, to be incorrect."

Those assertions are very obviously wrong, and the conclusions deduced from

---

* This event is narrated also in the "Life and Works of Robert Burns," by Mr R. Chambers.

them are most unwise and irrational. In my letter of 7th February 1873, I said that William Petrie was "*of our* Lodge." I repeat the statement, and have proved it. I *never* said that he was a member of Canongate Kilwinning in 1787. He *may* have been a member notwithstanding. He did not need to be a member to have been present at the inauguration.

Continuing the quotation from page 67 of "the printed correspondence," we are told :—

"If Brother Petrie was ever a member of Lodge Canongate Kilwinning, of which there is no evidence (?)," "his intimate acquaintance with that Lodge, if it ever existed, had ceased for many years prior to his death (?)."

At this point I suspend quoting further on purpose to contradict, as I do most emphatically, the *unauthorised assertions* by Brother Mackenzie's correspondent that there is *no* evidence of William Petrie having been a member of Canongate Kilwinning, and that if he had been, "his intimate acquaintance with that Lodge had ceased for *many years prior to his death.*"

I have proved that William Petrie was one of the Tylers of Canongate Kilwinning till 24th June 1845,—within a few months of his death.

I continue the quotation from previous paragraph, thus :—"for he held the humble office of Outer Guard—or Tyler—of the Lodge of Edinburgh for the long period of eighteen years, from December 1827 until his death in December 1845 ;—it being thus shown that the fundamental statement that Petrie was a member of the Lodge Canongate Kilwinning *when Burns visited it and was inaugurated as its Poet Laureate*, is untrue, the whole story, in so far at least as Petrie is concerned, is discredited, and falls to the ground." (!)

I have established all that is stated in my letter of 7th February 1873 relative to William Petrie having been a member "of *our* Lodge," and to his having been present at the inauguration of Burns as Poet Laureate.

4. *In re* THE EXTREME BREVITY OF CANONGATE KILWINNING MINUTES PRIOR TO THE YEAR 1789.

The statement made in my letter of 7th February 1873 regarding the extreme brevity of the Minutes during many years of last century will be found at page 60 of Part II., and need not be quoted here.

The remarks in that part of my letter are well supported by the testimony of Brother D. Murray Lyon in his excellent History of the Lodge of Edinburgh (Mary's Chapel) ;—in page 333 he says :—

"Our statement regarding what appears in the Minutes" [of Lodge Canongate Kilwinning] "on the subject of the Laureateship is founded upon a *personal* examination of the minute-book. But while deeming it proper to give the result of that examination, it is equally right that we should state that *the commonly received report of the circumstances connected with the Inauguration has never been discredited.* The Lodge Canongate Kilwinning is not singular in the omission from its records of facts which

e

have come to be regarded as interesting features in its history. *Its minutes at and for many years prior to the period of Burns's attendance at its communications are brief to a degree; and this may account for the infrequency of their allusions to Burns,* who was not then the distinguished poet he afterwards became. It was only after his death that Robert Burns and his works were esteemed at their proper value, and only after many years that his memory was regarded with anything like the veneration accorded to it now."

Another masonic author, in the year 1880,—who published an ably-written sketch of the chequered career of a well-known old lodge,—while endeavouring " to recall a few facts relative to its early history," said as follows :—

" The materials for such a purpose are unfortunately scarce, and those which exist are brief. *It is, indeed, questionable if Masonic Lodges two centuries ago, and down to a comparatively recent date, kept any record of their proceedings* IN THE SENSE OF THE MODERN MINUTE-BOOK, and it is clear that *if they did, it was not with very scrupulous care,* either as to their completeness or their preservation."

This same grievance of defective minutes had been similarly dealt with three years previously in the second of two lectures * which I delivered in connection with the Festival held 20th December 1877, commemorative of the bi-centenary of Lodge Canongate Kilwinning. I quote the following passages from that second lecture :—

" As we advance in the second century (1810 and onwards) of Canongate Kilwinning, there is observable over a very extended period, in the Minute-books, a marked improvement in recording the minutes; they are of greater length, more liberal in details, superior in penmanship and composition. Each Secretary in turn, for the time being, *appears to have been thoroughly impressed with the fact that he was writing the history of the Lodge,* and seems to have done his duty with rigid scrupulousness."† . . . "They (the minutes) stand forth in singular and instructive contrast to the curious laconism of *eighteen words* (sometimes less) which occurs so frequently as the record of a meeting *during the previous generation.*"

In evidence of the absolute truth of what is affirmed in those three quotations, on the brevity of Lodge minutes *prior " to a comparatively recent date,"* I quote the following instances *verbatim* from the minute books of Lodge Canongate Kilwinning :—

[29 words.] "EDINB^{R.} 5 *June* 1777

" The Lodge met this Evening agreeable to the above adjournment and was properly constituted—After *having gone thro' their usual business* the Lodge was adjourned to the 24 Current.

[What business?]

---

* One of these lectures, delivered shortly previous to the bi-centenary night, was on " The First Century of Lodge Canongate Kilwinning "; the other was on " The Second Century of Lodge Canongate Kilwinning," delivered shortly after that occasion. Lectures were given by other members, one each monthly meeting. The session was extended a month earlier and a month later than the usual period of November to April. A musical evening began the course, and, so far as I can remember, a musical evening closed it.

† *Ex gr.,* Bro. Taylor's compositions in 1815. *Vide* Part II. pp. 30, 31, and 32.

[19 words.]   "St John's Chapel.   6 *July* 1780

"The Lodge being duly constituted *& the usual business being done* was adjourned to the first Wednesday of August."

———

[16 words.]   "6 *Sept.* 1780

"The Lodge duly constituted *& the usual business over* they adjourned to their next monthly meeting."

———

[16 words.]   "4 *Oct.* 1780

"The Lodge was constituted *& the business ended as usual* adjourned to their next monthly meeting."

———

[17 words.]   "6 *Febry* 1782

"The Lodge having met *& the business being finished* it was adjourned to the next monthly meeting."

———

[18 words.]   "6 *Novem.* 1782

"The Lodge having met *& the usual business being finished* it was adjourned to the next monthly meeting."

———

[18 words.]   "4 *Decem.* 1782

"The Lodge having met *& the usual business being finished* it was adjourned to the next monthly meeting."

———

[24 words.]   "October 2nd, 1783

"The Lodge having met and being duly constituted *and having gone through the usual business* it was adjourned to the first Thursday of November."

———

[25 words.]   "Nov. 5, 1783

"The Lodge having met and being duly constituted *and having gone through the usual business* it was adjourned to the first Thursday of next month."

———

[30 words.]   "7 *Oct.* 1784

"The Lodge having met Brother Darling was elected Grand Steward for the year ensuing *& the other business of the Lodge being finished* it was adjourned till Thursday 11th November."   "Chas. More, D.M."

Those quotations may be deemed enough of *one* kind; therefore I pass on.

From the extraordinary similarity of the laconic minutes above quoted, it seems as if a printed form would have been specially useful in saving an indolent or incompetent secretary the seemingly great trouble of writing much more than the date heading;—but it shows that the secretary of those times was simply following the example of the high authority set forth in the pages of his own minute-books by the minute engrossed therein on behalf of Grand Lodge recording a visitation. The formula rigidly followed on such occasions is facetiously and truthfully described by Brother James Marshall at page 67 of "A Winter with Robert Burns," [and is referred to by Brother Mackenzie's disputant of *The Freemason* in his undated letter at page 45 of "the printed correspondence"] thus:—" It was the duty of the Grand Secretary and Grand Clerk of Grand Lodge to accompany the Grand Master in Visitations of Lodges, and on those occasions 'to insert in the books of the Lodge visited a minute of the fact, and this they did as if they copied it from a *style-book* in a regular *stick-to-the-form* manner.' Hence, you may "*witness our hand*" for a series of years in every Edinburgh Lodge, whoever was Grand Master, or whoever were present, or whatsoever were the sayings or doings or occurrences of the night.'"

The word *business* stands prominently in each of the brief minutes now quoted as an unmeaning term, as signifying anything or nothing, *perhaps* comprehending a great deal, *but* perhaps comprehending nothing. No doubt, several plausible interpretations may be put upon the word. Certainly, it is surprising that men of business habits, who had occasion to write the minutes of those times, could have so expressed themselves, or could have continued using the stereotyped phrase in which the word "business" predominates, and is so misapplied. Hence do I say that the phrase introduced by an indolent and incompetent secretary, as a conclusion to the minute of 1st March 1787 — "No other *business* being before the meeting the Lodge adjourned"—*has no special signification;* it is of no value whatever to Grand Secretary in his vain endeavour to prove a negative by claiming, as he does, such statement as evidence that the election and inauguration of Poet Laureate *did not* take place on that date. All the preceding matter of the minute is a brief report—in the usual hackneyed phraseology—of members initiated, passed, and raised "since last meeting." That was professedly all the *business* before the meeting. There was "*no other* business." In the estimation of the model [?] Lodge Secretary of that time,[*] the inauguration of Robert Burns as Poet Laureate was an event altogether *outside* the routine work or "business" of registering the names of new members (which, apparently, he considered was all the "business" needful to be recorded), and was no more needing to be mentioned in the minutes than any of the other notable, social, and convivial events which were continually occurring during that very lively period of the Lodge's history.

Quite akin to this branch of the subject are the following extracts from other records of those times, and these afford further evidence of the singular laxity that existed in the mode of recording minutes of Lodge Canongate Kilwinning during the period now under notice.

Extract from Minute—[concluding Paragraph and Postscript.]

"St. John's Chapel, 5 *Decem.* 1781.

*   *   *   *   *   *

"The Lodge *was closed* with the proper ceremonies & adjourned to the first Wednesday of January next.

> James Hamilton, M., *p.t.*
> Chas. More, S.W., *p.t.*
> Robert Hope, J.W., *p.t.*

"*Thereafter, before closing the Lodge,* Brother Thos. Brodie, of the Lodge of St. Luke, was assumed a member of this Lodge."

---

[*] The model [?] Lodge Secretary of 1787 was the "practising solicitor" who comes in for so much unfounded laudation at page 33 of "the printed correspondence."

The worthy brother who composed this postscript, which exhibits such a very amusing contradiction in terms, was quite a prototype of the Canongate Kilwinning Secretary who recorded the minute of 1st March 1787, and, like him, would also have ignored the Inauguration of Robert Burns as not being "business."

Copy of Minute—[complete in 49 words.]

"St John's Chapel 21st Augt. 1783

"The Lodge having met and being duly constituted the following Gentlemen vizt. Jas. Fortescue Esq, Mr. R. Wilson, and Lieut. McKenzie were all entered app^{ces} and paid their dues to the Treasurer."

Here occurs a considerable blank space in the minute; after which comes the final paragraph, as follows :—

" *The usual business* of the Lodge being done it was adjourned to the first Wednesday of October.

"Thomas Hay, M."

What was the usual business?
In the original minute, the word "October" is written over the word "November."

Extract from Minute—[concluding Paragraph and Postscript.]

"St. John's Chapel 5 *Feb.* 1789

•   •   •   •   •   •   •   •

"The Lodge was visited on this occasion by several brethren from the different Lodges in this City & particularly by Brother Symes, Master of the Mary's Chapel.

"Robert Moir Secry

"Will Dunbar M.

"Henry Jardine

"N.B.—At this meeting Brother Adair presented the Lodge with a new sword to be used at entering Brothers which was accepted with thanks."

This is an exceedingly apt illustration of the positive indifference which existed during last century to matters being recorded in the minutes, which, *now-a-days*, would at once be included in the regular " *business* " of a Lodge meeting.

Brother Adair himself, however, was quite wide-awake to the need of keeping the Secretary up to his work, and made it understood that his gift to the Lodge should have been recorded in due form as part of the evening's business—hence the " N.B."

5. *In re* The Testimony Recorded in the Work entitled "A Winter with Robert Burns," regarding Lodge Events of 1786-7, "was widely circulated, and never contradicted."

The above heading is a very brief *résumé* of one of the statements contained in my 1873 letter. The full text will be found in Part II., page 58, first and second paragraphs. I adduce the following facts in support of the statement:—

On 24th June 1802, the approval by Committee, and "the approbation of the Brethern," expressed with regard to the framed print—which had been "got for the Lodge"—of "Robert Burns the Scottish Bard, Poet Laureat, Lodge No. 2 Cannongate Kilwinning," were transactions not done in a corner. The membership at that special time was large and influential ; the meetings of the Lodge were frequent, and the attendance was usually very numerous,—many visiting brethren from other Lodges here and in distant lands being among the company,—as is testified by the records : therefore, that quaint-looking framed print was very well known among the Craft *then*, bearing the above-quoted inscription in large characters upon it. It has been prominently displayed in the Lodge-room for very nearly a century, and the truth of that inscription has never been called in question by any one of the very many thousands of members and visiting brethren who have seen it during that long period.

In the year 1815 the lists for subscriptions to the mausoleum fund were distributed throughout the brotherhood of Lodge Canongate Kilwinning, *because* of "*the Lamented Bard,* Robert Burns," having been "*a member and* Poet Laureat of this Lodge." Those subscription-lists were specially directed to be presented *to* "*every member*" of the Lodge, as the records testify. Such instruction was carried out, and every publicity was given to the object for which the subscriptions were being collected ;—and the fact was thereby proclaimed far and wide that Robert Burns had been Poet Laureate to the Lodge,—such "Subscription, in order to contribute towards the erection of that work [the mausoleum], being the only manner in which they [the brethren] can testify their respect for the Memory of a *Public Character so immediately connected with them,* and who, *on so many occasions,* contributed so generally to the harmony of the Masonic Order, *and to that of the Lodge Canongate Kilwinning in particular.*" * Assuredly, such testimony as to the Laureateship which was published with those subscription-lists "*was widely circulated, and never contradicted.*"

In the year 1835, when James Hogg was elected successor to Robert Burns in the Laureateship, and when, three years later, a committee of highly influential brethren of the Lodge was formed on purpose to glean materials for a history of the Canongate Kilwinning, not a word was uttered against the fact of Robert Burns having been Poet Laureate.

In 1845, when a picture of the Inauguration of Robert Burns was proposed to be painted, "authenticated particulars" relating to the Inauguration were asked for on occasion of the Lodge meeting held 12th November. The whole question was

---

* Extract from Minute, 9th February 1815, Part II., page 30.

discussed at that meeting and at the following one, when the said authenticated particulars were produced. These particulars had been so satisfactory that the R.W. Master himself seconded the motion, and it was "unanimously carried," empowering Brother Stewart Watson to proceed with the painting. The result was the production of that magnificent and justly-celebrated picture of the Inauguration, which for the past thirty-one years has been on view in the Board-room of Grand Lodge. Throughout this period, no brother mason, and no one else, has ever recorded a doubt regarding the Inauguration.

Grand Secretary, in his newly-conceived opinions regarding Robert Burns and the Laureateship, does not appear to have considered that if the election and inauguration of Robert Burns never took place, or if there had ever existed any doubt on the subject during the early years of this century, there were always on the alert a few brethren sufficiently fond of a little lively discussion to have caught hold of any such suggestion, and to have made themselves heard regarding it,—but no one ever raised such a question.

There is evidence in the minute books, and in letters possessed by the Lodge, proving that throughout the first and second decades of this century several events occurred which disturbed the usual harmony of Can. Kil. Especially was this the case during the period from 1807, when the secession differences of Canongate Kilwinning and sister Lodges in Edinburgh with Grand Lodge began, till these were smoothed down. As one instance during that period, I may mention that, on 24th June, 1809, on a motion by Past Master ALEXANDER JAFFRAY, upwards of *seventeen* brethren were visited with masonic censure "until they make satisfactory apologies for their conduct," for having "on many occasions behaved in a disrespectful manner towards this Lodge."

A few other curious and unwelcome events occurred during those times, as appears by the minute books, letters, and other records still extant. On 3rd April 1817 one brother was "expelled the Lodge" for his "unmasonic conduct," and others suspended from masonic privileges for a time.

Several of those occurrences took place while the lists were being circulated for subscriptions to the mausoleum fund, and while the money was being collected in the years 1815, 1816, and 1817, yet not an objection had ever been heard of, and not a word was ever recorded against the universally-accepted fact that Robert Burns had been Poet Laureate of Lodge Canongate Kilwinning.

I bring forward those unpleasant narrations merely as aids to illustrating one special fact, namely,—that, during the early years of this century, *when there were very many living witnesses of Lodge events which had occurred during the Burns period* to refer to,—had there been the slightest room for doubt of the Laureateship of Burns, it is very certain that some industrious, well-meaning member, and his seconder, would have discovered it to be their duty to put a motion on record for an enquiry into the question of the Laureateship. In such case, the matter would assuredly have been discussed and recorded ; but no such business has ever appeared on any of the minute books of Lodge Canongate Kilwinning.

Past Master Alexander Jaffray, above mentioned, along with his intimate friends, Brothers Charles More, William Ballantyne, and Alexander L. Robertson, took very active part in promoting the subscription towards fund for erection of the mausoleum to the memory of Robert Burns in the years 1815 and 1816, because Robert Burns had been Poet Laureate of Lodge Canongate Kilwinning.

Those brethren, and their connecting links and associations with the present time, form a strong chain of interesting and conclusive evidence in favour of the main fact set forth in " A Winter with Robert Burns," thus :—

Past Master ALEXANDER JAFFRAY, Advocate, 1795 to 1820,* was initiated while the Poet was yet alive, and on same night as Brother Robert Moir, W.S., was installed R.W.M. of Can. Kil. Said Brother Robert Moir had been initiated 1st Feb. 1787, same evening the Poet was affiliated ; the last trace of him in the records is in 1806.

Brother CHARLES MORE, of the Royal Bank, 1769 to 1818, was Depute Master when Robert Burns visited the Can. Kil. in 1786 and 1787. He took part in all the lodge events of that time ; appears to have attended every meeting ; and was on Committee from then till 1817. *Vide* page 12, *ante.*

Brother WILLIAM BALLANTYNE, W.S., 1799 to 1819, was re-elected Depute Master 24th June 1802, when Brother William Campbell, W.S., was re-elected Senior Warden, and when the framed print of Robert Burns as " Poet Laureat of the Lodge" met with "the approbation of the Brethern."

Brother WILLIAM CAMPBELL, Writer to the Signet, 1801 to 1849, son of Sir James Campbell, Baronet of Aberuchil, Perthshire, whom Burns visited. Brother William Campbell spent two of his "most happy days " with Robert Burns at Auchtertyre, the seat of Sir William Murray, Baronet, and, at Lodge meeting on 12th November 1845, Brother Campbell seconded motion for painting Inauguration picture. *Vide* page 14, *ante.*

Past Master ALEXANDER LAMBE ROBERTSON, Writer to the Signet, 1814 to 1863, was R.W.M. from June 1819 to June 1830, and again from June 1860 to June 1862 ; he was elected a member of Committee 24th June 1835, when James Hogg, the Ettrick Shepherd, was elected Poet Laureate in succession to Robert Burns. Past Master Alex. L. Robertson was an intimate friend and associate of Past Master Alex. M'Neil, Past Master Sam. Somerville of Ampherlaw ; Past Master W. N. Fraser of Tornaveen ; Past Master Thomas Drybrough, and Brother Thomas Elder MacRitchie.

Past Master ALEXANDER M'NEIL, Advocate [not recorded], 1824 to 1855.

Past Master SAMUEL SOMERVILLE, of Ampherlaw, M.D., 1840 to 1876. He was present as Immediate Past Master, along with the R.W.M. and other office-bearers, at meeting of 12th November 1845, when Brother William Campbell seconded the motion approving of the Inauguration picture being painted.

Brother WILLIAM PETRIE, 1787 to 1845. *Vide* page 19, *ante.*

---

* The two years noted immediately after each name, indicate the brother's masonic career.

Brother Thomas Elder MacRitchie, of Craigton and Dunork, W.S., 1818 to
1875, was on the Lodge Committee along with Past Masters Sam. Somerville, W. N. Fraser, and Thomas Drybrough, when, as Secretary to the
Lodge, I wrote, with their approval, the letter dated 7th February 1873, to
Brother D. M. Lyon, the statements in which are now being substantiated.

Brother Stewart Watson, Portrait Painter, 1828 to 1870. *Vide* Part II.,
page 48.

Past Master Thomas Drybrough, 1843 to the present time. *Vide* Part II.,
page 54.

Past Master William N. Fraser, of Findrack and Tornaveen, 1849 to the
present time. *Vide* Part II., page 53.

The above series of names presents the question, as it were, in a nutshell. Each
of the brethren has testified to the Laureateship and Inauguration of Robert Burns, and
each was more or less constantly in touch with the others, according to the duration of
his masonic life, as indicated by the years noted immediately after each name; all which
is proved by the notes and other references given.

Therefore, having all these facts on record, it is safely affirmed that the testimony
afforded in the work entitled, " A Winter with Robert Burns," and by the brethren who
gave their evidence in 1845, WAS WIDELY CIRCULATED AND NEVER CONTRADICTED.

---

6. *In re* "It would be palpably wrong to suppose," "that the men of acknow-
LEDGED WORTH AND STATUS IN SOCIETY," WHO, AT THE MEETINGS HELD 9TH
FEBRUARY AND 8TH JUNE 1815, TESTIFIED TO ROBERT BURNS HAVING BEEN
"POET LAUREAT OF THIS LODGE," HAD BECOME FOR THOSE OCCASIONS "MOST
UNSCRUPULOUS AND UNTRUTHFUL."

The statement, of which the above is a brief rendering, appears at pages 58 and
59 of Part II., as it was given in my letter of 7th February 1873.

Part of the letter written by Brother Allan Mackenzie to *The Freemason*, on 4th
March 1889,[*] specially merits reproduction now, by reason of his appropriate remarks
on this branch of the subject, and because of the significant reply given to it, which
reply also I shall now reproduce.

Brother Mackenzie—having quoted in his letter the paragraph from Lodge
minute of 12th November 1845, containing the words used by Brother William
Campbell, Writer to the Signet, when he (Brother Campbell) seconded the motion in
favour of having a picture of the Inauguration painted—goes on to say:—

" And this is a specimen of the testimony which is characterised as 'baseless
assertions.' Besides, he [Bro. Mackenzie's controversialist in *The Freemason*] virtually
asserts that all the correspondence which was carried on between men occupying the
highest legal status in society at and before 1815, and all conferences and committee

---

* *Vide* " the printed correspondence," pp. 40 and 41.

f

meetings of the Lodge downwards, were concocted or 'promoted' to launch and keep afloat a piece of imposition on the entire Craft; that even all the men of honour and integrity who were connected with the Lodge, at the time, and for many years after 1815, 'purposely suppressed' all particulars of the "*tragic scene*." *

"The list of subscribers to the fund in 1815 contains the names .of some distinguished lawyers, and I am confident that" . . . "unless good cause was shown, no member of this profession would be likely to contribute, and therefore they must have known or believed that Robert Burns was umquhile Poet Laureate of Canongate Kilwinning Lodge."

The statement of similar import contained in my letter of 7th February 1873, and the above observations in Brother Mackenzie's letter of 4th March 1889, remained unnoticed by Brother D. Murray Lyon.

It was reserved to Brother Mackenzie's correspondent of *The Freemason* to reply, which he did as follows :—†

"Brother Mackenzie appeals to me to say whether I think that the brethren, members of the Lodge, who subscribed in 1815 towards the erection of the Burns' mausoleum, would have given such subscriptions unless in the belief that he was the Laureate of their Lodge. *My answer is that I think they would have done so !*"

Such is this modern Freemason's estimate of the conscience possessed by each of his distinguished brother masons—of the Lodge Canongate Kilwinning—in the year 1815! Nevertheless, in a subsequent letter to *The Freemason*, the same writer found it convenient to refer to those worthy brethren in the following manner :—"*They were all men of high social and professional position.*"

I have much pleasure in also contributing the following extracts from Brother Mackenzie's able letter, dated 6th July 1889, which appeared in the columns of *The Freemason*, as well deserving of careful consideration. ‡

"I may be permitted to add just one very important fact, which, it must be admitted, confirms and supports the question at issue. It is, *that out of about one hundred members* whose names appear on the records as having frequented Canongate Kilwinning Lodge for years prior to, and at, Burns' affiliation, and also subsequent to the year 1815,—'when it was resolved to open a public subscription by the INDIVIDUAL MEMBERS of the Lodge in aid of the general subscription by the friends and admirers of THE LAMENTED BARD, ROBERT BURNS [WHO HAD BEEN POET LAUREAT OF THIS LODGE], for the erection of a mausoleum to his memory ' (*vide* minute, 8th June 1815),§—search may be made in vain for the record of any exception having been taken to this proceeding,

---

* This ludicrous reference to Burns' Inauguration as a "*tragic scene*," occurs in the letter from Brother Mackenzie's correspondent of *The Freemason*, dated 12th January 1889, reproduced at page 28 of "the printed correspondence." The word "tragic" signifies—"relating to tragedy—mournful—sorrowful—calamitous—fatal ; " but why the word is made to do duty in relation to the Inauguration scene is a mystery.

† What follows is quoted from undated letter in " the printed correspondence," pp. 50 and 51.

‡ Copied from "the printed correspondence," pp. 62 and 63.

§ *Vide* also Part II., p. 31, also p. 30, and pp. 32 to 38.

or of any discredit having been thrown on the Laureateship, and there is no contemporaneous evidence of any sort or kind to be found against the proposal [*i.e.*, to open a subscription by members of the Lodge]—in recognition of the office.

"*Amongst the members referred to above, mention may be made of*—

Lord Balcarres,*	.	.	. initiated 1775,	died 1825
Louis Cauvin, Burns' French teacher,†			„ 1778,	„ 1825
Alexander Nasmyth, painter of the only authentic portrait of Burns in existence,	.	.	„ 1777,	„ 1840
Dugald Stewart,	.	.	„ 1775,	„ 1828
Sir John Sinclair of Ulbster,	.	.	„ 1771,	„ 1835
Sir Ilay Campbell, President of the Court of Session,	.	.	„ 1758,	„ 1823
Dr Andrew Duncan, Founder of the Edinburgh Dispensary,	.	.	„ 1774,	„ 1828
Sir Henry Jardine Advocate, R.W. Master, 1790,			„ 1782,	„ 1851
Sir Charles Hope of Granton, President of the Court of Session,	.	.	„ 1784,	„ 1851

and many others to whom circulars containing the above resolution were sent."

Of the many others referred to by Brother Allan Mackenzie, I need only name the following :—

Charles More, of the Royal Bank, Member of Committee, 1783 to 1817,	.	. initiated 1769,	died 1818
Francis, seventh Lord Napier,‡	.	.	„ 1775,	„ 1823
Bailie George Spankie, Merchant, Treasurer, 1783 to 1803,	.	.	„ 1778,	„ 1820
James Sandilands, ninth Lord Torphichen, R.W.M., 1787-8,	.	.	„ 1782,	„ 1815
David Steuart, Earl of Buchan, . affiliated or			„ 1783,	„ 1829
Honourable Henry Erskine§ (initiation not recorded), R.W.M., 1780-81,	.	.		„ 1817
Honourable William Gordon of Kenmure, afterwards Earl of Kenmure,	.	. affiliated 1786,	„ 1840
Honourable Fletcher, Baron Norton, ‖ .	. initiated 1787,		„ 1820
And,				
William Campbell, Writer to the Signet,¶	.		„ 1801,	„ 1849

* Alexander, the sixth Earl of Balcarres.

† Son of Louis Cauvin, teacher of French, initiated 1752, died 1778.

‡ Lord Napier laid the foundation stone of Edinburgh University, 16th November 1789 ; *vide* Laurie's "History of Freemasonry," p. 141.

§ The Hon. Henry Erskine introduced Burns to the Canongate Kilwinning Lodge 1786, and to the *élité* of Edinburgh Society about the same time.

‖ Baron Norton, P. and R., 1st February 1787, same night Burns was affiliated.

¶ William Campbell was second son of Sir George Campbell of Aberuchil, Baronet ; was Senior Warden, 1801-2-3. Advocated painting of the Inauguration Picture, 12th November 1845.

7. *In re* "THE LODGE WAS A STRONG ONE IN THOSE DAYS [1815], AND, HAD EITHER THE MATTER OF BURNS' POET LAUREATESHIP, OR OF HIS FORMAL ELECTION·TO THE OFFICE OF POET LAUREATE—SO LONG AND WIDELY KNOWN—BEEN UNTRUE, THE CONTRADICTION WOULD ASSUREDLY HAVE BEEN KNOWN ALSO."

The above statement and relative matter will be found in copy of my letter at page 59 of Part II.

In support of such statement, I need only refer to section 5 of this chapter. The facts and arguments therein given apply equally to this section.

---

8. *In re* JAMES HOGG, THE ETTRICK SHEPHERD, SUCCESSOR TO ROBERT BURNS, POET LAUREATE, LODGE CANONGATE KILWINNING.

The complete statement on this part of the subject, which occurs in my letter, can be seen at page 59 of Part II., last paragraph.

The minute of meeting of Committee of the Lodge, held 16th January 1835, quoted at page 38 of Part II., affords incontrovertible proof that my statement is true; nevertheless, Grand Secretary, without any discrimination, commits himself to the sweeping assertion that "the statements" contained in my letter to him of 7th February 1873 are "unfounded."

In connection with this matter, I shall now quote a letter from Grand Secretary, dated·13th December 1886, as it appeared in the *Scotsman* newspaper, wherein he gives an extract from his history of Lodge No. 1, published in 1873. Giving such extract in that letter, proves that down to a comparatively recent period—the date of his letter— he believed *that what he wrote in* 1873, *and as far back as* 1863, acknowledging Robert Burns to have been Poet Laureate of Lodge Canongate Kilwinning, *was founded on absolute fact.*

The letter with its headline is as follows :—

"*Was the Ettrick Shepherd a Freemason?*"

"FREEMASONS' HALL, EDINBURGH,
"*December* 13, 1886.

"SIR,—A writer in a leading masonic journal has this week raised a curious question as to Hogg's connection with the craft. He says—'It has been generally understood that the celebrated Scottish poet, James Hogg, the Ettrick Shepherd, was a Freemason, in consequence of his having held the office of Poet Laureate of the Lodge Canongate Kilwinning, No. 2.' And to prove that Hogg never joined the fraternity, the writer quotes a letter from the poet to a member of that lodge, in which, writing from Altrive Lake, under date January 25, 1835, he says—'I am sixty-five years of age this night. I am not a mason, and never have been, having uniformly resisted the entreaties of my most influential friends to become one. I am, however, intensely sensible of the high honour intended me, which, coming to my hand on the morning of my birthday, has, I feel, added a new charm to the old shepherd's life. My kindest respects to the hon. master and members of the lodge, and say that I cannot join them, nor be initiated into the mysteries of the art, for I know I should infallibly . . . And alas! my dear John (Forbes), I am long past the age of enjoying masonic revels. I shall, however, be most proud to become nominally the poet laureate of the lodge, to have my name enrolled as such, and shall endeavour to contribute some poetic trifle annually.'

"Hogg did become a freemason, and his association with the Lodge Canongate Kilwinning is at once peculiar and interesting. In treating of Burns' connection with this ancient and distinguished lodge in my 'History of Freemasonry in Scotland,' 1873 I wrote—'The Laureateship is again referred to in the minute of 16th January 1835, which records the restoration, in the person of James Hogg, the Ettrick Shepherd, of the honorary office of Poet Laureate of the Lodge, which had been in abeyance since the death of the immortal brother, Robert Burns.'" The minute shows that while yet beyond the pale of the mystic tie, Hogg had been elected to office in Canongate Kilwinning *—an unprecedented proceeding on the part of a Lodge of Freemasons, and one that exposed its members to the highest masonic censure. Alarmed at their position,† the officers of the lodge renewed their efforts to induce Hogg to exchange a nominal for a real connection with the craft, and they succeeded, under a dispensation from the then Grand Master—Lord Fincastle, afterwards Earl of Dunmore. A deputation from the Canongate Lodge proceeded to Innerleithen on the 7th of May 1835, and in a special communication, held in the Cleikum Inn at St Ronan's, initiated their poet laureate into the mysteries of the 'royal art.' The shepherd is reported to have enjoyed with zest the harmony that followed his initiation, and delighted the brethren by singing one of his own songs—' When the kye comes hame.'

"It is unfortunate that, while in May 1836, enrolling some two hundred entrants in the books of the Grand Lodge of Scotland, the lodge should have omitted to return the name of Hogg.

"The Lodge Canongate Kilwinning will in a few days hold the third jubilee of the consecration of St. John's Chapel. It might then very properly pay a tribute to the memory of the Ettrick Shepherd, by having his name recorded in the official register of the Scottish craft.

"Hogg died in November 1835.—I am, etc., etc.,

"D. MURRAY LYON,
"Grand Secretary."

Grand Secretary is mistaken in the statements which follow the quotation from his History. There is no indication whatever of the officers of the Lodge having become "alarmed at their position." That is a mere unsupported assertion by Grand Secretary. There was no cause for alarm. When the motion was passed at the meeting of Lodge Canongate Kilwinning, on 16th January 1835, relative to the Poet Laureateship, "Brother John Forbes,‡ in consequence of his being personally acquainted with Mr Hogg, was instructed to communicate to him this resolution." Nobody dreamt of James

---

* The minute in question contains no mention of Hogg having been *elected* to office—*Vide* Part II., p. 38.

† An extravagant assertion.

‡ Brother John Forbes, Writer, E.P. and R. August 12th, 1825, was elected Treasurer in 1831, and was thereafter a member of committee till 1839.

Hogg being elected Poet Laureate *unless* he were to be previously admitted a member of the Lodge. Everybody knew that the idea of proposing James Hogg as Poet Laureate, carried with it as a *sine qua non* his admission to membership, to precede his election to such office. The office-bearers of Canongate Kilwinning were all able lawyers, most of them very old masons. The admission to membership of the R.W. Master Alexander M'Neil, Advocate, happens to be unrecorded; but he is mentioned in the minute of *24th June* 1824 as having been *then* elected a member of committee; therefore, he must have been an experienced member of the Craft at that early time :—he had been five years R.W. Master of the Lodge—no one should in such case look on *him* as a novice in masonic law or custom. Brother John Forbes, Writer, the intimate friend and adviser of James Hogg, had been initiated, passed, and raised in the Canongate Kilwinning *as early as the year* 1825. Brother John Leslie, S.W., and Brother John Abercromby, J.W., had both been admitted members in 1828, and Brother Francis G. Souter, Treasurer, joined the Lodge in 1826—*every one of them* experienced masons. Brother Charles Mac-dougall, Advocate, the Depute-Master, and Brother W. B. D. D. Turnbull, Advocate, the Substitute Master, appear to have been constant in their services ever since joining the Lodge. These are a few of the officers of the Lodge in 1835; *all* of them, with one exception, experienced men of law: they were of high social as well as professional standing; most of them were also old members of the Craft, and not one of them was likely to be caught napping over a small matter of masonic law and procedure with which any tyro in masonry is familiar. The reputation of those very worthy masons on such a point of masonic jurisprudence is not likely to be damaged by the strictures of any critic of the present day.

Grand Secretary is quite wrong in asserting, as he does in his letter of 13th December 1886 now quoted, that "the officers of the lodge renewed their efforts to induce Hogg to exchange a nominal for a real connection with the craft." Hogg never could have had a "nominal" connection with the craft, therefore to "exchange" it "for a real connection" was not in his power. The correspondence proves what I say. The tenor of James Hogg's reply, dated 25th January 1835, to the letter from his valued friend John Forbes, dated the 16th of same month and year, clearly shows that Brother Forbes had invited him to join the craft in Lodge Canongate Kilwinning—and *that invitation* had been the special point in the letter from Brother Forbes to his friend the Ettrick Shepherd—the Laureateship had been secondary, or made dependent on the first point being conceded. *The offer at the close of James Hogg's letter was very obviously his own,* spontaneously made in ignorance of Masonic law, and from a desire to oblige his friend and correspondent, John Forbes. Grand Secretary is in error also, asserting that the deputation " initiated their poet laureate into the mysteries of the ' royal art;' " —they initiated James Hogg.

There is no evidence whatever in the Canongate Kilwinning records of there having been [as Grand Secretary asserts] "any dispensation from the then Grand Master Lord Fincastle, afterwards Earl of Dunmore," granted to empower a deputation from the Canongate Kilwinning Lodge to proceed to Innerleithen on purpose to initiate James Hogg. Lord Fincastle was not "the then Grand Master," as is shown in page 41.

The procedure which was observed on such very memorable occasion is well expressed by Brother Allan Mackenzie in his "History of the Lodge Canongate Kilwinning," thus :—

"It will be seen that the refusal of Mr James Hogg, at this date,* even to join the Order, arose chiefly from a resolution to withdraw himself from public society. Nevertheless, what cannot be considered otherwise than a most graceful compliment to the Craft, Mr Hogg, after mature consideration of the value of freemasonry, about three months afterwards, declared his willingness to join, and subsequent to becoming a member, frequently expressed himself more than satisfied with the fraternity, and looked upon the circumstances attending his initiation as marked by complimentary exceptions in his favour.

"As circumstances prevented Mr Hogg from attending a meeting of the Lodge in Edinburgh, a masonic excursion was determined on, to go to Peebleshire for the purpose of initiating him into the order; but previous to doing so, a warrant, or dispensation, to constitute a Lodge there was obtained, and it is minuted that—

"'At a meeting of the Committee of the Lodge Canongate Kilwinning, held on the first day of May 1835. The which day it was moved and unanimously approved of: That in consideration of the eminent character and acknowledged worth of James Hogg, the Ettrick Shepherd, he be admitted a member of this ancient Lodge, and for that purpose a deputation, headed by Bro. Jas. Deans as acting Master, assisted by Bros. Anthony Trail and Alex. Mackie, as his Wardens, and other Brethren, do proceed to Innerleithen, or any other convenient place there, to open and hold a meeting of the Lodge Canongate Kilwinning, and to initiate the said James Hogg, or other gentlemen present on that occasion : *For doing whereof this shall be your Warrant.*

"'Given under our hands and seal at St. John's Chapel, Edinburgh, this 1st day of May 1835, and of Masonry, 5835.

"'(S^d) CHARLES MACDOUGAL, *D.M.*
"'W. B. D. D. TURNBULL, *S.M.*
"'JOHN LESLIE, *S. W.*
"'A. MACKIE, *Secy.*'

"The ceremony was accordingly fixed for 7th May 1835, and on the morning of that day two of the Brethren, Messrs Adam Wilson and William Pringle, drove to Mr Hogg's House at Altrive Lake, when they found him prepared to mount his steed for the occasion. After being hospitably welcomed to the Banks of Yarrow, the party started on a short fishing excursion. Having arrived at the Cleikum Inn, St Ronans, the expectant Brethren were all introduced to him, and the proper paraphernalia having been brought from the city, the Lodge was duly constituted, and the three degrees conferred upon the 'Shepherd'; after which the Brethren sat down to a sumptuous repast in the Cleikum Inn, kept by Meg Dods. After the usual masonic toasts, the R.W.M. proposed the health 'of the newly initiated Brother JAMES HOGG,' and in so doing alluded to the remarkable circumstance of *Burns having been the Poet Laureate of the Lodge Canongate Kilwinning,* and said, that as the '*Ettrick Shepherd*' was universally

---

* 25th January 1835.

looked upon as the successor of that immortal poet in his poetic fame, so the members had felt the greater anxiety to enrol the name of *James Hogg, Poet Laureate of the Lodge.*'"

Passing over Brother Hogg's reply, and other particulars of this famous event in Scottish masonry—which is so graphically told in Brother Mackenzie's History—I conclude the quotation therefrom as follows :—

"Many other toasts were drunk, among which was 'the health of Brother Professor Wilson, the friend and patron of the Yarrow bard.'

"The Ettrick Shepherd sang some of his own sweet lays, such as 'When the Kye comes hame.' Next day three of the Brethren went home with Brother Hogg, with whom they dined, returning delighted with his hospitality, and agreeable family and fireside.

"Under the above date (7th May, 1835) it is minuted that—

"'IN VIRTUE OF THE ABOVE DISPENSATION, WE, the undersigned Brethren, did this day meet within the Cleikum Inn, at Innerleithen, and there held a Lodge, at which James Hogg of Altrive Lake, the Ettrick Shepherd, was regularly initiated as an Entered Apprentice, passed a Fellow-Craft, and raised to the sublime degree of a Master Mason.

"'Given under our hands and seal this 7th day of May, in the year of our Lord, 1835, and of Masonry, 5835.

"'(S^d)   JAS. DEANS, *M.*

"'ANTH. TRAIL, *S.W.*

"'A. MACKIE, *J.W.*

"'James Hogg.

"'James Burnes, M.D., H.E.I.C.S.;

"'Adam Wilson, Dan. M. Davidson, R.A.;

"'John Donald, Wm. Jeffries Dowlin, And. Sievwright,

"'Pat. Sandeman, Wm. Pringle,

"'John Forbes, C. Neaves,

"'Rob. Boyd, A. Mackie, *Secretary.*'"

From these quotations it is clear that the deputation from Canongate Kilwinning did not have occasion to proceed to Innerleithen to initiate James Hogg, "under a dispensation from the then Grand Master," as Grand Secretary asserted, *but*, the deputation *did* proceed on such errand under a warrant or dispensation granted by Lodge Canongate Kilwinning herself, dated 1st May 1835, which is duly recorded in the minute book. The concluding line is very definite, thus—"*For doing whereof this shall be your Warrant.*"

Again, it is chronicled in the minute book of that time, that, "*In virtue of the above dispensation,*" certain brethren who had formed the deputation, duly recorded the fact that on the 7th May 1835 they had met at the Cleikum Inn, and there held a Lodge, in which the three degrees had been conferred on James Hogg, the Ettrick Shepherd. The minute is signed by fifteen of the brethren, and by James Hogg.

Not a word occurs anywhere in the minute book, of "a dispensation from the then Grand Master."

Grand Secretary made another unfounded statement in his extraordinary story about James Hogg: because "*the then Grand Master*" *was not Lord Fincastle*, but the Marquess of Douglas and Clydesdale. The latter had been re-elected Grand Master on 1st December 1834. According to recognised authorities, the Right Hon. Alexander Edward, Viscount Fincastle, was not elected Grand Master till 30th November 1835 *— six months after James Hogg had been made a Freemason.

Further details regarding the initiation of the "Shepherd" will be found instructive and agreeable reading, at page 200 and onwards of the "History of Lodge Canongate Kilwinning."

In relation to this matter, I should mention that Brother George Cumming, Writer to the Signet,—not recorded, like very many more brethren—but who was elected Junior Warden, 24th June 1835,—in the course of one of his many letters to me regarding interesting events which occurred in Lodge Canongate Kilwinning during those old days, gave some valuable particulars relative to James Hogg; among others, he mentioned the special invitation from the Ettrick Shepherd's friend, Brother John Forbes, requesting the Shepherd to become a member of Lodge Canongate Kilwinning, and various circumstances connected with such an auspicious occasion. The gist of Brother Cumming's remarks may be here aptly expressed in his own words, thus :—" *His* [the Shepherd's] *initiation was quite an event in Scottish masonry.*"

Returning to Grand Secretary's letter, above quoted, of 13th December 1886, and, in view of all the circumstances now detailed, it would be of much interest to know his authority for asserting that " a dispensation from the then Grand Master" was ever granted to, or ever acted on, by the Lodge Canongate Kilwinning with respect to the admission of James Hogg as a member of the Lodge.

---

9. *In re* " AUTHENTICATED PARTICULARS" RELATIVE TO THE ELECTION AND INAUGURA-
TION OF ROBERT BURNS AS POET LAUREATE, WERE ASKED FOR AND SUPPLIED
DURING NOVEMBER 1845.

This statement, as given in my letter, will be found at page 60 of Part II., and the Lodge Minutes to which it refers are quoted at pages 41, 42, and 43 of Part II.

No other proof of my statement being well-founded is necessary.

The "authenticated particulars" produced at the Lodge Meeting held 19th November 1845—pursuant to the requisition expressed at the meeting held a week previously—*were so very satisfactory that the R. W. Master, Archibald David Campbell, seconded the motion* made on that date in favour of having a picture painted of the Inauguration of Robert Burns as Poet Laureate, and it was "unanimously carried."

The question may be asked—Why were those "authenticated particulars" not

---

* *Vide* W. A. Laurie's "History of Freemasonry," pp. 216, 217; also, "The Constitution and Laws of Grand Lodge," edition MDCCCLXXXVI., p. 139.

recorded in the minute book? My answer is, that the authenticated particulars produced to the Lodge meeting on 19th November 1845 were so copious, that the brethren would never expect their Secretary to engross them in the Lodge minute book. It is enough to know by the minute of that date that those particulars were approved, and that the motion was " unanimously carried."

It is not by any means probable that the particulars—all duly authenticated—which are *now* produced will ever be recorded in the minute book of the Lodge.

―――――――――

These are "the statements" of which my letter to Brother D. Murray Lyon, dated 7th Feb. 1873, mainly consist. They are the only statements that are essential to the question, and are herein proved beyond any doubt or cavil.

VI.

Brother D. MURRAY LYON'S FLUCTUATIONS OF OPINION

WITH REFERENCE TO

ROBERT BURNS

HAVING BEEN POET LAUREATE OF LODGE CANONGATE KILWINNING.

———

Brother Mackenzie's correspondent of *The Freemason*, in his letter dated 15th October 1889—reproduced in "the printed correspondence" which was submitted to Grand Committee by Grand Secretary, 29th December 1892, asserts that I "misled our eminent historian" by the statements relative to Brother William Petrie, as contained in my letter of 7th February 1873.

Grand Secretary himself makes assertions of a similarly depreciative nature in the extract from Grand Lodge Proceedings, 29th December 1892, *vide* Part II., page 1; as also in "the printed correspondence" therein referred to, regarding "the statement laid before him," and "the statements made to him," by me in that letter of 7th February 1873, "which (he asserts) he unfortunately accepted as true, and, *in his History modified the opinion which he had originally formed.*"

It would be matter of some interest to know who had "misled" [?] Brother D. Murray Lyon ten years previously to my writing him, when he announced to the world, in *The Scottish Freemason's Magazine* of 1st December 1863, very distinctly and impressively, his belief in Robert Burns having been Poet Laureate of Lodge Canongate Kilwinning.

The passage I refer to occurs at page 206, year 1863, of that magazine, and it is a very edifying quotation in the light of events, because therein Brother D. Murray Lyon truthfully, pithily, and eloquently asserts—

"The Royal Arch of St. Abb, under whose warrant Scotia's Bard was exalted; Tarbolton St. David, within the walls of which he first beheld the light; Kilmarnock Kilwinning St. John, with whom he was linked by the tie of Honorary Membership, and to whom were addressed the stanzas beginning—

"'Ye sons of Old Killie, assembled by Willie;'

AND THE CANONGATE KILWINNING, WHOSE POET LAUREATE HE WAS, may all feel justly proud of their connection with Robert Burns."

In that quotation Brother D. Murray Lyon designates Robert Burns as Poet

Laureate of Lodge Canongate Kilwinning. As a rule, historians do not make such unqualified statements without proper investigation, and without being satisfied as to their truth. I am disposed to believe that Brother D. Murray Lyon, before lending the character and weight of his name to such an assertion, and committing his thoughts to an article in a public magazine, must have thoroughly sifted all available information on the subject. I will not assume that he accepted of the information he obtained regarding it without a belief that he had proof of its authenticity.

What trust, what reliance, can be placed on the other assertions of Brother D. Murray Lyon, if I am compelled to believe that the assertion in question was made without due investigation?

It might be curious, if not useful, to briefly state the various changes or fluctuations of opinion which have taken place in the worthy historian's mind before he has arrived at the conclusion which he now holds on this important subject. To any one who considers this matter with care, it must strike him as a remarkable circumstance, that the "eminent historian" has had frequent occasion to change his mind. In fact, his changes of mind have been so sudden and so often as to be perplexing to his readers.

In order to be exact, and to show the fluctuations alluded to, it may be as well to narrate those changes in detail.

FIRST.—The Grand Secretary himself informs us, in the "Extract from Grand Lodge Proceedings, 29th December 1892," that *his original opinion was*, "that Burns never was elected to, and never held the office of, Poet Laureate of the Lodge, and never was installed into such an office."

SECOND.—On 1st December 1863, in *The Scottish Freemason's Magazine*, Brother D. Murray Lyon wrote to the following effect:—"*The Canongate Kilwinning, whose Poet Laureate he was*, may feel justly proud of their connection with Robert Burns."

THIRD.—Brother D. Murray Lyon, by his letter to me, dated 24th January 1873, in a qualified manner threw doubts upon the question of Robert Burns having been Poet Laureate, and challenged me to produce evidence in support thereof.

FOURTH.—On 7th February 1873, as requested by Brother D. Murray Lyon, I furnished him with the evidence required as to the Election and Inauguration of Robert Burns as Poet Laureate of Lodge Canongate Kilwinning; and on 11th February 1873, he replied to me, making the following statement:—"I recognise the *satisfactory nature of the evidence* you have submitted, and shall have pleasure in giving effect to it in my forthcoming work."

In the work referred to—the History of Lodge No. 1—Brother D. Murray Lyon acknowledges, *at the very commencement* of his notice of "Burns and the Laureateship of Canongate Kilwinning," * that—

"Mr Fergusson of Craigdarroch was Master of Canongate Kilwinning at the date of Burns's appointment to the Laureateship of that Lodge. *The Inauguration of the Poet to this office is the subject of a painting well known to Scottish Freemasons*, executed by a member of the Lodge, the late Bro. Stewart Watson; it also forms the subject of a

---

* A title quoted from the Index of the History of No. 1.

small volume entitled, ' A Winter with Robert Burns,' * containing biographical sketches of the Brethren whose portraits appear in the painting."

Brother D. Murray Lyon must admit that such language is *entirely his own*, and that he is not indebted to me for any part—either of the text matter or of the footnote relating to it—from my letter of 7th February 1873. In that letter of mine I did not mention the name of " Mr Fergusson of Craigdarroch." Copy of the letter can be seen in Part II., page 57. More than that, Brother Lyon, in his reply, dated 11th February 1873, acknowledging receipt of that letter from me, warned me thus:—" I would take the liberty of saying, that while I shall embody the facts you have put me in possession of, *I will not require to* ALTER *a single sentence of what I had previously written.*"

Therefore, one portion at least of that which he " had previously written " must consist of the opening sentences of the notice now referred to of " Burns and the Laureateship of Canongate Kilwinning," with which sentences my statements had no connection whatever.

Further, as showing Grand Secretary's long-continued faith in Burns as Poet Laureate of Lodge Canongate Kilwinning, I quote the following passage from a letter of his dated 13*th December* 1886, to *The Scotsman* newspaper.† He therein refers to " the restoration, in the person of James Hogg, the ' Ettrick Shepherd,' of the ' honorary office of Poet Laureate of the lodge, which had been in abeyance since the death of the immortal Brother, Robert Burns.'"

FIFTH.—The latest confession of faith on the subject by Brother D. Murray Lyon, so far as I am aware, is that contained in the " Extract from Grand Lodge Proceedings, 29th December 1892," wherein we find that after all those changes of opinion, he has travelled back to " *the opinion which he had originally formed*," which he asserts is— " that Burns never was elected to, and never held the office of, Poet Laureate of the Lodge, and never was installed into such an office."

---

* " The author of this work, Bro. James Marshall, was a Solicitor in the Supreme Courts of Scotland, but afterwards emigrated to Australia, and carried on the business of an attorney in the city of Melbourne, Victoria, where he died in 1870."

† Quoted in full at pp. 36 and 37.

VII.

ERRORS

IN

"THE PRINTED COPY OF THE CORRESPONDENCE"

WHICH WAS SUBMITTED BY GRAND SECRETARY TO GRAND COMMITTEE,
29TH DECEMBER 1892, IN SUPPORT OF HIS CONTENTION.

In previous chapters I have exposed a few of the errors, both of assertion and argument, that occur throughout the letters written by Brother Allan Mackenzie's two controversialists, as reproduced in "the printed copy of correspondence."

The errors are very numerous. I have no intention to load this work with a refutation of them all—that would be too big a task at this time—but, in what now follows, I shall exhibit and controvert a few of the most prominent of them which have not yet been referred to.

---

1. PROCEDURE ALLEGED TO BE NECESSARY IN "CREATING AN ADDITIONAL OFFICE-BEARER."

As a specimen of the plausible but erroneous style of controversy typical of the letters written by one of Brother Mackenzie's disputants, I quote the following lines from page 43 of "the printed correspondence," letter No. VI., written to *The Freemason* by the Past Master of Lodge No. 1, who described himself as such in the "Prefatory Note" to that collection of letters.

"I have set forth well-established contemporary facts and circumstances, in my opinion clearly showing that the office (of Poet Laureate) had no existence till 1835. . . .

"The office could only have been created by a written resolution passed by the Lodge creating an additional office-bearer, which would have been an alteration on its laws and constitution requiring the approval of Grand Lodge; and had such a change been made, it would have been recorded not only in the minutes of the Lodge No. 1, but also in the minutes of Grand Lodge itself. *The minute book* in which that resolution ought to have been found *is in existence. It is well and continuously kept,** and contains no record either of the creation of the office, of the Poet's election to fill such an office, or of his inauguration into it, nor of Grand Lodge's approval of the step. The minute book of Grand Lodge is also ominously silent on the subject."

Was any law on the subject, as defined so elaborately in above quotation, "created" so far back as the times when the offices of Poet Laureate and Substitute Master were "created"?

Let it be specially noted that the important office of Substitute Master of Lodge Canongate Kilwinning was "created" 24th June 1788, *solely* by the very simple process of naming John Millar, Advocate, as Substitute Master, in his proper place, along with the other office-bearers elected on that date.

How is it then with other offices that have been "created" on equally short notice in Lodge Canongate Kilwinning?

By reference to the Chart of Office-bearers in Appendix hereto annexed, it will be found that the following offices have been "created" on the respective dates indicated, and *in no instance* has the creation been accomplished by the tedious and unwonted procedure above described in the quotation :—

Poet Laureate,	Robert Burns, the Scottish Bard,	1787, March 1.
Substitute Master,	John Millar, Advocate,	1788, June 24.
Organist,	Robert Purdie,	1800, June 24.
Chaplain,	Fras. M'Nab,	1808, June 24.
Senior Deacon,	Archibald Horn,	1816, June 24.
Junior Deacon,	Malcolm M'Neil,	1816, June 24.
Corresponding Member in London,	David Plenderleath,	1819, June 24.
Convener or Chairman of Committee	John Wilson, Advocate, "Christopher North,"	1835, June 24.
Architect and Superintendent of Works,	David Rhind,	1836, Jany. 27.
Master of Ceremonies,	Andw. Dunlop, W.S.,	1836, June 24.

In like manner, *pipers* were introduced in the year 1889, and have been regularly allotted a place in the list of office-bearers elected each year since then. No "written resolution passed by the Lodge, creating an additional office-bearer" on such occasion, was ever recorded in the Lodge minute-book, and it may be safely concluded that "the minute-book of Grand Lodge is also ominously silent on the subject."

Quoting further from "the printed correspondence," it will be seen in letter XI.— the last of the series—that Brother D. Murray Lyon, Grand Secretary, in respect of the Laureateship of No. 2, asserts that :—

"Hogg, the Ettrick Shepherd, was the first of its Poets-Laureate, and he was made so in 1835."

By such a pointed, but unsupported assertion, Grand Secretary quite ignores all the plausible story set forth in letter VI. of same series, descriptive of the procedure which

* An unfounded assertion ; *vide* pp. 6 and 7 *ante* ; also Part II., pp. 4 to 11, and pp. 12 to 19.

Brother Mackenzie's *other* controversialist asserts is necessary in creating a new office-bearer. Oddly enough, that other controversialist himself ignores it when asserting, as he does, that "the office of Poet Laureate had no existence till 1835."

Specially worthy of note in this connection is the fact that the *only* record of James Hogg having been elected Poet Laureate of Lodge Canongate Kilwinning occurs in the minute of meeting held 24th June 1835, and that entry occupies a single line in the list of office-bearers then elected,* thus :—

"James Hogg, the 'Ettrick Shepherd'...............Poet Laureate."

There is no evidence whatever of any communication having been made to Grand Lodge, nor of any sanction by Grand Lodge having been given to Canongate Kilwinning for "creating" the office of Poet Laureate in the year 1835. Such long-drawn-out procedure, involving "a written resolution passed by the Lodge creating an additional office-bearer," etc., etc., if it ever had been observed, was then quite un-necessary, for the good reason that Grand Lodge, and Freemasons generally who knew anything at all of Canongate Kilwinning, were quite well aware that ROBERT BURNS, the Scottish Bard [and not "Hogg, the Ettrick Shepherd], was the first of its Poets-Laureate."

---

2. INCONSISTENCY OF BROTHER MACKENZIE'S CORRESPONDENTS OF *The Freemason.*

The inconsistency exhibited by the Past Master of the Lodge of Edinburgh Mary's Chapel, No. 1, and by Grand Secretary in their letters since the year 1888 on the subject of the Inauguration of Robert Burns has been briefly referred to in pages 7 and 8 *ante.* I shall follow up that reference now.

The Past Master of the Lodge of Edinburgh Mary's Chapel, No. 1—who claims to have "rendered some help to Brother Lyon in the production of his History" of that Lodge, is the first of the two correspondents who, shortly after the publication of the "History of Lodge Canongate Kilwinning," wrote to *The Freemason,* taking exception to the reference in that work to Robert Burns having been Poet Laureate of Lodge Canongate Kilwinning.

Grand Secretary is the other correspondent : he contributed two letters to the series, one dated 12th February 1889, and the other dated 18th August 1891.

Robert Burns and the Lodge St. Andrew, Edinburgh.

The Past Master of the Lodge of Edinburgh in his first letter to *The Freemason* —at page 16 of "the printed correspondence "—expresses himself as follows regarding the visit of Robert Burns to Lodge St. Andrew, Edinburgh, No. 48 :—

"The Poet was proud of honours paid him, and took frequent notice of them. On his visit to the LODGE ST. ANDREW, EDINBURGH, shortly prior to the alleged inauguration, he writes that the toast was given of 'Caledonia and Caledonia's Bard,

---

* *Vide* Part II., p. 40.

Robert Burns,' and proudly records his gratification at the compliment. In like manner he records his honorary affiliation a few months later by the Eyemouth Lodge; but, singularly, neither he nor the Lodge Canongate Kilwinning, nor any one else, make any contemporaneous record of the great and exceptionable (*sic*) honour said to have been conferred on him by a Lodge of foremost distinction, at a special gathering of upwards of sixty of the most distinguished Scotsmen of the age."

The above reference to that famous meeting of the Lodge St. Andrew, Edinburgh, which took place "shortly prior to the alleged inauguration," is appropriately supported by testimony contained in the "History of the Lodge of Edinburgh (Mary's Chapel)." In that valuable work the talented author—the second of Brother Mackenzie's correspondents—gives interesting details of certain Grand Lodge visitations to Lodge No. 1. At pages 331 and 332, he mentions a visit to No. 1 which occurred towards the close of 1786, and follows that with a telling narrative of the "special gathering" which took place in the Lodge of St. Andrew on 12th January 1787, thus :—

"1786 : *December* 12.—Francis Charteris, younger of Amisfield (afterwards Lord Elcho), the Grand Master 36th in succession, was accompanied by Alexander Fergusson of Craigdarroch, Provincial Grand Master of the Southern District. This was one of a series of Grand Visitations that were being made at the time of Burns's visit to Edinburgh. Through his attendance at some of these, and other Masonic meetings, the Poet made the acquaintance of the Earls of Glencairn, Buchan, Balcarres, and Eglinton; Lords Elcho, Napier, Torphichen, and Monboddo; Sir William Forbes, Sir James Hunter Blair, Professor Dugald Stewart, Henry Erskine (the celebrated lawyer), Henry Mackenzie ('The Man of Feeling'), William Smellie (the printer of the second edition of Burns's Poems), William Creech, and other luminaries in that galaxy of Scottish Craftsmen, of which he for a time formed the centre of attraction.* Writing to his friend and patron John Ballantine, the brother to whom he inscribed the beautiful allegory of 'The Twa Brigs,' Burns gives the following graphic account of his reception at one of these Communications, held in THE LODGE ST. ANDREW, ON THE 12TH OF JANUARY 1787 :—'I went to a Mason Lodge yesternight, where the Most Worshipful Grand Master Charteris, and all the Grand Lodge of Scotland visited. The meeting was numerous and elegant; the different Lodges about town were present in all their pomp. The Grand Master, who presided with great solemnity and honour to himself, as a gentleman and a Mason, among other general toasts, gave 'Caledonia, and Caledonia's Bard, Brother Burns,' which rang through the whole assembly with multiplied honours and repeated acclamations. As I had no idea such a thing would happen, I was downright thunderstruck, and trembling in every nerve, made the best return in my power. Just as I had finished, some of the Grand Officers said, so loud that I could hear, with a most comforting accent, 'Very well, indeed!' which set me something to rights again.' Mr Charteris, during his Grand Mastership, succeeded to the title of Lord Elcho, his father

---

* Canongate Kilwinning was the mother Lodge of all those distinguished brethren, except two, and those two were affiliated members. Alexander Fergusson of Craigdarroch was at this time also R.W. Master of Lodge Canongate Kilwinning.

h

having inherited the Earldom of Wemyss. He belonged to the Lodge Haddington St. John, and was also an affiliated member of Canongate Kilwinning."

[Then follows the notice regarding "Burns and the Canongate Kilwinning," the first two sentences of which are quoted at pp. 44-45 *ante*, and the whole of it in Part II., page 63.]

Those are very interesting narratives of the well-known visit of Brother Burns, "Caledonia's Bard," to the Lodge St. Andrew, Edinburgh, No. 48, on the 12th January 1787, but there is *no record* in the minute book for the year 1787 of Robert Burns having ever visited that Lodge.

The minute book is before me while I write, and I remark that the Secretary of the Lodge *has not recorded any minute of the proceedings* on the 12th January 1787.

The only memorial of events which took place in the Lodge on that date is the minute recorded on behalf of Grand Lodge, accurately reproduced as follows :—

"Edin". 12 Jan"'. 1787.

" This evening the Lodge being duly constituted by the Right Worshipful Master Thereafter the most Worshipful Francis Charteris Esq'. junior of Amisfield Grand Master Mason of Scotland The Right Worshipful Fletcher Norton Esq'. Depute Grand Master P.T. The Right Worshipful Thomas Hay Esq Substitute Grand Master James Home Esq' and Gillies Grand Wardens *p.t.* William Mason Grand Sec'. & Robert Meikle G'd Clerk preceded by the Lodge of Grand Stewards in their proper clothing were pleased to favor this Lodge with a visit when he was received with that respect due to the dignity of his high office & distinguished rank and having taken the chair delivered a suitable charge to the brethren which was received with the highest tokens of applause & approbation. The Lodge on this occasion was visited by Brethren from the following Lodges, viz'.—Canongate & Leith, Leith & Canongate, S'. James, Ruglen Royal Arch, & S'. Stephens Edin'., To all whom the proper compliments were paid and due returns made."

WILL. MASON G. Sec'.   FRANCIS CHARTERIS G.M. *
Ro. MEIKLE G. Clk.   FL^R. NORTON D.G.M. *p.t.*
                                      THOMAS HAY S^t. G.M.
                                        JAMES HOME S.G.W. *p.t.*
                                        ADAM GILLIS J.G.W. *p.t.*"

It may seem extraordinary that Lodge St. Andrew—which has acquired much fame by the Bard's visit—possesses no record of that highly appreciated episode in his life. But even the Grand Lodge officials present on such an extraordinary occasion did not consider the presence of Burns, or the toast given of " Caledonia and Caledonia's Bard, Robert Burns," as *business* needing to be put on record, and possibly the Secretary

---

* Francis Charteris was affiliated to Lodge Canongate Kilwinning in 1779—seven years before he became M.W.G.M. ; and Canongate Kilwinning was the mother Lodge of Fletcher Norton, Thomas Hay, and James Home, whose signatures are appended to above minute.

of No. 48 might think, that, with such an example before him, there was no necessity for *him* to be at any trouble making a record of the proceedings.

Evidently the Grand Lodge minute of 12th January 1787 has been held to include all that was needful to be recorded—" No other *business* being before the meeting." *

Be that as it may, there can be no doubt that the Secretary of Lodge St. Andrew, on 12th January 1787, like the Secretary of Lodge Canongate Kilwinning, on the 1st March of same year [when the Inauguration of Robert Burns took place], must have been very easy-going, even neglectful, of his duties, as we view those matters now-a-days. Each of the two Secretaries seems to have considered the whole affair, wherein Robert Burns appeared such a conspicuous figure on these respective occasions, simply as a social event in which no " business" of a customary kind had been transacted, and therefore that it had no need to be mentioned in the minute.

There is no minute recorded by the Secretary of Lodge St. Andrew after the one dated 27th December 1786, till that of the monthly meeting held 9th February 1787.

In passing, and while on this subject setting forth the perfunctory style of work accomplished by some secretaries of last century, and especially about the time of Burns' visit, it may be shown by the following illustration that Lodge St. Andrew could almost match Lodge Canongate Kilwinning for brevity of minutes.

[23 words.]   . " 1786, ED^R· 20th *November.*

" The Lodge Ed^r· St. Andrew Being legally met & constitute Mr John Cummin was entered an Apprentice Mason & paid his fees Accordingly.

> GEO. MONTGOMERY, Master.
> AND^w· SMITH, S.W.
> JA^s· SAGE, Junr· J.W.P.T."

Towards the close of Grand Secretary's letter to *The Freemason*, dated 18th August 1891,—last of the series of letters contained in " the printed correspondence" (p. 71), he pretentiously displays a copy of the Canongate Kilwinning minute, dated 1st March 1787, with the following introduction :—

" In all statements and discussions in support of the story of the inauguration, the minute of the meeting at which the event is alleged to have happened *has been studiously kept out of sight.* It had better be published, and here it is :—[See Part II., page 14.].

As I happen to be one of the brethren who made certain statements † in support of the fact that Robert Burns had been elected and inaugurated Poet Laureate of Canongate Kilwinning, which statements are fully substantiated in pages 12 to 42 *ante*, I feel privileged—without further noticing the ill-advised and unfounded taunt—to ask Grand Secretary why he, as an eminent historian, should commit himself to the adverse

---

* *Vide* Can. Kil. minute of 1st March 1787, Part II., page 14.
† My " statements " were made in a letter to Brother D. Murray Lyon, as long ago as 7th February 1873, copy of which will be found at page 57 of Part II.

assertions which he now does relative to "Burns and the Canongate Kilwinning," after having published in his history of No. 1 such a very attractive story about Burns and the Lodge St. Andrew, Edinburgh, as is quoted in page 49 *ante, for which story there is no authority in the minute book of that Lodge?*

The little work which Grand Secretary refers to as "the printed copy of the correspondence," and which contains the narrative about Burns and the Lodge St. Andrew, quoted at pp. 48-49 *ante,* was submitted by Grand Secretary to Grand Committee as substantiating his contention about Burns and the Canongate Kilwinning so lately as 29th December 1892,* which testifies that *at that date,* he continued to believe the said narrative as quoted from his History of Lodge No. 1.

A very few days previous to that meeting of Grand Committee, Grand Secretary wrote [12th December 1892] to Brother George Crawford, Right Worshipful Master of Lodge Canongate Kilwinning, a letter from which I am permitted to make the following quotation :—

"1st March 1787 is the date given as that on which Burns was 'inaugurated' as Poet Laureate of Can. Kil. The Minute of the Lodge of that date shews that no such inauguration took place.

"Your Lodge does not require to perpetuate a *myth* in connection with its historical recollections."

Will Grand Secretary show a valid reason for taking so much trouble vainly trying to sever the connection of "Burns and the Canongate Kilwinning"—so far as the Poet-Laureateship is concerned—while he is "ominously silent"† about the very obvious discrepancies in his eloquent narrative of Burns and the Lodge St. Andrew?—

The two cases are quite parallel, in respect that neither on the 1st March 1787, in the minute book of Lodge Canongate Kilwinning, No. 2, nor on the 12th January 1787, in the minute book of Lodge St. Andrew, No. 48, is there any mention of Robert Burns!

On the question of discrepancies in the very interesting narrative regarding Burns and the Lodge St. Andrew, it is well to point out that in his letter to John Ballantine,—which is quoted both by the Historian and the Past-Master of the Lodge of Edinburgh,—Robert Burns did not say that he visited the Lodge St. Andrew. He begins his reference to the event thus :—"I went *to a mason-lodge* yesternight, where the most Worshipful Grand Master Chartres and all the Grand Lodge of Scotland visited."‡

Further, it cannot fail to be observed, as an odd coincidence, that the date of Burns' letter is omitted by both correspondents from their versions of the narrative. The letter was dated 14th January 1787, which was a Sunday, and the statement made by Burns as to time and place was merely that he "*went to a mason-lodge yesternight,*"—

---

* Part II., page 1.

† This is one of the happy expressions invented by Bro. Mackenzie's correspondent, the Past-Master of No. 1, and is given in his undated letter, marked VI., in the "printed correspondence," page 44.

‡ Quoted from the "Prose Works of Robert Burns." W. & R. Chambers, 1839. Letter XXXIII., page 17.

implying the night of Saturday, the 13th January 1787. The meeting in Lodge St. Andrew took place on Friday, 12th January 1787.

By the 14th November 1888—when the first letter of "the printed correspondence" was written to *The Freemason*—there had been time for the author of it to discover that some difference of opinion might exist regarding the precise date of this visit "to a mason lodge," because our poet's letter was dated the 14th January 1787, therefore the writer of that first letter, like a "wary controversialist,"* adroitly avoids naming any specific date, and refers to the presence of Burns on such occasion thus :— "On his visit to the Lodge St. Andrew, Edinburgh, *shortly prior to the alleged inauguration*, he [Burns] writes that the toast was given, 'Caledonia and Caledonia's Bard, Robert Burns,' and proudly records his gratification at the compliment."

Those observations are not made in any captious spirit ;—they are not made with any idea of casting any discredit on the universal belief in the narrative of proceedings which it is *understood*† took place in Lodge St. Andrew, Edinburgh, on 12th January 1787, although the Secretary has omitted to record them, and even Grand Lodge minute of that date contains no reference to "Caledonia's Bard." No one, so far as known, has ever expressed any doubt whatever of the events having taken place as narrated.

Such discrepancies or defects as I have noted in the attractive narrative of Burns and the Lodge St. Andrew, Edinburgh, demonstrate that Grand Secretary and the Past Master of Lodge No. 1 have written on that subject in a much more liberal and friendly spirit than is characteristic of their references to the Inauguration of Robert Burns in the Lodge Canongate Kilwinning on the 1st March 1787, while *the two instances*—so far as the main fact of each is concerned—*are precisely similar.*

Gavin Wilson and the Lodge St. David, Edinburgh.

The extraordinary inconsistency exhibited by Grand Secretary and Brother Mackenzie's other correspondent of *The Freemason*, in their treatment of the well-known narratives, respectively, of Burns in Lodge St. Andrew, on 12th January 1787, and the Inauguration of Burns in Lodge Canongate Kilwinning, on 1st March 1787, becomes more conspicuous according as the minute books of other Lodges are examined, and as attention is given to the careless manner in which, during last century, certain

---

* The author of that phrase is the Past Master of Lodge No. 1—Brother Mackenzie's correspondent—who used it very erroneously in his undated letter to *The Freemason*, marked VI. in "the printed correspondence," page 47, as follows :—" I cannot help expressing the fear that he (Bro. Mackenzie) is not so *wary a controversialist* as the author of 'A Winter with Robert Burns,' for Brother Mackenzie gives particulars which enables one to check the accuracy of the statements in the minute which Brother Marshall more adroitly suppresses."

† The inauguration of Robert Burns as Poet Laureate of Lodge Canongate Kilwinning was *understood* to have taken place on 1st March 1787, as stated in my letter, dated 7th February 1873, set forth in Part II., page 59, line 24, and erroneously commented on by the Past Master of No. 1 in his letter to *The Freemason*, dated 12th January 1889, reproduced in "the printed correspondence," page 29.

Lodge matters were recorded, while others were left unrecorded, precisely as is observable throughout the eighteenth-century minutes of the two Lodges above named.

In this connection, my attention was drawn some time ago to a very interesting article which appeared in Part III., Vol. V., of the Transactions of the "Ars Quatuor Coronatorum." It is headed "Gavin Wilson, a forgotten Masonic Worthy," and is quoted from *The Gentleman's Magazine*, of 17th April 1793. The article is valuable as affording another parallel to the Canongate Kilwinning minute of 1st March 1787, by its references to the Lodge St. David, Edinburgh, No. 36, of which Lodge the said Brother Gavin Wilson was a highly-valued member.

I shall merely quote the following sentences regarding Brother Wilson from the article as it appears in page 156 of the work above-mentioned :—

"He was a regular attendant at the Lodges of the Freemasons, and a warm friend of the fraternity. By his propensity for versifying and composing songs and short stories in rhyme, he contributed much to the social mirth and enjoyment of their meetings, and to the good humour and amusement of all companies where he came. He frequently sang and recited his own productions in the Lodge meetings—from this circumstance he was elected Poet Laureate to the Lodge of St. David, at Edinburgh, of which he was a member.* After receiving this distinguished mark of honour, in the year 1788 he published a collection of his poetical performances under the title of ' A Collection of Masonic Songs and entertaining Anecdotes for the use of all the Lodges. By Gavin Wilson, Poet Laureat to the Lodge of St. David, Edinburgh.' To this publication is prefixed a portrait of the author decorated with Masonic insignia. By people who were acquainted with him, I have been told that it is a very good likeness. It is drawn and etched by a very ingenious artist, Mr John Kay, engraver and portrait painter in Edinburgh." †

Brother Gavin Wilson's book of Songs was advertised as being "In the Press" in the year 1787, and published shortly afterwards. His portrait by Kay, facing the title-page, is dated 1787, and that appears to be something more than a mere coincidence—it suggests the very obvious conclusion that, as Gavin Wilson "was a regular attendant at the Lodges of the Freemasons, and a warm friend of the fraternity," he met Robert Burns during his frequent visits to the Canongate Kilwinning, and knew of Burns as her Poet Laureate.

A copy of Gavin Wilson's "Collection of Masonic Songs" is in the Advocates' Library, Edinburgh, and it contains many pieces of interest. One is of special value to Lodge Canongate Kilwinning, being a dirge composed by Brother Gavin Wilson to the memory of Past Master George Drummond, which was sung at "a Funeral meeting" of Lodge Canongate Kilwinning, held in the Lodge-room, 7th January 1767, "in honour of the memory of George Drummond, Esq., once Grand Master for Scotland, and late Master of this Lodge." An interesting report of this funeral meeting is given in the Canongate Kilwinning minute of 7th January 1767, portion of which is quoted at page 92 of the history of that Lodge.

---

* No mention of such election occurs in the minutes of Lodge St. David.
† Below the likeness, on left side, is engraved, " K. Fect." ; on the right, " 1787."

No. X. (written in the year 1771) of Brother Gavin Wilson's "Collection of Masonic Songs," contains a laudatory reference to "the organ," and to the inspiriting effect of music as given forth from that effective instrument. The organ* in Canongate Kilwinning has for nearly a century and a half been a special attraction in the Lodge, and evidently was so to Brother Gavin Wilson, who found that it could "discourse most eloquent music."

From these and other circumstances above mentioned it is evident that the Poet Laureate of Lodge St. David, No. 36, was a frequent visitor at meetings of the Canongate Kilwinning.

In connection with these references to Bro. Gavin Wilson and his having been Poet Laureate of Lodge St. David, Edinburgh, I beg to subjoin the result of an examination of the minute books of that Lodge, made in order to glean such information regarding him as those records afford. The first allusion to him is in the year 1766, as follows :—

"21 *October* 1766.—*Monthly Meeting.*

"'The Lodge being convened and properly formed Br Peter Smith in name of " Br Gavin Wilson of St. Paul's Glasgow presented this Lodge with two handsome " large Leather mugs, of his own workmanship for which the Brethren unanimously " expressed their thanks by drinking his health, and also assumed him as a member " of this Lodge." (*No signature.*)

The minutes of the annual election of office-bearers on St. John the Evangelist's days in 1767, 1768, and 1769 record that he was elected on each occasion one of the Stewards of the Lodge. The next reference is :—

"*Monthly Meeting.*—16 *October* 1770.

. . . . "The Brethren were entertained with vocal music from Brs Esplin, " Pillam, Downie &c and the new song of St. David by Particular desire from " Brother Gavin Wilson. After the visitors were gone the Lodge unanimously made " choice of Br Gavin Wilson to be their General Stewart for the ensuing year."
"(Signed)   ANDREW BALFOUR, Mr."

Brother Gavin Wilson was re-elected one of the Lodge Stewards on 27th December 1770; "contd Grand Stewart for the ensuing year," on 15th October 1771; re-elected one of the Lodge Stewards on St. John's Day in December 1771; and, finally, at an "Emergency" meeting on 9th October 1772, it is recorded that he acted as Junior Warden *pro. tem.* With these exceptions, Gavin Wilson's name does not appear in the minutes of St. David's Lodge, and it is certainly a noteworthy circumstance that his Laureateship was published to the world a few months after the date that Burns had been elected to a similar office in Canongate Kilwinning.

---

* The organ, built by Sneitzler, of London, still in first-rate condition, was placed in the Lodge-room, in 1757, within a niche prepared for it opposite the R. W. Master's chair, by Brother James Fergus, Architect of the Royal Exchange, etc. By the time Robert Burns visited Can. Kil., the organ had been placed within the more convenient recess shown in the Inauguration picture, where it now is.

Proof of this is found in the following advertisement, which appeared in the *Edinburgh Evening Courant* newspaper of Saturday, 15th December 1787 :—

> "*In the Press, and speedily will be Published.*
> "DEDICATED BY PERMISSION
> "To the RIGHT HONOURABLE AND MOST WORSHIPFUL
> LORD ELCHO
> "GRAND MASTER OF FREEMASONS IN SCOTLAND
> "A COLLECTION OF MASONIC SONGS
> "AND
> "ENTERTAINING ANECDOTES
> "For the Use of all the Lodges
> "Ornamented with a Print of the Author taken from the Life by J. Kay
> "By GAVIN WILSON
> "POET LAUREAT TO THE LODGE OF ST. DAVID
> "Leg, Arm, and Boot Maker :
> "Inventor of Hardened and Polished Leather."

Hence it is seen that very shortly after Robert Burns had been elected "Poet Laureat" of Lodge Canongate Kilwinning—in the very same year, 1787—the news had been proclaimed to the world through the press in the above manner and otherwise, that Brother Gavin Wilson was "Poet Laureat to the Lodge of St. David,"—*nevertheless, there is no record in any minute of the Lodge that Brother Gavin Wilson had ever been elected to that office.* Evidently such appointment had been considered outside the "usual business," as appears to have been the case on other occasions.

Leonard Horner and the Lodge Kirknewton and Ratho.

Through the kindness of Brother George Innes, a respected Past Master of the Lodge Kirknewton and Ratho, I am enabled to exhibit another parallel to the very incomplete minute of Lodge Canongate Kilwinning, dated 1st March 1787, in the minute of a meeting held by the Lodge Kirknewton and Ratho, No. 85, on 30th September 1803. By that minute it appears that even in 1803 there was a Lodge Secretary quite as forgetful of his duties as was the "practising solicitor" who was understood to be Secretary of the Canongate Kilwinning in the year 1787.

Before reproducing the minute, I take occasion to explain that Brother Leonard Horner, a distinguished citizen of Edinburgh during the early part of this century, and who is specially referred to in page 18 *ante* as a friend of Brother William Campbell, Writer to the Signet, Senior Warden of Canongate Kilwinning, 1801 to 1803,* was affiliated a member of Lodge Kirknewton and Ratho on 30th September 1803, as is very distinctly stated by Brother Horner in the inscription on a bible which he presented to that Lodge, and which is quoted in said page 18 *ante.* Copy of a letter from

---

* The same Brother William Campbell who, on 12th November 1845, seconded the motion as to painting the picture of the Inauguration of Robert Burns as Poet Laureate.

Brother Horner, and extract from subsequent minute of the Lodge, relative to this matter, are herein given under the head of *Notanda.*

The odd part of the business is that Brother Leonard Horner is not recorded in the minute of 30th September 1803, nor in any other minute, as having been affiliated from Lodge Canongate Kilwinning.

The minute referred to of Lodge Kirknewton and Ratho is as follows :—

"RATHO *Sept*. 30ᵗʰ 1803

"The Lodge met and Constitute when James Kraft Simonsen of Norway, Abraham Henderson, William Weir, & Geo. M⁰Laren were admitted Members, & paid their dues accordingly.

Brother Simonsen paid . . . . o 13 6
Brothers Henderson, Weir, & M⁰Laren, 10/6 each."

(*No Signature.*)

Were Grand Secretary's illogical assertion regarding the Canongate Kilwinning minute of 1st March 1787 for a moment to be entertained, then, by a parity of such reasoning, "*the foregoing minute proves beyond question that no such event as the*" affiliation of Brother Leonard Horner to the Lodge Kirknewton and Ratho "*took place at the meeting of*" * 30th September 1803,—which reasoning is manifestly absurd and untrue.

Robert Burns and the Royal Burgh of Linlithgow.

The inconsistency of those two brethren, the Historian and an industrious Past-Master of the Lodge of Edinburgh (Mary's Chapel), in ignoring the fact that the visit of Robert Burns to the Lodge St. Andrew, No. 48, on 12th January 1787, is not recorded in the minute book of that Lodge,—while, by their vaunting reference to the Canongate Kilwinning minute of 1st March 1787, they try hard to persuade their readers that *the omission* from that minute of any record concerning Robert Burns "*proves beyond question*" that no such event as the Inauguration of Burns as Poet Laureate of Canongate " Kilwinning took place at the meeting of 1st March 1787,"—is further demonstrated by the following narrative of an episode in the Poet's life which is not generally known.

This narrative comes as a very complete parallel to the Inauguration episode above mentioned, in respect that the great honour conferred upon Robert Burns on the special occasion in question was not minuted on the date of its occurrence, "and yet, " *neither he, nor any of his friends, nor any of his biographers, take any notice of such an* " *event.*" †

The narrative is as follows :—

On the 16th day of November 1787, Robert Burns of Mossgeil, Ayrshire, was made a Burgess and Guild Brother of the Royal Burgh of Linlithgow, but the easy-going

---

* The two quotations in above paragraph are from Grand Secretary's letter to *The Freemason,* dated 18th August 1891.

† A statement *in re* the Inauguration quoted from the letter written by Brother Mackenzie's correspondent to *The Freemason,* dated 14th November 1888.

Town Clerk of that ancient and renowned burgh took no notice in his minute of the Town Council's business on that day, of the unusual occurrence he had witnessed, in which Burns figured so prominently. The Town Clerk doubtless considered the rare honour conferred on Burns was quite a *complimentary* or *social* affair—quite outside the usual routine, and not "*business*," according to his acceptation of the term,—just as the Secretary of Lodge St. Andrew, Edinburgh, appears to have thought of the Burns' incident on 12th January 1787, and as the Secretary of Canongate Kilwinning thought regarding the Inauguration of Burns as Poet Laureate on 1st March 1787.

That Robert Burns had been made a Burgess and Guild Brother of Linlithgow on 16th November 1787—that no record of such event had been made in the minute of the Linlithgow Town Council Meeting of said date—and that his Burgess Ticket, bearing same date upon it, was produced and verified at a meeting of the Town Council of Linlithgow held on 4th January 1859 are indisputable facts, satisfactorily shown in the following copy of Excerpt from Minute of Council Meeting held on the latter date :—

"*Excerpt from Minute of Meeting of the Town Council of the Royal Burgh
of Linlithgow, held on 4th January* 1859.

" Alexander Thomas, Esquire, residing in Linlithgow, having been introduced to the meeting, exhibited a Burgess Ticket to instruct that our great National Poet, Robert Burns, the Centenary of whose birth is to be celebrated with such universal acclaim throughout the length and breadth of the land upon the 25th of January current, was duly admitted a Burgess of this Burgh upon the 16th of November 1787. Mr Thomas stated that this interesting and valuable relic was now the property of Neilson Mitchell, Esq., Merchant in Glasgow, a native, like himself, of the good town.

" The Council, having inspected the Ticket and the impression of the Burgh Seal attached to it, and *being fully satisfied of their genuineness,—altho' no notice is taken of the admission in the Council Minute of the date it was made,*—arising, doubtless, from the practice that prevailed in the Burgh down to a comparatively recent period of parties being admitted by the Magistrates without any record of the circumstance being preserved in the Council Minute Books,*—instruct the Clerk to subjoin a copy of the Burgess Ticket to this minute, and also to insert a Memorandum on the Minute Book of the date it took place that such an admission had been made, and that the Burgess Ticket had this day been produced to and verified by the Council.

" The meeting further passed a vote of thanks both to Mr Mitchell and Mr Thomas for thus enabling them to preserve such gratifying evidence of the connection that existed betwixt the Burgh and Scotland's own Immortal Bard."

---

* From this singular explanation, made in the year 1859, it is evident that the bestowal of a Burgess Ticket, even upon so distinguished a poet as Robert Burns, was not considered "*business.*" *Vide* minute of Lodge Canongate Kilwinning, March 1st, 1787, Part II., page 14.

"COPY OF BURGESS TICKET granted by the Town of Linlithgow to ROBERT BURNS.

"AT LINLITHGOW, *the Sixteenth day of November One thousand seven hundred*
"*and Eighty-seven years.*

"The which day, in presence of James Andrew, Esq., Provost of the Burgh of
"Linlithgow; William Napier, James Watson, Stephen Mitchell, and John Gibson,
"Baillies, and Robert Speeden, Dean of Guild,—COMPEARED, Mr Robert Burns,
"Mossgeil, Ayrshire, who was made and created Burgess and Guild Brother of the
"said Burgh, having given his Oath of Fidelity according to the form used thereanent.

"*EXTRACTED BY*

"(Signed) JA. TAYLOR, *Clk.*"

*The
Burgh Seal
attached.*

Notwithstanding the very plausible explanation given in the year 1859 by the
Town Council of the ancient burgh of Linlithgow, as to the singular omission from
their minute of meeting, dated the 16th November 1787, of any reference to Burns—
it does seem very odd that the Burgess Ticket should appear as if it had been
"*Extracted* by Jas. Taylor, Clk.," from some record of the said Town Council.

That all shows how indifferent even a Town Clerk could be during last century
in rendering an account of what occurred at one of his most important meetings.

———

3. EXCURSIONS OF ROBERT BURNS DURING THE SUMMER AND AUTUMN, 1787.

The Past-Master of the Lodge of Edinburgh (Mary's Chapel), No. 1, in his
undated letter to *The Freemason*, pp. 48 and 49 of "the printed correspondence," has
expended much time and labour unnecessarily in his references to a "journey" which
Burns made in the year 1787. Throughout pages 14 to 19 *ante*, I have shown that, in
the letter referred to, he has made most absurd and unfounded assertions concerning
the boy William Campbell and "this journey." At this point I shall only quote the
following words from it :—

"But Brother Campbell's statement is contradicted by all the biographers of
Burns, who state that he made this journey in company with Dr Adair only."
[Continuation of this quotation will be found at page 14 *ante*.]

Brother Mackenzie's correspondent cannot prove the assertion with which he
begins that paragraph. Brother Campbell's statement is a very simple one; it is quoted
in the last paragraph of page 14 *ante*, and, instead of being "contradicted by *all* the
"biographers of Burns," it is not mentioned by any one of them.

Further, "all the biographers of Burns" *do not* "state that he made this journey "in company with Dr Adair only," as will now be shown.

On this subject of the excursions made by Robert Burns during the summer and autumn of 1787, I quote from "The Life and Works of Robert Burns," by Robert Chambers, appendix to vol. II., page 319, published 1886, as follows :—

"In previous narratives of Burns's life the events of the summer and autumn of 1787 are to a serious extent incorrectly arranged.

"Dr Currie represents Burns as returning from Mauchline to Edinburgh in June, and thence setting out on the West Highland ride which terminated at Dumbarton. There is no apparent evidence for his having returned at this time to Edinburgh."

    *   *   *   *   *

"The learned biographer is certainly wrong in placing the tour by Stirling to Harvieston with Dr Adair in August. Burns was at Mauchline till the 7th of that month, and on the 23rd he wrote a letter, dated from Nicol's house in Edinburgh. On the 25th he and Nicol set out on their post-chaise journey to the Highlands. It is very unlikely that Burns would have a ten days' tour between the 7th and 23rd of August, and so early as the 25th set out again over the same ground—ground, too, which Currie represents him as having passed over for a first time in June."

    *   *   *   *   *

"What finally sets it at rest is a document, lighted upon since the above was written, and alluded to in the text, showing that Burns was a subject of legal proceedings, and made a personal appearance in Edinburgh on account of them on the 15th of August. Arriving in Edinburgh from Mossgiel on the 7th, engaged in these legal matters on and perhaps *before* the 15th, writing to Robert Ainslie from Nicol's house on the 23rd, and setting out on the post-chaise journey with Nicol on the 25th, there is no time for a ten days' tour with Dr Adair during this month. No such tour, therefore, took place at that time. The early and middle part of October is the first clear space of time which will suffice for a ten days' tour; it is also the first sufficient space of time prior to the setting in of winter, after which any such tour was not likely to have taken place."

The foregoing is only one authority on the subject of the August and October excursions of Robert Burns in the year 1787 at variance with statements in "the printed correspondence," and, as already stated, that authority was published in the year 1886. In the following information, published so far back as 1871, I find a similar account of the circumstantial narrative of the several journeys as traced by Robert Chambers. It is quoted from "Chronological Summary of the Life and Writings of Burns," a chapter contained in "The Complete Poetical Works of Robert Burns," by William Scott Douglas.

"MORE EDINBURGH LIFE, AND SUNNY-DAY RECREATIONS,
[1787—AGE 28].

"AUG. 25.—*Northern Tour.*—[Sets out from Edinburgh in a chaise, along with Wm. Nicol, for Stirling and the North.]

"AUG. 27.—[The poet leaves Nicol for one day in Stirling, and proceeds to visit Gavin Hamilton's relatives at Harvieston, on the Devon.]

" Aug. 28.—[Journey resumed by way of Crieff, Taymouth, Aberfeldy, Dunkeld, Blair-Athole, Killiecrankie, Fort-George, Inverness ; and back by Nairn, Forres, Elgin, Fochabers, Castle-Gordon, Cullen, Aberdeen, The Mearns, Montrose, Arbroath, Dundee, Carse of Gowrie, Perth, Strathearn, Invermay, Kinross, Queensferry to Edinburgh, where the travellers arrived on 16th September, after three weeks' absence.]

" *Final Excursion in October.*—[Re-visits Stirling and Harvieston in company with Dr Adair; Cauldron Linn, Rumbling Brig. Visits Mr Ramsay of Ochtertyre on Teith, and Sir William Murray of Ochtertyre in Strathearn ; also Mrs Bruce of Clack-mannan Tower.]

" Oct. 20.—[Returns to Edinburgh, and makes his residence with Mr William Cruickshanks, teacher, High School.]"

A third authority is " The Complete Works of Robert Burns, with a Memoir by " William Gunnyon," published in 1873 by William P. Nimmo. It affords precisely the same information as do those two authorities already quoted,—quite in opposition to the erroneous assertion of Brother Mackenzie's correspondent, regarding what he asserts is said by " *all* the biographers of Burns."

A fourth authority to similar effect on the subject of the August and October excursions in 1787, is " The National Burns," edited by the late Rev. George Gilfillan.

But,—independently of all those testimonies,—evidence exists from so far back a period as the year 1846 in the " Dedication " [Preface] of " A Winter with Robert Burns," where it is stated that Brother James Marshall, the compiler of such work, testified to the fact of Brother William Campbell, W.S., having said that he had been in " the company of Burns at Auchtertyre House, *during the autumn of* 1787." Brother Marshall was present at the meeting of Lodge Canongate Kilwinning when his friend Brother William Campbell so expressed himself. Further evidence, therefore, on this head is unnecessary to confute the reckless assertions of Brother Mackenzie's correspondent, the Past Master of the Lodge of Edinburgh, No. 1.

---

4. Attendance of Robert Burns at Meetings of Lodge Canongate Kilwinning.

The Past Master of the Lodge of Edinburgh (Mary's Chapel), No. 1, in his " Prefatory Note " to " the printed Copy of the Correspondence," dated June 1892, concludes his assertions thus :—

" It may be added, *for what it may be worth*, that, in the opinion of the writer,—formed after an exhaustive examination of every available source of information, and a careful consideration of the associations and movements of the Poet during his visits to Edinburgh,—there is nothing to lead one to believe that the Poet visited the Canongate Kilwinning Lodge on any occasion other than the *one* on which he received honorary affiliation."

In his first letter on the subject, dated 14th November 1888, the same writer said :—

"It is seen that he (Burns) could have attended, at the most, only *three* meetings of the Lodge Canongate Kilwinning during the season 1786-87."

A few lines further on, in same letter, he writes :—

"He (Burns) thus, during the Masonic season 1787-88, could not have attended more than *two* such meetings, *if he attended any.*"

In his letter to *The Freemason*, dated 6th July 1889, the correspondent made the following assertion :—

"I have already shown that Burns could have only attended the Lodge Canongate Kilwinning on *two*, certainly not more than *three*, occasions."

But afterwards, *in same letter*, the correspondent assured his readers as follows:—

"From my own researches *I* am satisfied that Burns attended *one* meeting only —the February meeting—of the Lodge in 1787."

As a direct and effectual contradiction of those assertions made by the Past Master of Lodge No. 1 (Brother Mackenzie's correspondent of *The Freemason*), I shall do little more than refer to the extract from Minute of Lodge meeting, held 9th February 1815, to be found herein at page 30 of Part II., in which the lamented Poet Laureate is referred to as "*a public character so immediately connected with them* [the brethren of Canongate Kilwinning], *and who on so many occasions contributed so generally to the harmony of the Masonic Order, and to that of the Lodge Canongate Kilwinning in particular.*"

Further, as showing how very quickly after arriving in Edinburgh Robert Burns began his attendances at Canongate Kilwinning, the following extract will prove of interest. I quote it from page 282 of "Biography of the Hon. Henry Erskine, Lord Advocate for Scotland, by Lieut.-Colonel Alex. Fergusson," 1882 :—

"*It was Mr Erskine who introduced Burns, on his coming to Edinburgh, to the Canongate Kilwinning Lodge of Masons.* He had himself joined it about six years previously, and since that time had frequently occupied the chair at the meetings of this Lodge, which was especially resorted to by many of the leading Whigs at that time. Mr Erskine was the more ready to present his friend to the brethren, as he had, it is stated, 'seen by his poems that he was a person who would be quite at home in a Lodge.'"

Robert Burns arrived in Edinburgh, 28th November 1786.

"On the 7th December 1786, Burns wrote to his friend, Gavin Hamilton :—'My Lord Glencairn and the Dean of Faculty, Mr Henry Erskine, have taken me under their wing.'"

There is a minute of the Lodge meeting held 7th December—first of the season 1786—also a minute on behalf of Grand Lodge on same date, but in neither of them is there any mention of Burns being present. That is not surprising after what we learn of the neglect elsewhere in the Canongate Kilwinning records, also in the minutes of Lodge St. Andrew, Edinburgh, because the minute-book of the latter body shows no mention of Robert Burns as being present at the great meeting of 12th January 1787.

At page 278 of same work quoted, it is said :—

"The year 1786 is memorable as that in which Robert Burns made his *début* in Edinburgh, an event closely connected with more than one member of the Erskine family."

* * * * * *

"The extreme cordiality of the reception which awaited Robert Burns on his arrival in Edinburgh, from a small group of congenial souls, is not difficult of explanation—there was more in it than mere admiration for genius. Mr Erskine's sister had, as has been stated, been married in the preceding year to the Earl of Glencairn's brother."—(Page 280.)

* * * * * *

"Creech the bookseller, too, who had been the travelling tutor of Lord Glencairn, and who was to be Burns' publisher, was not the least important of those whose acquaintance he made by means of this family coterie at the earliest stage of his Edinburgh career." (Page 281.)

In my Review of the minutes of years 1786-7-8, at pages 4 to 11 of Part II., abundant proof is given *out of the recorded minutes themselves*—reproduced in the eight pages which immediately follow that Review—*that very many other meetings* of Lodge Canongate Kilwinning *had taken place* during the two-and-a-half years referred to, *of which no record has been preserved.*

It will be obvious to any impartial reader of that Review, and those minutes of the years 1786-7-8, that there had been very many meetings of Lodge Canongate Kilwinning besides the very few recorded during that period, and, consequently, there is no reason to doubt what was said by the R.W. Master, George Simson, and acquiesced in by all the brethren present, at the Lodge meeting, held 9th February 1815, that Burns on "*many occasions contributed to the harmony* of the Masonic Order, and to that "*of the Lodge Canongate Kilwinning* in particular."

---

5. Alleged First Mention in Canongate Kilwinning Records of Robert Burns having been Poet Laureate.

The Past-Master of the Lodge of Edinburgh (Mary's Chapel), No. 1—Brother Mackenzie's correspondent of *The Freemason*—in his first letter, already referred to, said :—

"Until 1835 there was no such office in the Lodge Canongate Kilwinning as that of Poet Laureate."

In same letter it is said :—"The Poet is claimed not only as having been elected its first Poet Laureate, but as having held that office from 1787 until his death in 1796. The records of the Lodge, which I some years ago examined, give no countenance to this assertion."

And, further on, it is added :—" It was not until 1815, twenty-eight years after the alleged occurrence, and nineteen years after the Poet's death, that any mention is made of the event."

In answer to those misleading assertions, I will briefly remark that it is quite evident that the records of Lodge Canongate Kilwinning did not receive a very "exhaustive" examination by the said Past Master of Lodge No. 1, otherwise he would have learned, if anxious about it, that the earliest record in Lodge Canongate Kilwinning of Robert Burns having been Poet Laureate, so far as yet discovered, is the framed print of our first Poet Laureate, bearing the following inscription :—

" ROBERT BURNS, THE SCOTTISH BARD,
" *POET LAUREAT,*
" *LODGE No. 1, CANNONGATE*
" *KILWINNING.*"

further, that the said Past Master of Lodge No. 1—had he been careful in his examination of Canongate Kilwinning records, and desirous of the information—should have discovered also, as I did, that the above-mentioned print was one of "four prints which were got for the Lodge," and which on 24th June 1802, "met with the approbation of the Brethern."

Such entry in the record of Lodge meeting, held 24th June 1802, constitutes it the earliest reference in the minute books of Canongate Kilwinning to Robert Burns as Poet Laureate of the Lodge.

The said Past Master of Lodge No. 1 should have also learned that the above noted print of Robert Burns, " Poet Laureat," contains the year of publication, 1798, engraved upon it, and, consequently, that it may have been exhibited in the Lodge-room even earlier than on 24th June 1802, though only approved on that date by "the Brethern." See frontispiece, also pages 11 and 20 *ante*, and Part II., pages 20 to 25.

---

6. GARBLED QUOTATIONS.

Brother Mackenzie's principal correspondent of *The Freemason*—the industrious Past Master of the Lodge of Edinburgh (Mary's Chapel)—in his anxiety to underrate the argument contained in my letter of 7th February 1873, has made some extravagant assertions, and has mixed and misquoted passages from that letter in a most arbitrary manner.

I shall confine my comments on this point to a certain portion of the letter written 14th November 1888 by the above-designated correspondent to *The Freemason*.

The portion to which I refer appears in pp. 12 and 13 of " the printed copy of correspondence." In reproducing the same as follows, I also reproduce alongside it two paragraphs—from widely separate parts of my letter of 7th February 1873—

out of which the misquotations in question have been adroitly woven. These show at a glance how the garbling process has been accomplished :—

EXTRACTS from LETTER to Brother D. MURRAY LYON from Brother HUGH C. PEACOCK when the latter was Secretary of Lodge Canongate Kilwinning.

7th February 1873.
[*Vide* Part II., pp. 57 and 59, also History of Lodge Canongate Kilwinning, pp. 117 and 120.]

[*Paragraph from beginning of Letter.*]

"Had any doubt ever been previously thrown on the universally accepted connection of Robert Burns with the Canongate Kilwinning, the nature of your reference to it might be looked for in such a comprehensive work as you propose to publish; but, when it is considered that only *now*, when few of the living links‡ remain, *connecting us with those* who had often borne testimony to their personal acquaintance with Burns, and to their having been at meetings of the Lodge when he was there as its Poet Laureate, the tenor of your notice appears extraordinary."

[*Paragraph from nearly the end of Letter.*]

"It may be reckoned comparatively slender evidence to add to the foregoing, yet it may be remarked as some satisfaction to know, that there are members of the Lodge at the present time who associated for years with those members who had the privilege of Burns' company in the Lodge when he wore the jewel of his office as Poet Laureate; that, *further, that jewel was also worn by the Ettrick Shepherd as Poet Laureate of Canongate Kilwinning,* and it had the name of Robert Burns engraved upon it when the Poet Laureateship was conferred on him."

EXTRACT from LETTER to *The Freemason* by Brother MACKENZIE'S chief correspondent—the Past Master of the Lodge of Edinburgh No. 1.

14th November 1888.

"The allegation that Burns was elected Poet Laureate of the Lodge is further sought to be supported by letters written by Brother Peacock, the Secretary of the Lodge, to Brother Murray Lyon so recently as 1873, in consequence of hearing that Brother Lyon was, in his then forthcoming 'History of Freemasonry,' 'to discredit' the fact.[*] The reasons given in these letters amount to little. They are mostly assumed inferences from alleged facts, the accuracy of which is not known, and is not instructed. The chief reasons founded on are that Brother Marshall 'believed' in the inauguration, that his statement of the occurrence had not until then (1873) been questioned, that Brother M'Neill, the Master of the Lodge—1830–1837—'had *no doubt* whatever of the fact,' and that un-named old members of the Lodge [†]

' had often borne testimony to their personal ac-
' quaintance with Burns, and to their having been
' at meetings of the Lodge when he was there as
' its Poet Laureate,

and that there are
' members of the Lodge at the present time (1873)
' who associated for years with those members who
' had the privilege of Burns' company in the Lodge
' when he wore the jewel of his office as Poet
' Laureate,'

which 'had the name of Robert Burns engraved
' upon it *when the Poet Laureateship was conferred*
' *on him*'."
(The concluding eight words were *not* printed in italics in the paragraph from which the quotation is made. The correspondent italicised them in his perverted extract, as above.)

---

* It was a mistake to discredit "*the fact*."

† Many of those, whom the correspondent designates "un-named old members of the Lodge," are faithfully portrayed in the Inauguration picture, and they are duly named and described in the instructive handbook to that picture, entitled "A Winter with Robert Burns."

‡ A "few of the living links," in the year 1873, "connecting us with those who had often borne testimony to their personal acquaintance with Burns" are named in *Notanda.*

The foregoing contrasted quotations clearly show that the correspondent, in what is professedly a quotation from my letter, connects a portion of one paragraph with a portion of another totally different paragraph, by adroitly introducing between them the conjunction "*and*" within the quotation marks *as if it were mine*. Not only so, but he has "*studiously kept out of sight*"[*] an essential clause of the second paragraph with regard to the Ettrick Shepherd, totally perverting the sense and meaning of the matter so misquoted, and he ingeniously connects the disjoined portions of that paragraph by the convenient pronoun "which." This appears to have been done "for his own purposes,"[†] just as the same correspondent asserts when charging the late Brother James Marshall—author of "A Winter with Robert Burns"—with having been guilty of using a misquotation.

Other misquotations, which have been arranged with equal ingenuity, so as to convey quite a different signification from what the author intended, are referred to elsewhere in these pages.

7. Conclusion.

The Laureateship.

. . . "Until 1835 there was no such office in the Lodge Canongate Kilwinning as that of Poet Laureate."

> P. M. of Lodge No. 1 in Letter I., 14th November 1888.

. . . "It is only in 1815 that the claim was, for the first time, put forward of his (Robert Burns) having been the Poet Laureate of the Lodge."

> Grand Secretary in Letter IV., 12th February (presumably 1889).

Neither of those correspondents of Brother Mackenzie in *The Freemason* appear to have made adequate use of their boasted opportunities of examining Canongate Kilwinning records, otherwise they would have known of the framed print of Robert Burns our first Poet Laureate, which has been prominently exhibited in the Lodge-room for nearly a century,—that it is one of "four prints" mentioned in the minute of 24th June 1802 as having "met with the approbation of the Brethern,"—and that in all probability it had been placed in the Lodge-room before that date, because it was published in the year 1798. Those facts clearly confute the correspondents' misleading assertions. *Vide* frontispiece, also pp. 11, 30, and 32 *ante*, and p. 20 of Part II.

The Inauguration.

"It was not until 1846—fifty-nine years after the alleged Inauguration—that it was for the first time made known to the public."

> P. M. of Lodge No. 1 in Letter III., 12th January 1889.

"The 'Inauguration' was never heard of until then."

> P. M. of Lodge No. 1 in Letter VI., undated.

---

[*] That is a phrase which occurs in Grand Secretary's letter to *The Freemason*, dated 18th August 1891;—p. 17 of "the printed correspondence."

[†] In Letter VI., undated.

"While preparing my 'History of Freemasonry' in 1873, it became known that I discredited the story of the Inauguration. Statements were then made to me by the office-bearers of the Lodge, which I unfortunately believed—assertions which subsequent investigation showed had no foundation in fact."

Grand Secretary in Letter XI., 18th August 1891.

To expose such unfounded assertions—in addition to what is already advanced herein on the subject—I need only now refer to the minute of Committee meeting, held 16th January 1835, an extract of which will be found at page 38, Part II. It will there be seen that the brethren were desirous that James Hogg should join the Lodge, and be appointed Poet Laureate in succession to Robert Burns. At the request of the Committee this resolution was communicated to the "Ettrick Shepherd" by his personal friend Brother John Forbes, as is proved by James Hogg's answer, wherein he says that he "cannot join them, nor be initiated into the mysteries of the Art" (*vide* page 39, Part II.). The minute goes on to say that Bro. Forbes was instructed "*at the same time,* " in name of the Master, Office-bearers, and Members, to invite his (the Shepherd's) " attendance at a full meeting of the Lodge" on an early date, "TO HAVE HIS BROW " ENCIRCLED WITH THE LAUREL WREATH, THE INSIGNIA OF HIS OFFICE."

Those graphic concluding fourteen words prove most effectively that the Inauguration was no invention or "concoction," perpetrated in either 1845 or 1846, as is alleged by the correspondent. They prove that in the year 1835, *ten years* at least before the Inauguration picture was proposed to be painted—and before the artist, Bro. Stewart Watson, had returned from Italy—*eleven years* before the admirable companion-work, entitled "A Winter with Robert Burns, was written—the brethren of Canongate Kilwinning had ample knowledge of the laurel wreath having been a prominent feature in the installation of Robert Burns as Poet Laureate, and quite warrantably looked forward to James Hogg joining the Lodge, and being elected and inaugurated Poet Laureate, in same manner as had been his predecessor in that office.

In the foregoing quotation from Grand Secretary's letter of 18th August 1891 to *The Freemason* he refers to "assertions which subsequent investigation showed had no " foundation in fact," as having been made to him in 1873 by the Office-bearers of Canongate Kilwinning. It would doubtless have been interesting to his readers had they been informed what was the nature of the "subsequent investigation" and *when it was made,* because, in a letter dated so recently as 13th December 1886, and published in the *Scotsman* newspaper, Grand Secretary distinctly expressed his belief in Robert Burns having been Poet Laureate of Canongate Kilwinning (*vide* pp. 36, 37 *ante*).

The allegations have already been confuted which Grand Secretary makes against the "statements" said to have been made to him in 1873 "by the Office-bearers of the Lodge."

Unfounded Charges.

. . . "It was not until Brother Marshall directed his ingenuity to the matter that it was said that Burns had been 'elected' and 'inaugurated' into that office! It was

Brother Marshall and Brother Stewart Watson, the painter of the picture illustrating the alleged event, who, in 1845, conceived and originated the grand gathering of 1787."

P. M. of Lodge No. 1 in Letter VI., undated.

"We, besides, find him [Brother Marshall], *for his own purposes*, misquoting the minute of the Lodge of 12th November 1845, and making many assertions manufactured for his story. It is thus impossible to acquit him of the charge of wilful and gross concoction."

P. M. of Lodge No. 1 in Letter VI., undated.

The industrious correspondent appears to have thought those serious charges could safely be made *now* against Brothers Stewart Watson and James Marshall, after forty-eight years have elapsed since their respective works—*The Inauguration Picture*, and "A Winter with Robert Burns"—were published, and after twenty-four years have elapsed since each of the worthy brethren had been laid in his grave.

Did the correspondent reckon on there being no brethren in the Canongate Kilwinning Lodge now who would say a word in defence of those loyal and distinguished members and their services to the Lodge?

The charges are utterly preposterous. They are all bare assertions, and are obviously untrue. Brother Marshall's narrative of the Lodge meeting held 12th November 1845 was evidently written from his own recollection of the proceedings, and is doubly valuable on that very account—by reason of him having been present on the occasion. He vouches for Brother William Campbell having then said that "he (Brother Campbell) had himself spent *three* of the happiest days of his life in the company of Burns at Auchtertyre House during the *autumn* of 1787." Brother Marshall is quite as likely to be correct in that portion of the narrative as the Secretary who minuted the statement that Brother Campbell said "he spent *two* of the most happy days with him (Burns) at Auchtertyre Castle."

Burns had a busy time when enjoying, together with several other guests, Sir William Murray's hospitality at Auchtertyre House in October 1787. While being entertained on that occasion he was shown around the vicinity, and especially he was shown Loch Turit, which visit inspired him to write the sympathetic poem, entitled, "On Scaring some Water-fowl in Loch Turit, a wild scene among the hills of Oughtertyre." Among the company whom Burns met while under Sir William Murray's roof was the lady in whose praise he composed the song "Blythe, Blythe and Merry was She,"—a young cousin of his host, Miss Euphemia Murray of Lintrose, who eventually became the wife of Lord Methven, one of the judges of the Court of Session. During his stay at Auchtertyre Burns also wrote several letters. All such entertainment and literary work may easily have occupied more than *two* days. Brother Marshall's statement above quoted is better expressed and more explicit than that of the Lodge Secretary in the minute, and is perhaps more nearly correct.

"It is impossible to believe that those convening and carrying through such a demonstration (Inauguration of Burns) would have purposely suppressed all mention of it. But, singularly enough, this is what Brother Marshall asserts they did."

P. M. of Lodge No. 1 in Letter I., 14th November 1888.

"Indeed, the propounders of the theory in 1846 alleged that" . . . "it was resolved to suppress all record of the occurrence!"

P. M. of Lodge No. 1 in Letter III., 12th January 1889.

. . . "and yet we are asked to believe that this *tragic scene* occurred, and that all record of it was purposely suppressed by its promoters!"

P. M. of Lodge No. 1 in Letter III., 12th January 1889.

"The minute was thus, according to Brother Marshall, purposely suppressed." . . . . "Had such a demonstration occurred it is impossible to believe that it could have accidentally escaped notice in the minutes of the meeting, which are still extant."

P. M. of Lodge No. 1 in Letter VI., undated.

By the frequent repetition of above charge against Brother Marshall and the Lodge Canongate Kilwinning, the correspondent appears desirous of ignoring the very obvious raillery contained in Brother Marshall's reference, in "A Winter with Robert Burns," to the Inauguration minute. Any impartial reader may see that a vein of playful sarcasm, at the expense of the illustrious trio, namely, Grand Secretary, Grand Clerk, and the facile, easy-going Secretary Mercer, of Lodge Canongate Kilwinning, runs throughout all that Brother Marshall says concerning it. In his valuable handbook of the event, at page 66, he chronicles the following amusing particulars:—

"William Mason, Grand Secretary," . . . "was a writer at the Bowhead, and held the situation of Extractor of the Decisions of the Supreme Court." . . . "Mr Meikle, by this time [1st March 1787] promoted as Assistant-Clerk of Court, was Grand Clerk of the Grand Lodge. *This fat pair* were, in their *legal* official capacity, accustomed to the use of words of strict style in all their writings, and they transferred the same dry formality in the exercise of their *masonic* duties. On the occasion of the grand visits, it fell to their province to insert in the book of the Lodge visited a minute of the fact, and this they did as if they copied it from a *style-book* in a regular *stick-to-the-form* manner. Hence you may 'witness our hand' for a series of years in every Edinburgh lodge, *whoever* was Grand Master, or *whoever* were present, or *whatsoever* were the sayings or doings or occurrences of the night. *Wherever* they happen to be for the time, you have invariably their grand scratchitaryships telling the identical tale that they told in *St Andrew's Lodge on Friday, the 12th January* 1787, when Charteris pleased the Poet so much by acknowledging him as Caledonia's Bard.* Here it is:—" [The minute has already been quoted at page 50 *ante*, and need not be repeated here.]

---

* A specimen of similar kind of record—proving Brother Marshall's words regarding the severe uniformity in style adhered to by the "fat pair"—is given under the head of *Notanda*, being copy of minute of Grand Lodge visitation to Lodge Canongate Kilwinning on 7th December 1786.

It is worthy, however, of special remark—as corroborating Brother Marshall's humorous statements—that the Grand Lodge minute contains no mention whatever of Robert Burns having been present. After that instance of omission of the name of Burns from the Grand Secretary's minute of this celebrated meeting, the assertions quoted above from the correspondent's letters are worthless by way of argument.

"A Winter with Robert Burns" is absolutely silent regarding any "*tragic scene*"[*] as having occurred 1st March 1787, and in no part of that excellent work did the author, Brother Marshall, assert "that all record of it [the Inauguration] was purposely suppressed by its promoters," or even assert anything resembling such an absurd statement, as is erroneously maintained in above quotations by Brother Mackenzie's indefatigable correspondent.

Brother Marshall had a complete knowledge of his subject, and appears very properly to have felt privileged to treat this particular incident jocosely relative to Brothers Mason, Meikle, and Mercer. He concludes his observations thus :—

"Brother Mason is characteristically represented viewing the Inauguration as rather calculated to 'hold up *Adam's* profession,' and *anti*-masonic, and something *for which there is no precedent in the books*. It may be readily *supposed* that after a consultation with the Grand Clerk and with Secretary Mercer as to a STYLE for recording such a fact, it would be finally resolved 'by three' that the *least said's soonest mended*."

"This fat pair"—according to the drift of Brother Marshall's lively narration—appear to have thought that, as there was neither law nor precedent for their guidance in preserving any record of the visit which it is *understood* "Caledonia's Bard" paid to the Lodge St. Andrew, Edinburgh, on 12th January 1787, they were justified in making no record of the visit in their minute of the proceedings in that Lodge; nevertheless, "it may be readily supposed" that ere very long they had misgivings as to the propriety of their omission from that minute of all reference to "Caledonia's Bard;" therefore, when Robert Burns was again the hero of the hour at a lodge meeting—and that lodge the Canongate Kilwinning, on 1st March 1787—the said "pair" were not likely to allow the Secretary of a daughter Lodge to score a point against them, by recording anything about Burns or the Laureateship, especially seeing his election was accompanied by such an "anti-masonic" ceremonial as that wherein the Poet had "his brow encircled with the laurel wreath, the insignia of his office." [†]

In the pages immediately foregoing, there have been exposed only a few of the errors which occur in letters written by the Past Master and the Historian of the Lodge of Edinburgh (Mary's Chapel), No. 1, as contained in "the printed copy of the correspondence," submitted to Grand Lodge by Grand Secretary, "in the interests of truth," on 29th December 1892. Other errors in those letters are disposed of elsewhere throughout this evidence, and especially in the sections, at pp. 14 to 25 *ante*, relating to Brothers William Campbell, W.S., and William Petrie, also pp. 44 and 48 of Part II.

---

[*] A special reference to this peculiar expression occurs at page 34, *ante*.
[†] Quoted from Lodge minute, page 38, part II.

PART II.

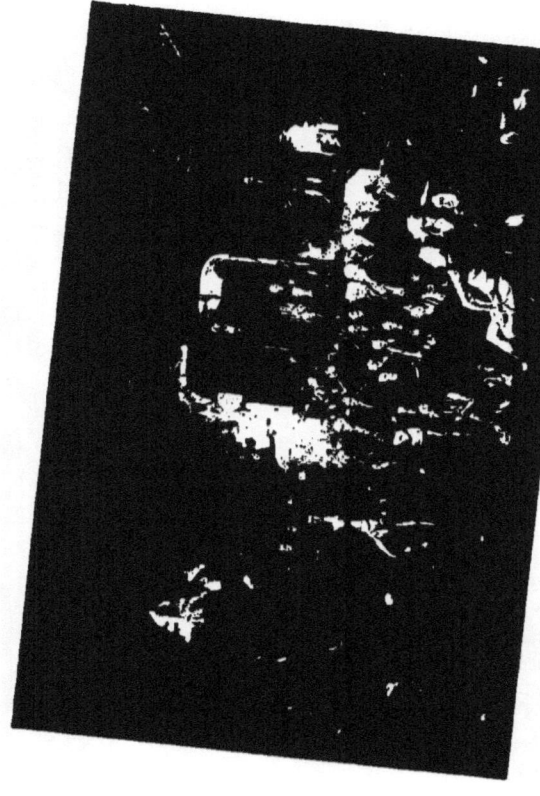

THE INAUGURATION OF ROBERT BURNS AS POET LAUREATE OF LODGE CANONGATE KILWINNING

1 MARCH 1787

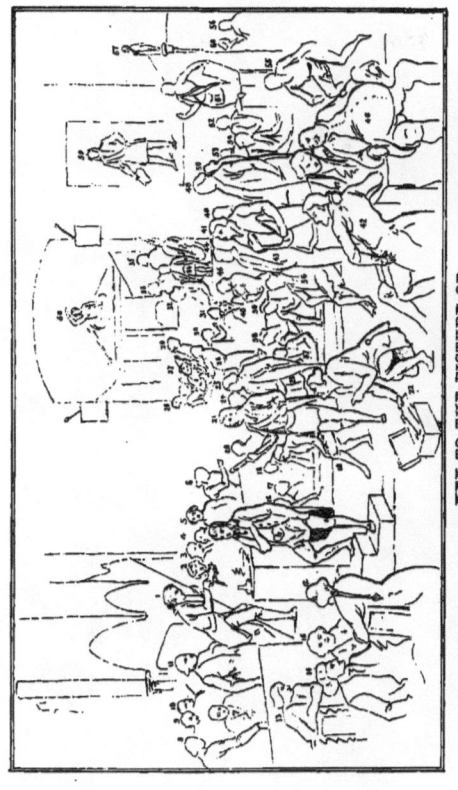

KEY TO THE PICTURE OF

THE INAUGURATION OF ROBERT BURNS AS POET-LAUREATE OF THE CANONGATE KILWINNING LODGE, 1787.

LINES

On Viewing Bro. STEWART WATSON's Picture

OF

THE INAUGURATION

Contributed 30th March 1846,

By WILLIAM PRINGLE.

———

I.

Bard of our hearts, beheld again on earth!
Not now, indeed, as oft through fancy's eye,
Following the plough, or by the rustic hearth,
Or 'mid the woods—warbling thy melody:
But in the shrine of Ancient Masonry,
Among "the favour'd, the enlighten'd few,"
Who, by its "hieroglyphic bright," descry
The wisdom hidden from the world's dim view.

II.

Oh, ever blessed be that art divine,
Which, with creative power, can back restore
The living look, each lineament and hue,
Of lov'd familiar faces now no more!
Honour'd the pencil that hath traced before
Our eyes the imaged presence of the Bard,
Whose name and fame have filled all space, and o'er
His brow renewed the *wreath*—fond Masonry's award.

———

The author of the foregoing testimony to his faith in the Inauguration, and to his admiration of Stewart Watson's talented work, was Brother William Pringle, whose name appears on the Lodge roll as "William Pringle, Jun., Writer," E.P. & R., 1824, Feb. 5. He had been, therefore, an old and constant member of the Lodge in 1846. He was a member of Committee as early as 1827, Senior Deacon 1827-8, and Poet-Laureate 1854-1859.

EXTRACT

FROM

GRAND LODGE PROCEEDINGS, DECEMBER 29, 1892.

"Grand Secretary drew the attention of Grand Committee to the Painting in the Board Room purporting to represent the Installation of Burns as Poet-Laureate of Lodge Canongate Kilwinning, No. 2. This picture came into the possession of Grand Lodge on 2nd February 1863 as a present from the family of the late Chevalier James Burnes, and was acknowledged by Grand Secretary as a handsome donation.

"The gift was accepted without question as to whether the event portrayed therein were real or imaginary. The story of the inauguration was never challenged until 1873, when the present Grand Secretary, while preparing his 'History of Freemasonry in Scotland,' and after a minute examination of Canongate Kilwinning's records, formed the opinion that Burns never was elected to, and never held the office of, Poet-Laureate of the Lodge, and never was installed into such an office. His views having become known to its office-bearers, by their instructions the Secretary of the Lodge questioned the soundness of his opinion, and laid a statement before him embodying alleged facts which he unfortunately accepted as true, and in his History modified the opinion which he had originally formed. As will be seen in the printed copy of the correspondence between Brothers Allan Mackenzie, the historian of No. 2, and William Officer, now submitted, Grand Secretary asserts that the statements made to him were unfounded, and that it is clearly established that the story of the Installation of Burns as Poet-Laureate is a myth.

"Attached to the original painting presented by the Burneses is the inscription, 'The Inauguration of Robert Burns as Poet-Laureate of Lodge Canongate Kilwinning, 1st March, 1787.' This date is accepted by the Lodge as correct. In all statements and discussions in support of the story the minute of the meeting at which the event is alleged to have happened has been kept out of sight. It is as follows :—

"St John's Chapel, 1st March 1787.

"The Lodge being duly constituted, it was reported that since last meeting R. Dalrymple, Esq. ; F. T. Hammond, Esq. ; R. A. Maitland, Esq., were entered apprentices and the following brethren passed and raised.—R. Sinclair, Esq.; A. M'Donald, Esq.; C. B. Clive, Esq.; Captain Dalrymple; R. A. Maitland, Esq.; F. T. Hammond, Esq.; Mr Clavaring, Mr M'Donald, Mr Millar, Mr Sime, and Mr Gray, who all paid their fees to the Treasurer. *No other business being before the meeting*, the Lodge adjourned.

" Enteries,	.	£3 13 6	" Alexr. Fergusson, M.
" P. and R.,	.	6 6 6	" Chas. More, D.
" Collected,	.	1 1 0	" Jo. Millar, J.W."
		"£11 1 0"	

" Grand Secretary submits that, in the interests of truth as set against a fable, it is necessary that steps should be taken by Grand Committee to have the inscription on the picture amended.

" Brother Mackenzie said that it would be well for Grand Committee to ascertain whether the event really took place or not, and questioned its right to alter the inscription on any painting bequeathed to Grand Lodge. He explained that the friendly correspondence between Brother Officer and himself was, so far as he was concerned, undertaken on his own responsibility, and had not been officially recognised by Canongate Kilwinning, but that his history was only a compilation of some of its records. Further, that since Grand Secretary had brought the matter before Grand Committee, he had seen a document which bore strong evidence of the installation having taken place, and he knew that the Lodge No. 2 was in possession of other documentary evidence of a like nature.

" On the motion of Brother Christie, Brothers William Officer, David Sneddon, and Allan Mackenzie were appointed to consider and report upon the whole question—Brother Officer, Convener."

ROBERT BURNS,

Poet Laureate of Lodge Canongate Kilwinning.

This matter being of supreme importance to Lodge Canongate Kilwinning as well as to the Craft in general, and as it is most desirable that a full and complete Report of the evidence now available be submitted to Grand Lodge, Brother Allan Mackenzie, P.M., of No. 2, having conferred with the R. W. MASTER AND OFFICE-BEARERS of the Lodge begs to lay the following statements and particulars before the Special Committee appointed by Grand Committee to report.

ROTHER D. MURRAY LYON mentions in his "History of Free-masonry in Scotland," p. 333, that in the year 1873 he made a *minute* examination of Canongate Kilwinning records, and found that the Laureateship is referred to on 9th February and 9th June 1815, and again on 16th January 1835. In point of fact, it is referred to in at least thirteen different Minutes and other Records, from 1802 to 1845, of which the dates are—24th June 1802, 9th February and 8th June 1815 (there is no Minute of 9th June 1815), 11th and 24th June 1816, 2nd and 2nd also 8th and 8th January 1817, 16th January and 24th June 1835, and 12th and 19th November 1845. Copies of those references are reproduced here, together with copy of inscription on portrait of Burns dated 1798.

Grand Lodge remit mentions that Brother Lyon now asserts that the communication received by him from the Secretary of the Lodge in 1873 contained "unfounded statements" and "alleged facts." A reply to this extraordinary assertion is given herewith.

The only other Office-Bearers now alive who took an active part on the Executive in 1873, namely, W. N. Fraser, Esq., of Findrack and Tornaveen, and ex-Councillor Thomas Drybrough, Past Masters, have also been communicated with, and copies of their replies are appended.

Brother Mackenzie would here explain that the document he referred to in Grand Committee alludes to 1st March 1787, and its contents are embraced in the communication received from Past Master W. N. Fraser. The word "installation," used by Grand Secretary, does not occur in the records of the Lodge during the period of Burns' lifetime.

REVIEW

MINUTES OF LODGE CANONGATE KILWINNING

From 24th June 1786 to 12th December 1788 inclusive.

The various references to Robert Burns having been a member and Poet Laureate of Canongate Kilwinning, which occur in the minutes of the years 1802, 1815, 1816, and 1817, and in relative documents, were testified to by many worthy brethren of those times.

A number of those brethren had been for many years active and constant members of Canongate Kilwinning. One of them had been admitted a member as far back as the year 1760, others respectively in 1767, 1769, 1774, 1778 (two), 1781, 1784, 1787, 1795, 1799, 1800, and 1801, while Charles More—still on committee during the years 1815, 1816 and 1817—and William Dunbar ("Rattlin' Roarin' Willie") had been successively Depute Master while Robert Burns was attending meetings of the Lodge in the years 1786 and 1787.

With such evidence as is found in the minutes of 1802 and 1815 to 1817 regarding Burns having been Poet Laureate of this Lodge, it may at first appear strange that no reference to his election as Poet Laureate occurs in the minutes of 1787. On carefully inspecting the very few, imperfect, and brief minutes of this period, a *verbatim* copy of which is annexed hereto—the omission may be quite easily accounted for.

Those minutes show extraordinary negligence on the part of some one during the period 24th June 1786 to 12th December 1788. Within that time— two and a half years—eleven meetings only have been recorded. The Secretary signed only one of those eleven minutes :—two of them *have not been signed by any person*. Conspicuously enough, one of those *unsigned minutes* is that of the *Annual Election, 25th June* 1787. Several of the minutes contain indications of *other meetings* than those engrossed having taken place, of which there is no record. Two whole pages of the minute-book have been left blank,—evidently with the intention of entering certain minutes therein at some more convenient season. Those blank pages occur between the minute dated 2nd August 1787 and that of 24th June 1788—a proof that minutes of, at least, the six usual monthly meetings, November to April, of the session 1787-88, have been lost through most unaccountable laxity.

In this connection my attention has been drawn to the following extract from page 33 of the printed correspondence referred to in the remit from Grand Lodge :—

"The minutes of the Canongate Lodge at the period in question were " kept by a practising solicitor. They appear to have been kept with care and " ample fulness of detail. The very minute, assuming Burns a member of the " Lodge, illustrates this fact, for it bears evidence of careful revision, being " partially erased in at least two places;"—the erasement, however, being evidently made to allow of the change of two words in a slovenly-written report.

No doubt the Secretary, who was elected in June 1786, was a solicitor— or writer, as he is designated in the records—and, no doubt the minute assuming Brother Burns a member of the Lodge is partially erased in at least two places, but the other statements in above quotation are erroneous—very probably from an incomplete or hurried examination of the minute-book.

By reason of such omissions as those referred to, very many brethren have never been recorded. This has been more notably the case in respect of several brethren who, successively, during the years 1788 to 1798, were elected to the Chair of Lodge Canongate Kilwinning. There is no evidence whatever to show at what date the following Right Worshipful Masters became members of the Lodge.

Bro. William Dunbar, W.S., R.W.M., 1788-89-90.
„ Dr Thomas Cochrane, R.W.M., 1792-93.
„ Dr William Farquharson, R.W.M., 1793-94-95.
„ Hugh Smith Mercer, R.W.M., 1798-99, 1800-1.

Other office-bearers of those times were likewise unrecorded.

Much of this very gross negligence in minuting the business of Lodge Canongate Kilwinning is clearly traceable to the period 1786 onwards to end of the year 1788.

Matters had evidently reached a climax when, at a meeting on December 12th 1788, at which Brother Dr Thomas Hay presided, a new Secretary was appointed. That Secretary was Brother Robert Moir, initiated 1st February 1787, on same night Brother Burns was affiliated. A marked improvement is observable in the minutes from the time Brother Moir accepted office. He signed all minutes while Secretary, which none of the brethren who had officiated as Secretary or Acting-Secretary during the years 1786, 1787 and 1788 had cared to do.   His faithful services were rewarded.   He advanced through the several offices to the Chair, to which he was elected in 1795, remaining till 1798, then re-elected 1804.

Ordinarily, it is expected that the Secretary of a Lodge is responsible for the minutes during the time he holds office, and that he acknowledges such responsibility by signing the minute of each meeting he attends ; but, throughout all that period of two years and a half—24th June 1786 to 12th December 1788—the only minute signed by any one of the several brethren who respectively acted as Secretary, is that of 24th June 1786, which was signed by Brother John Mercer, who had been same day elected Secretary.   By signing such minute Brother Mercer showed he was quite well aware of that part of his duty.   His signature does not appear again anywhere in the minutes.

1786 June 24.

In the opening paragraph of the Minute, dated 24th June 1786, readers are informed " that the Committee had passed Mr Spankie's Account from 21st " June 1783 to 24th June 1786,—the Ballance in favour of the Lodge being " £10, 15s. 4d."   I beg to call attention to the fact that *no minute of the Committee meeting when such account was passed has been recorded,* and no comment is made, nor is any explanation given as to Bailie Spankie's long-winded account. Practically the Lodge has been left quite in the dark about that business.

The first monthly meeting of the season 1786-87 was doubtless held in November as usual, but has not been recorded.

1786 December 7.

The second minute of this series is headed " St John's Chapel " 7th Decemr. 1786," when " It was reported that since last meeting John " Cathcart Esq., Jno. Hepburn Esq., Mr Burn and Mr Jones were entered " Apprentices."   Those words are undoubted evidence that since previous recorded or monthly meeting there must have been at the least *one* meeting of the brethren when degrees were conferred, and when, perhaps, other events occurred, of all which *no record has been preserved.*

Surely such mode of writing the minute of a meeting—" Mr Burn and Mr Jones were entered Apprentices "—is not creditable in a professional man, if it really was written by Brother John Mercer, solicitor, the Secretary.   Who were " Mr Burn " and " Mr Jones " among several others of like surnames, but without christian names, on the roll ?

1786 December 7.

In the next minute, dated 27th December 1786, a similar announcement is made as to members admitted " *since last meeting,*" showing that a meeting or meetings of the Lodge had certainly been held, of which no record has been made.

1787 February 1.

The fourth minute is the well-known one of February 1st 1787, when " it " was reported that since the 27th of Decemr. last, Mr Burns, Mr Speid, " Mr Haig, Mr Maule, Mr Wotherspoon, Mr Moir," and others, were entered Apprentices, and that certain brethren, named in similar manner, were passed and raised—" who all paid their dues to the Treasurer as also Mr Alexr. Boog."

The Secretary's ideas appear to have become very much confused as he wrote those words :—such clumsy composition surely could not be the work of a professional man.

"Mr Burns," "Mr Speid," "Mr Haig,"."Mr Maule," "Mr Wotherspoon "Mr Moir"!—no christian name affixed to any one of those patronymics, nor intended to be affixed, because no space has been left for it !—no designation and no address given of any one of the new members mentioned in the minute! Verily, the writer of this model minute of 1st February 1787—whether he was a practising solicitor or not—could not have felt impressed with the idea that he was "writing history."

The well-known paragraph containing statement relative to the affiliation of "Brother Burns, a great Poetic Writer," is another instance of the inability of the author of this minute to fulfil adequately the duties of a Lodge Secretary. "Brother Burns" appears without a christian name, although a "Mr Burns" is mentioned in preceding paragraph, but the easy-going Secretary or his deputy saw no need to waste valuable time filling in christian names :—it was obvious to the meanest capacity that as "Mr Burns" had just been initiated, and "Brother Burns" affiliated, they were different men, and that was sufficient for him.

It is fortunate that "Brother Burns" is distinctly identified as "a great Poetic Writer." The Lodge is not named from which he was affiliated—a very culpable omission.

The minute "being partially erased in at least two places" may be "evidence of careful revision," as has been alleged ; so may be the word "for" which appears interpolated in the fourth line of the paragraph referred to, and so also may be the "&" introduced between the names "Mr Craigie" and "Mr L. Carnegie" in the preceding paragraph, but, notwithstanding all these evidences of the author's carefulness in trimming his laboured composition, it has a poor appearance in the end. What an extraordinary production it must have been before these emendations were made! No wonder that the author of it, who-ever he was, did not acknowledge the work by appending his signature.

We are informed that at this meeting of 1st February 1787 "it was Reported that Since the 27th of Decemr" certain thirteen gentlemen were entered apprentices and six brethren were passed and raised—enough work for half-a-dozen meetings in the interval, but no record of them has been made.

1787 March 1. The minute of 1st March 1787 opens with a similar announcement to the effect that "Since last meeting" certain three gentlemen were entered apprentices and eleven brethren were passed and raised. In this, as in previous instances, the words "Since last meeting" obviously mean since previous *monthly* or *recorded* meeting. Therefore, it is clear that the brethren of Lodge Canongate Kilwinning in those days had a lively time of it with occasional or special meet-

ings, although *no record whatever has been preserved* of them except the names
—*often only the surnames*—of new members reported at the monthly or other
recorded meeting following admission.

With such repeated evidence that meetings other than those recorded
were continually taking place at short intervals, why is it contended in the
printed correspondence that Burns "could have attended at the most only three
"meetings of the Lodge Canongate Kilwinning during the season 1786-87?"
And this is asserted notwithstanding that in the minute dated 9th February
1815 referring to "*Robert Burns, who was a Member and Poet Laureat of this
Lodge,*" he is spoken of as "*a Public Character so immediately connected with
them*" [the brethren of Canongate Kilwinning] "*and who on so many occasions
contributed so generally to the harmony of the Masonic Order, and to that of the
Lodge Canongate Kilwinning in particular.*"

I have a similar criticism to make on the minute of 1st March as on
previous ones respecting the curt mention of new members, to wit,—"*Mr*
Clavaring, *Mr* M'Donald, *Mr* Millar, *Mr* Sime, and *Mr* Gray, who all paid their
dues to the Treasurer." This manner of recording business by any one acting
as Lodge Secretary was slovenly in the extreme, and shows that the author
of the minute was tired of the whole business and wanted to be done with
it as speedily as possible. Hence, in this, as in other minutes, he abruptly
finished by repeating the convenient and stereotyped conclusion—"No other
business being before the meeting the Lodge adjourned." The Secretary's
signature is awanting.

It would be interesting to know what the Secretary or his deputy at those
meetings considered as "business."

Certainly, on this occasion the brother who acted as Secretary omitted to
record that on a motion by Bro. Alexander Fergusson of Craigdarroch, Right
Worshipful Master, Brother Robert Burns was appointed Poet Laureate of the
Lodge. This statement has been attested by Past Master William Nathaniel
Fraser of Findrack and Tornaveen, who was informed of the event by his
brother-in-law the late Brother James Veitch, of Elliock, Dumfriesshire, who
got the information from his cousin, Brother Cutlar Fergusson, of Craigdarroch,
H.M. Judge-Advocate-General. The latter gentleman was assumed a member
of Canongate Kilwinning on 25th June 1787, same evening that his father,
Alexander Fergusson of Craigdarroch, R.W. Master, vacated the chair, and
Lord Torphichen was elected his successor.

The minute of Monthly meeting, held in April 1787, had been omitted—
The regular session was then, and is now, *six months, November to April inclusive.*
Sometimes an additional monthly meeting was held in October, and sometimes
one in May.

1787, June 25

The next record is that of 25th June 1787, when, we are told, "It was reported that since last meeting" certain five gentlemen were entered apprentices, and eight brethren were passed and raised. Here is another instance of negligence on the part of the office-bearer who had charge of the minute-book, in the fact that, since previous recorded meeting, there had certainly been meetings of the brethren when the business of conferring degrees had been transacted, and other events deserving mention had undoubtedly occurred, yet no record thereof had been made in the minute-book.

The minute of Annual meeting, for election of office-bearers, dated 25th June 1787, remains in the minute-book *without any signature.*

1787, August 2

Following the minute, dated 2nd August 1787, *two whole pages of the book have been left blank*—presumably with the intention of writing therein the arrears of minutes on some other occasion.

No other minutes were engrossed for nearly eleven months.

Therefore, it is perfectly obvious that records of the following meetings of the Lodge—whatever others, extra-monthly, or occasional—were omitted, viz. :—

Monthly meeting . . . . November 1787.
           " . . . . December 1787.
Festival of St John the Evangelist . . December 27th 1787.
Monthly meeting . . . . January 1788.
           " " . . . February 1788.
           " " . . . March 1788.
           " " . . . April 1788

and no record has been kept of the Quarterly meetings of Committee during that long interval.

1788, June 24

The first record which occurs after the two blank pages in the minute-book is that of the Annual meeting, on 24th June 1788, when "It was reported " that, since last meeting, Brother Daniel Stroble, junior, from Charleston, South " Carolina, was duly entered an apprentice, & Brother William Lehrie, of the " Roman Eagle, assumed as a member."

At this meeting, "Brother Dunbar was elected Master, Brother Jardine " Depute Mastr *Brother Millar Substitute Mastr.* Brother Andrew Forbes " Senr Warden Br John Mercer, Junr Warden, B. Spankie, Continued Trea-" surer, Brother William Lehrie, Secretary."

This is a very curious record immediately following the great *hiatus* in the minute-book—and, consequently, in the history of the Lodge—of almost ELEVEN MONTHS.

" It was reported that since last meeting," &c.! Did the author of that stereotyped and hackneyed phrase refer to the meeting held August 2nd in previous year? or, to some unrecorded meeting held only a short time previous to minute of this date?

"B. Spankie Continued Treasurer Brother William Lehrie Secretary!"—Hence it appears probable that Brother Lehrie, at some previous time within the period under review, must have been appointed Secretary, of which there is no record.

If so, his being *assumed a member* must be a much older affair than it seems to be from this minute of 24th June 1788. The author of this historical record was very much to blame in not trying to express himself more clearly.

Among the elections of this date is that of "*Brother Millar Substitute* "*Mastr*"—a curt and unceremonious mode of recording a noteworthy event.

This is the *first mention of such an office* in the minutes of Lodge Canongate Kilwinning, and,—like the election of Robert Burns to the office of Poet Laureate—the work was accomplished, and the office was effectually "created" and established without the process detailed so carefully in pages 43 and 44 of the printed correspondence.

1788, November 6

The minute of meeting, held November 6th 1788, is composed of very few words, and needs little comment. Brief as it is, the acting Secretary took special care to mention in addition to other "business" that "They, after "spending a most social evening, adjourned till Festival of St Andrew."

But the eventful Festival of St Andrew passed into oblivion—no allusion to the proceedings is in the book. Perhaps the acting Secretary had only another "most social evening" to record, and "there was no other business." Perhaps, as was the fact with regard to many other occasions during the period 1787 and 1788, the "business" of the meeting, and the acting Secretary's business to record it were alike forgotten.

1788, December 4

Several defects in the brief minute dated December 4th 1788 are so palpable, they will readily be discerned at a glance, and need no comment.

Committee Meeting, 1788, December 12

The minute of committee, dated December 12, 1788, contains the announcement, that "they elected Brother Lehrie to be Junior Warden in place "of *Brother Mercer, who had gone abroad,* and Brother Robert Moir to be "Secretary, in place of Brother Lehrie."

Brother Mercer seems to have been very much "abroad" ever since accepting office in 1786 as Secretary, and at no time altogether at home in that position. The time when he took his departure is not mentioned.

This, the last minute of the series under review, is without any signature.

It is the only minute of a committee meeting recorded within the long period of two years and a-half.

From this analysis of the minutes of 1786, 1787, 1788, may be deduced the following conclusions, viz. :—

1. *That*, although the narrations in those minutes are extremely meagre and otherwise very imperfect, nevertheless, *for the information contained in them—so far as it goes*, and so far as the language used is clear and unequivocal *—the minutes are quite reliable.—exampli gratia*—The Affiliation of Robert Burns on 1st February 1787.

2. *That*, in place of being an accurate and complete record of business and noteworthy events, *those minutes are remarkably deficient, inaccurate, and incomplete :*—therefore,—the mere fact that certain business or noteworthy events *have been omitted from those defective minutes is no evidence whatever that such business or events did not occur*,—more especially when indisputable evidence to the contrary is produced from other sources.—*ex. gr.*—The Election and Inauguration of Robert Burns as Poet Laureate on 1st March 1787.

Respectfully submitted by

HUGH C. PEACOCK,
Past Secy. and Past Depute Master Lodge Can. Kil.
Proxy Master No. 476.

COPY MINUTES

OF

LODGE CANONGATE KILWINNING

From 24th June 1786 to 12th December 1788.

Festival of St John the Baptist

  The Lodge having met to celebrate the Anniversary of St. John the Baptist It was reported that the Committee had passed Mr. Spankie's Accot from 21st June 1783 to 24 June 1786. The Ballance in favour of the Lodge being £10. 15. 4. : the Vouchers were delivered and lodged in the Charter Chest.

  That at the Meeting it was proposed That Brother Ferguson should be continued Master, wch being unanimously agreed to, he accordingly being re-elected. Proposed Brother More be Continued Depute Master Br Wm Dunbar Wr to Signet, Senr Warden, Jno Millar Advocate, Junr Warden, Geo. Spankie Contd Treasurer & Jno Mercer Secy. The usual Business of the Meeting being finished and after having spent the Evening with that fun and Good Humour which always attends the Meetings of that lodge they adjourned the Meeting.

Alexr Fergusson of Craigdarroch
 admission not recorded
Charles More of the Royal Bank
 E. 1769 Feby 8
William Dunbar, W.S.
 not recorded
John Millar Advocate
 E.P.R. 1786 March 2
George Spankie Merchant
 E. 1778 March 2
John Mercer Writer
 E.P.R. 1784 Novr 11

ALEXR FERGUSSON M

CHAs MORE D.M.

WILL DUNBAR Senr Ward

JO MILLER Jun War

GEO SPANKIE Treasurer

JOHN MERCER Secry

St Johns Chapel, *7th Decemr.* 1786.

The Lodge being duly Constituted, it was Reported that since last Meeting John Cathcart Esqr Jno Hepburn Esqr Mr Burn and Mr Jones were entered apprentices, and Mr Spence, Mr Jones and Lord Torphichen were passed as fellow Craft and raised to the High degree of Master Masons and paid their dues accordingly.

The Lodge was afterwards visited by the Most Worshipful Grand Master and other Officers of the Grand Lodge of Scotland.

At this Meeting the undermentioned were assumed Members, viz:—

The Right Honble The Earl of Errol, The Honble Mr Gordon of Karemuir, Mr John Newal of Earlston, Capin Rollo Gillespie, & Wm Campbell Esqr of Fairfield.

After passing the Evening in a sociable and agreable manner the Lodge adjourned till St Johns Day.

4 Entries £4. 18/.
3 P and R f. 14/6
Collected 7. 15.
£14. 7. 6.

Alexr Fergusson
not recorded
Chas More
E 1769 Feb 8

ALEXR FERGUSSON M.

CHAS MORE D.M.

Minute
of the Grand Lodge

[The next minute is that of the visitation, above noticed, by the M W Grand Master and other Officers of Grand Lodge, apparently written by Robert Meikle Grand Clerk. The following Signatures are attached to the Minute.

Francis Charteris Junr of Amisfield
shortly afterwards Lord Elcho
Affd from Haddington Lodge 1779 March 3
Lord Torphichen E 1786 March 2
Dr Thomas Hay E 1774 Octr 12
RWM 1781 to 1784 Junr Gr Wn 1782 to 1784
Subte Gr Master 1784 to 1798
Dr James Home E 1778 Decr 2

WILL MASON G. Secy.
RO MEIKLE Gd Clk

FRANCIS CHARTERIS Junr G.M.

TORPHICHEN D.G.M.
THOMAS HAY St G.M.

JAMES HOME S.G.W.p.t.
Wm. MACKILLOP J.G.W.p.t.]

St Johns Chapel, 27 *Decr.* 1785.

The Lodge being Constituted, it was Reported that since last Meeting Mr J. Seton & Mr J. Hobman were Entered Apprentices and Mr. J. Hobman Passed and raised, who paid their dues accordingly.

This being the festival of St John the Evangelist the Lodge received and returned Visitations to the different Lodges in Edinburgh, and, after the usual compliments were paid the visiting Lodges the Lodge adjourned till the next Monthly Meeting.

2 Entries £2 9 —
1 P. & R — 11 6
Collected — 19 —
£3 19 6

Alexr Fergusson
Admission not recorded
Chas More
E 1769 Feby 8
John Millar
E 1786 March 2

ALEXR. FERGUSSON M.
CHAS. MORE D.M.
JO MILLAR Junr. J.W.

There being no Meeting in January the Lodge met this Evening and being duly Constituted it was Reported that since the 27th of Decemr last the following gentlemen were Entered Apprentices vizt Mr Burns, Mr Speid, Captn Bartlet, Mr Haig, G. Douglas Esqr, E. B. Clive Esqr, Lloyd Lynn Norfolk, Mr Maule, Mr Wotherspoon, Mr Moir, Mr L. Carnegie, Mr Archd Miller, Mr James Buchan, and that the following Brethern were passed and Raised to the High Degree of Master Masons vizt Mr Haig, Capt Bartlet, Lloyd Lynn Norfolk, Baron Norton, Mr Craigie&Mr L. Carnegie who all paid their dues to the Treasurer as also Mr Alexr. Boog.

Assumed Br Burns the Poet

The Right Worshipful Master having observed that Brother Burns was at present in the Lodge who is well known as a great Poetic Writer and a for ∧ late publication of his Works which have been universally Commended And Submitted that he should be assumed a member of this Lodge which was unanimously agreed to and he was assumed accordingly.

13 Entries £15 18 6
7 Passed & Rd. 4 0 6
Collected 2 12 6
————
£22 11 6

Having spent the Evening in a very Social, Affect & Brotherly manner as the meetings of this Lodge always have been it was adjourned till next monthly meeting.

not recorded
E 1769 Feby 8

ALEXR FERGUSSON M.
CHAS MORE D.M.

E 1786 March 2

JO MILLAR Junr J.W.

The Lodge being duly Constituted it was Reported that since last meeting R. Dalrymple Esqr F. J. Hammond Esqr and R. A. Maitland Esqr were entered apprentices and the following Brethern Passed and Raised R. Sinclair Esqr, A. McDonald Esqr, E. B. Clive Esqr, Capt Dalrymple, R. A. Maitland Esqr F. J. Hammond Esqr, Mr Clavaring, Mr McDonald, Mr Millar, Mr Sime and Mr Gray who all paid their dues to the Treasurer. No other Business being before the Meeting the Lodge adjourned.

3 Entries 3 13 6
11 P & R 6 6 6
Collected 1 1 0
————
£11 1 0

not recorded
E 1769 Feby 8
E 1786 March 2

JO MILLAR, J.W.

ALEXR FERGUSSON M.
CHAS MORE D

Festival of St John the Baptist

The Lodge having met to Celebrate the Anniversary of John the Baptist. It was reported that since last Meeting the following Gentlemen were Entered Apprentices vizt Cornet John Hart of the 6th Dragoons, Mr Schinimen, Mr Jo Boader M.D. Mr Stewart and Mr C. Abercromby this Evening and the following Brethern passed and raised vizt Cornet Hart, Mr Schinimen, Mr Boader, Mr Gardner, Mr Speid, Mr Witherspoon, Mr Moir and Mr Maule who all paid their Dues to the Treasurer. It was also reported that the Committee had passed Mr Spankies Accounts from June 1786 to this date, the Balance in favour of the Lodge £6. 1. 8½, the Vouchers were delivered and lodged in the Charter Chest.

Lord Torphichen
E 1786 March 2
William Dunbar
not recorded
John Millar
E 1786 March 2
Lindsay Carnegie
E 1787 Feb 1
George Spankie
E 1778 March 2

The Meeting proceeded next to the Election of their Officers when Lord Torphichen was appointed Master, Mr William Dunbar Depute Master, Mr John Millar, Senior, and Mr Lindsay Carnegie Junr Wardens, Mr Spankie and Mr Mercer Continued, the former Treasurer and the latter Secretary. They also appointed the last with the present Officers together with Doctor Spense and Mr Thomas Hay to be a Committee to manage the Affairs of the Lodge.

Mr Fergusson Junr of Craigdarroch and Mr Frizzle of the Isle of Man were this night assumed Members.

There were Several Visitations from the different Lodges which were returned. No other Business before the Meeting the Lodge adjourned till August.

(No Signature to this Minute.)

St Johns Lodge, 2nd August
1787.

Dr Thos. Hay
E 1774 Oct 12

The Lodge being met and duly constituted Brother T. Hay reported last that since meeting he & some other Brethern of the Committee had taken

upon themselves to order £4. 4. to be paid to a Brother who was in such necessity as to admit of no delay, & therefore begg'd that he might receive the Sanction of the Master & Brethern of the Lodge for that order which the Master & Lodge highly approved of & returned thanks to the Gentlemen of the Committee and to Brother Hay in particular for his proper conduct and friendly attention to the Brother in distress.

There being no other business before the Lodge it was adjourned untill

not recorded
E 1769 Feby 8.

E 1782 Decr 4 RWM 1790 to 1792

Will Dunbar Mr. pt.
Chas. More S.W. P. T.
Henry Jardine J.W. p.t.

[*The succeeding two pages of the Minute-Book are wholly blank*].

First of two pages blank in Minute Book—immediately following the Minute dated 2nd August 1787

Second of two pages blank in Minute Book—immediately following the Minute, dated 2nd August 1787.

St Johns Lodge, 24 June 1788.

The Lodge having met to Celebrate the Anniversary of St John the Baptist — It was reported that since last meeting Brother Daniel Stroble Junr from Charleston, South Carolina was duly entered an Apprentice; & Brother William Lehrie of the Roman Eagle assumed as a Member.

The meeting then proceeded to the Election of Officers when Brother Dunbar was elected Master, Brother Jardine Depute Mastr., *Brother Millar Substitute Mastr.*, Brother, Andrew Forbes Senr Warden Br John Mercer Junr Warden B. Spankie Continued Treasurer Brother William Lehric Secretary. They also appointed the last with the present Officers together with Brs Hay, Ferguson of Craigdarroch & Chas. More to be a Committee to manage the affairs of the Lodge.

Thereafter Messrs Augustine Smith, James Box Young, James Moultrie, Thomas Marshall, Peter Ward from America, & Brothers James Robertson & John Dick, all of the Roman Eagle, with Brother John Bushby of St Lukes were assumed Brothers.

The Petition of John Clark an Indigent Brother was received—The Lodge allowed him Five Shillings. No other Business before the Lodge. They adjourned untill the first Thursday July.

HENRY JARDINE D.M.

Wm Dunbar, W.S.
Not recorded
Henry Jardine,
    Advocate
E 1782 Dec 4
John Millar, Advocate
E 1786 March 2
Andrew Forbes
E 1786 March 2
John Mercer, Writer
E 1784 Nov 11
George Spankie,
    Merchant
E 1778 March 2
William Lehrie,
    Stud of Med.
Affd 1788 June 24
Dr Thos Hay
E 1774 Oct 12
Alexr Fergusson
Not recorded
Chas More
E 1769 Feb 8

E 1782 Dec 4

Edinburgh *Novr 6th* 1788

There being no meetings in July or August the Lodge met this Evening, and being duly Constituted Brother Darling was elected Grand Steward & Brother John Brown of the Lodge of St Davids was Assumed a Member. They after spending a most Social Evening adjourned till Festival of St Andrew.

HENRY JARDINE D.M.

Robert Darling
P & R 1776 Nov 6

E 1782 Decr 4

St Johns Lodge
Edinburgh *Decemr 4th* 1788

The Lodge having met, it was reported that Brothers George Pitt Stevenson & John T. Shoof both of Maryland, & Brother Thomas James Virginia North America, with Brother James Makethick Adair, Tichfield, Northamptonshire, England, were all duly entered as Apprentices.

Thereafter Brothers John Abercromby Senior Warden of the Union Kilwinning Lodge at Charleston So. Carolina, Herman Lion of the Antient Lodge No. 53 of Liverpool, James Dewar, James Hay, John Oliphant, &
all of the Thistle
William Robertson were all Assumed Brothers of
∧

No other Business coming before the Lodge, they after spending the Evening in a very Social Affect & Brotherly manner, as the meetings of this Lodge have always been, adjourned till

E 1782 Decr 4

HENRY JARDINE, D.M.

———————

EDINBURGH 12 *December* 1788.

Meeting of
the Committee

The Committee of the Lodge having met Brother Thomas Hay Master in absence of the Right Worshipfull, they elected Brother Lehrie to be Junior Warden in place of Brother Mercer who had gone abroad, and Brother Robert Moir to be Secretary in place of Brother Lehrie.
No other Business coming before the Committee they adjourned.

[No Signature to above Minute.]

———————

I certify that the foregoing is a true Copy of all the Minutes of Lodge Canongate Kilwinning, contained in the Minute-book from 24th June 1786 to 12th December 1788, inclusive.

GEO. CRAWFORD, R.W.M.,
Lodge Can. Kil. No. 2.

EDINBURGH, *April 12, 1893.*

FIRST REFERENCE

ROBERT BURNS

Having been POET LAUREATE of the Lodge.

On a prominent part of the east wall of Lodge Canongate Kilwinning—between the Master's chair and the Poet's corner—hangs a very antique-looking framed print of Robert Burns, and, on the blackened glass mount below his portrait, is displayed in bright golden characters, the following inscription :—

"ROBERT BURNS the SCOTTISH BARD

"*POET LAUREAT*

"*LODGE No. 2 CANNONGATE*

"*KILWINNING*"

That singularly attractive old print of our great national poet was published on the 29th day of October 1798.

It is one of four prints got for Lodge Canongate Kilwinning by the Committee, which were all duly approved by the Lodge on the 24th day of June 1802.

It has been there exhibited on one of the walls of the Lodge room in the full view of very many thousands of visitors *throughout the past ninety-one years*, and no one of the visitors during that long period has ever called in question the fact which is so conspicuously proclaimed by the inscription on the picture that "Robert Burns, the Scottish Bard," had been "Poet Laureat" of Lodge Canongate Kilwinning.

Naming them in the order of their publication the four prints are—

PROVOST GEORGE DRUMMOND, R. W. Master A.D. 1764 to 1766, published 17—.
DR NATHANIEL SPENS, R. W. Master A.D. 1778 to 1780, published 1793.
ROBERT BURNS, Poet Laureat A D. 1787 to 1796, published 1798.
H.R.H. GEORGE AUGUSTUS FREDERICK, PRINCE OF WALES, &c., "Grand
   "Patron of the Most Antient and Honourable Order of Free and
   "Accepted Masons" (Dedicated to the Grand Lodge of England), pub-
   lished 1802.

First Reference in Cas. Kil. records to ROBERT BURNS as "POET LAUREAT"

Minuted 5 years and 11 months after his death

In one of the following *excerpta* from the minute of Annual Meeting 1802 occurs the first reference to those prints. The Lodge Secretary—with that singular laxity which is so characteristic of his time in matters which had not been deemed strictly "business," and which therefore did not require special description—has quite omitted to name whom the four prints represent; but ample proof is hereinafter given that the *"four prints which were got for the Lodge,'* and which *"met with the approbation of the Brethern"* on 24th June 1802, are assuredly the four briefly described in above list.

EXCERPTA FROM MINUTE OF ANNUAL MEETING 1802.

Festival of St. John the Baptist June 24, 1802

ST. JOHN'S CHAPEL, 24th June 1802.

*   *   *   *

E 1787 Feb. 1, same night when Robert Burns was affiliated E 1795 June 24 Vide Minute dated 9th February 1815

"Brother ROBERT MOIR was called to the chair, and he proposed to the Brethern that Brother ALEXANDER JAFFRAY (late Rt. Worshipful Master) should be re-elected, which was agreed to with unanimous consent. Accordingly Brother Jaffray took the chair, and recommended to the Brethern that the other offices of the Lodge should be filled by the past Office-Bearers, which was unanimously agreed to. viz.—

P & R 1799 Nov 17 Vide Minute dated 9th February 1815 P & R 1801 June 24 E P & R 1801 April 1 Vide Minute of Nov 12 1845 E 1800 Dec 27 P & R 1778 Dec 2 E 1778 Dec 2 E 1760 June 23 Not recorded but 1780 June 24 was "continued as "Steward" E 1760 June 23 Not recorded

WILLIAM BALLANTYNE, Depute Master.
JOHN RUSSEL, Substitute Master.
WILLIAM CAMPBELL, Senior Warden.
JOSEPH DIXON, Junior Warden.
JOHN MORE, junr., Secretary.
GEORGE SPANKIE, Treasurer.
GEORGE MILNE, Grand Steward.
ALEXANDER FORBES, Steward.
GEORGE MILNE, Tyler.
ABRAM STRACHAN, Assistant Tyler.

"The Rt. Worshipful Master then proposed that the Committee for Managing the Affairs of the Lodge should consist of the Office-bearers with the addition of

E 1769 Feb 8
Vide minute of Feb.
1st, 1787, &c., also
minute of June 8th,
1815
E 1787 Feb 1
P & R 1795 June 24
Not recorded, but
was sec. 1790

Brother CHARLES MORE.
    „   ROBERT MOIR.
    „   ROBERT SCOTT MONCRIEFF, and
    „   HUGH SMYTH MERCER.

"The Committee recommend that a Seal should be got for the Lodge, and remit to Messrs Jaffray, Russel, and Curroll to project a proper device, likewise that the fee for a Diploma should be seven shillings and sixpence sterling. *They approve of four prints which were got for the Lodge*, and they recommend that the Lodge should be Painted, and that new coverings should be got for the Tables. *All the above mentioned has met with the approbation of the Brethern.*"

*   *   *   *

"A very numerous attendance of the Brethern took place this evening :—the Lodge was closed with regret after a night spent with the greatest harmony and delight, and to the heartfelt satisfaction of every Brother present.

P & R 1778 Dec 2
E 1795 June 24
E 1800 Dec 27

"JOHN MORE, junr., Sy.

"A. JAFFRAY, M.

Joseph Dixon, J.W."

In evidence that the picture of Robert Burns now under notice was originally as it appears at the present time, with the inscription on it as quoted, and is one of the four oldest framed prints or engravings in the Lodge-room of Canongate Kilwinning.—I beg to submit the opinion of Mr David Reed, Printseller, &c., Rose Street, Edinburgh, a competent authority in such matters, who has made a careful examination of all the said prints, and expresses his judgment thereanent in the following letter :—

OPINION OF EXPERT AS TO PRINTS.

94 ROSE STREET,
EDINBURGH, *12th June* 1893.

Mr HUGH C. PEACOCK,
    8 York Buildings.

Dear Sir,

With reference to my visits to the Lodge-room of Lodge Canongate Kilwinning and to the Examination, which, on request of yourself and other Members, I have made of certain framed engravings there, I beg to report as follows :—

The four oldest prints or engravings that I found hanging on the walls of the lodge-room are—

First:—The print of GEORGE DRUMMOND, bearing the following inscription in gold letters on the blackened glass mount:—

"GEORGE DRUMMOND ESQ., LORD PROVOST OF EDINBURGH
"*and*
"R.W.M. of CANONGATE KILWINNING LODGE
"A.D. 1764-65."

and, below the portrait, are engraved the words:—

"J. Alexander Pinxit 1752.   A. Bell, Fecit, Edinr.

"GEORGE DRUMMOND ESQ.

"Late Lord Provost of the City of Edinburgh, and one of the Honourable "Commissioners of His Majesty's Revenues of Excise in Scotland."

Note.—In Redgrave's Dictionary of Painters and Engravers I observe that "Cosmo Alexander, Portrait Painter, practised in Edinburgh about 1750," and "painted portrait of Provost of that time,"—*i.e.*—portrait of Provost George Drummond.

Second:—The celebrated print by John Beugo of Dr NATHANIEL SPENS, bearing the following inscription in gold letters on blackened glass mount:—

"NATHANIEL SPENS, M.D.
"R.W. MASTER of CANONGATE KILWINNING LODGE
"FROM A.D. 1778 to 1780.

and, below the portrait, are engraved the words:—

"Painted by H. Raeburn.   Engraved by Beugo."

According to *Catalogue of the Works of Sir Henry Raeburn, R.A.*, exhibited in the Royal Academy National Galleries, Edinburgh 1876, the portrait of Nathaniel Spens, M.D. was painted for the Archer's Hall in the year 1774. John Beugo engraved the portrait in 1793.

This portrait is specially referred to in a small 8vo book in my possession, entitled "Picture of Edinburgh," published 1805, wherein Mr John Beugo is mentioned as one of the principal Edinburgh Engravers of that time, and it is there said "His full length of Dr Spens as an Archer is a fine print." In "The New Scots Almanack" for 1803-4, page 113, Dr Nathaniel Spens is named as one of the Brigadiers-General of the Royal Company of Archers, also as Vice-President of the Council of same Company.

Third:—The print of ROBERT BURNS, bearing the following inscription in gold letters on blackened glass mount:—

" ROBERT BURNS the SCOTTISH BARD
" *POET LAUREAT*
" *LODGE No. 2 CANNONGATE*
" *KILWINNING*"

and below the portrait are engraved the words :—
" Painted by Naysmith, Drawn by Skirving, Engraved by Paton Thomson."
" ROBERT BURNS
" London, published as the Act directs, October 29th, 1798, and sold by R.
" Wilkinson, Cornhill, and A. Skelton, No. 23 Haymarket."

The glazing of each of these three pictures has been done with the original old-style crown glass, peculiar to the period ninety to a hundred years ago. It is bent and uneven in surface, unequal in thickness, greenish in tone, and varies in refractive quality. The blackening of the glass inside upon the broad gold bands in shape of a mount around the portrait, and on the gold lettering below it, was a style much in vogue about that time. Further, the gold leaf then employed was at the least two-and-a-half times thicker than what is generally in use now for such purposes, hence its continued extraordinary brightness in all the pictures under notice.

The three pictures above described are *thoroughly uniform* both in kind of glass, with which—nearly a century ago—they have been glazed, and in the artistically filled in gold lines around, and gold lettering below, each portrait on the blackened border within the glass.

Fourth :—Print of GEORGE AUGUSTUS FREDERICK PRINCE OF WALES, &c., published June 4th, 1802, by the well-known printseller, Wm. Walker, of 31 Old Bond Street, London.

This print has been very much neglected or wantonly defaced. It appears to have remained a long time without the protective covering of a glass or mount, and is therefore much begrimed by smoke and dust. The lower part of the portrait has at some time been torn across and the parts clumsily joined. There are evidences of more than one attempt at restoration or repair. The following quotation shews what remains of the inscription, and shews also, by the blanks, the parts in it that have been destroyed :—

" Drawn and Engraved by Edmund Scott.   Portrait Engraver to their.........
" HIS ROYAL HIGHNESS GEORGE AUGUSTUS...............PRINCE REGENT, &c. &c.
" GRAND PATRON of the MOST ANTIENT and HON......FREE and ACCEPTED MASONS.
" Dedicated by Permission to the Grand Lodge of England
" by their Obliged and Obedient Servant
" Edmund Scott

" Published June 4th, 1802, by W. Walker, 31 Old Bond Street, Forest, Piccadilly ;
" W. Austin, Russell Street ; and E. Scott, No. 7 Craven Buildings, Brighton."

The frame is obviously very old—quite as old as the print. The glass is also old, but not coeval with the frame and print. It is whiter and more regular on the surface than any glass in the other three pictures. From sundry evidences on the frame, I am of opinion that this print of George Augustus Prince of Wales was originally glazed and mounted in exactly the same manner as the other three pictures. One circumstance among others strongly supporting such conclusion is that all along the inside check or rabbet of the frame there are indications of a knife having been used to enlarge the space so as to admit a square of glass completed in same style as in the other three pictures, which glass had been rather large, and which—by reason of being painted black around the edges—could not be reduced in size by cutting with a diamond, as clear glass could have been.

With the exception of an engraving of the Earl of Moira—probably added to the collection after he came to Scotland in 1803—all of the above described four prints are older by many years than any other framed print or engraving in the lodge-room.

Yours faithfully,

DAVID REED.

BROTHER WILL^{M.} CAMPBELL,

AND A FEW OF HIS EARLY ASSOCIATES.

The attendance of brethren at meetings of the Lodge about this time was usually very large, as is shown at page 22 in the concluding lines of quotation from the minute of 24th June 1802, and the following brief extracts, signed by Bro. Campbell, from minutes of meetings held shortly previous to that date.——

"24th June 1801.

*　　　*　　　*　　　*　　　*

" The meeting was very numerous."

*　　　*　　　*　　　*　　　*

Alex^{r.} Jaffray
E 1795 June 24
John More junr.
E 1778 Dec 2
Willm. Campbell
E 1801 April 1

" JOHN MORE, junr., Sec^{y.}"

" WILL^{M.} CAMPBELL, Senior Warden."

" ALEX. JAFFRAY, M.

D

*   *   *   *   *

"Upwards of 100 of the brethren met at the Lodge this evening."

*   *   *   *   *

(*Vide Supra*)   "JOHN MORE, junr., Secr.   "ALEX. JAFFRAY, M.
" WILLM. CAMPBELL, Senior Warden."

Brother WILLIAM CAMPBELL, who signed the minutes above quoted, was re-elected Senior Warden, June 24th, 1802.

He and the other worthy Brethren who comprised the "very numerous attendance" at the meeting of that date, formally approved of certain "*four* "*prints which were got for the Lodge*," one of these being the well known engraved portrait of the Poet, having on its antique glass mount the inscription :—

" ROBERT BURNS the SCOTTISH BARD

" *POET LAUREAT*

" *LODGE No.* 2 *CANNONGATE*

" *KILWINNING*"

Several of the Brethren present on that occasion had enjoyed the company of the Poet Laureate at meetings of the Canongate Kilwinning. They all saw the picture of Robert Burns, with that bright attractive inscription appended to it as we see it to this day, and they all, by their ready approval of the "four prints which were got for the Lodge," as expressed in the minute of 24th June, 1802, acknowledged their belief in the fact, so prominently announced by the inscription, that he was "Poet Laureat" of their Lodge.

Thus far it is amply proved that Robert Burns had been "Poet Laureat."

There is ample proof also that Robert Burns, besides being duly elected to that office, was formally *inaugurated* "Poet Laureat," and that the Inauguration took place March 1st, 1787, notwithstanding that the minute of that date— written by an incompetent or indifferent Secretary—contains no record whatever of the event. The Secretary, we are informed, was "a practising Solicitor." If so, he did not import his good business qualities into the Secretaryship of Canongate Kilwinning. (*Vide* pages 4 to 19 hereof.)

In support of this statement relative to the Inauguration, I desire to draw special attention to the valuable fact that this Brother WILLIAM CAMPBELL, who was Senior Warden in the years 1801 to 1803, associated during that period with many brethren who had enjoyed the company of Robert Burns at Lodge meetings—they subsequently testifying that Burns had been "Poet Laureat" of this

Lodge, as is indisputably proved by the minutes of meetings held throughout the years 1801-2 and 3, also 1815-16, and 17—and that he was the same Brother WILLIAM CAMPBELL, who, at a meeting of the Lodge on 12th November, 1845, seconded the motion "That Brother Watson have access to sketch the antique " and picturesque interior of the Lodge, with a view to his painting the Inaugura- " tion of Robert Burns as her Poet Laureate,"—on which occasion he stated that " *he thought the proposition one deserving every support*,"—that " he had been forty- " five years a Mason, and connected with this Lodge,"—that he had travelled in company of Burns, "and spent two of the most happy days with him at Auchter- " tyre Castle, the seat of Sir William Murray,"—and "*he was happy that he had " lived to second such an admirable motion.*"

Brother Sam. Somerville of Ampherlaw, M.D.,—who was a member of Committee along with Past-Master Fraser, and Past-Master Thomas Drybrough, in the year 1873, when I was Secretary of the Lodge, and who took an active interest in my correspondence with Bro. D. Murray Lyon in January and February of that year—was Immediate Past-Master of the Lodge, and was present along with Bro. Willm. Campbell and other old members at this meeting of 12th November, 1845.

Further direct evidence that the Inauguration of Robert Burns as Poet Laureate of Lodge Canongate Kilwinning, took place March 1st, 1787, is given by Past-Master W. N. Fraser of Tornaveen.

In considering this question of the Inauguration and the picture repre- senting it, there is one part of the minute of 12th Nov., 1845, above referred to, relative to the motion so cordially seconded by Bro. Willm. Campbell, which deserves special notice. It runs thus :—"Brother Marshall was requested to " furnish the AUTHENTICATED PARTICULARS to a subsequent meeting, when the " motion should be disposed of. Meantime, it was unanimously entertained ;" and, in the minute of next meeting, 19th Nov., 1845, when the motion was brought up for disposal, the sequel is thus recorded :—"The motion was seconded " by the R.W.M. (Bro. A. D. Campbell), and unanimously carried."

Hence, it appears, that at those two meetings, held respectively on the 12th and 19th November, 1845, the whole subject of the Election and Inaugura- tion of Robert Burns as Poet Laureate was thoroughly sifted, and the AUTHENTI- CATED PARTICULARS—furnished to the meeting of 19th Nov. as directed— proved to be so satisfactory that the R.W. Master himself seconded the motion, relative to painting the Inauguration, and it was unanimously carried.

The signature of "WILL^M. CAMPBELL" appended to minutes of 1801, as above quoted, supplies *absolute proof* that that brother was the same William Campbell who was re-elected Senior Warden, 24th June, 1802, when the "four " prints which were got for the Lodge" "met with the approbation of the " Brethren"—*one of those prints being that of Robert Burns, "Poet Laureat*,"

already described, and absolute proof also that *he was the same* " WILL^M. CAMP-
BELL " *who signed the attendance book on occasion of the meeting, held 12th*
November, 1845, when *he cordially seconded the motion* (which was "unanimously
" carried ") to the effect *that the Inauguration of Robert Burns as Poet Laureate*
be painted by Brother Stewart Watson.

In this connection the following memoranda are particularly worthy of
notice, relative to a few of the office-bearers of the Lodge who were associated
with Brother William Campbell, in the election which took place 24th June, 1802 :—

> Brother ROBERT MOIR, who was called to the chair on said occasion, had
> been initiated in Canongate Kilwinning, February 1st, 1787, *same*
> *night Robert Burns was affiliated.* He became an active and valuable
> member of the Lodge :—Was appointed Secretary, December 12th,
> 1788, just when a good Secretary was urgently needed, the minute
> book having been much neglected for nearly two years. [*Vide* pages
> 4 and 12.] Brother Moir served in several other offices, and
> ultimately became R.W. Master in 1795.

> Brother ALEXANDER JAFFRAY was initiated in Can. Kil., June 24th, 1795,
> while Robert Burns was yet in life, and when the above named Robert
> Moir was R.W. Master of the Lodge. He was most active in the
> years 1815 and 1816 in promoting the general subscription towards
> the fund for the " *Mausoleum to the memory of Robert Burns, who*
> " *was a member and Poet Laureat of this Lodge.*" *Vide* minute,
> dated 9th February, 1815.

> Brother WILLIAM BALLANTYNE, Writer to the Signet, initiated 1799, was
> elected Secretary, Nov. 30, 1799, re-elected June 24, 1800 ; elected
> Depute-Master 1801, re-elected June 24, 1802,—when the Print of
> " *Robert Burns, the Scottish Bard, Poet Laureat, Lodge No. 2 Cannon-*
> " *gate Kilwinning,*" "met with the approbation of the Brethren,"—
> re-elected also Depute-Master in 1803, 4, and 5. He was a member
> of Committee until the year 1817, and, along with other old brethren
> now referred to, acknowledged the fact that Robert Burns *was a*
> *member,* " *and Poet Laureat of this Lodge,*" by promoting the Mau-
> soleum subscription in the year 1815. *Vide* minute, dated 9th
> February, 1815.

> Brother HUGH SMYTH MERCER, Writer to the Signet, has not been
> recorded. This omission from the minute book is doubtless one of
> the very many instances of gross neglect which I have proved to have
> occurred during the Burns period. *Vide* reference to Bro. Mercer at
> page 5 hereof. The first mention of Bro. Hugh Smyth Mercer in
> the Can. Kil. records is very shortly after the period referred to in
> the list of office-bearers elected June 24, 1790, when he was elected

Secretary :—was R.W. Master 1798, 1799, and 1800, and appointed a member of Committee at the meeting above-mentioned, June 24, 1802, when the Print of the "Poet Laureat" was approved.

Brother ROBERT SCOTT MONCRIEFF of Wellwood and Pitliver,—recorded as P. and R. June 24, 1795; was elected Secretary 1796, J. W. 1797, S.W. 1798, and Depute-Master 1799 and 1800. At the meeting of June 24, 1802, he was elected a member of Committee, and well aware, therefore, that Burns had been "Poet Laureat." He continued on Committee with Bro. Charles More, and other old members, for several years afterwards.

Brother JOHN MORE, jun., and Brother GEORGE SPANKIE, were both initiated December 2, 1778. The latter was continuously in office as Treasurer from 1784 and throughout the Burns' period, and had therefore been fully cognizant of all proceedings during the time Burns attended the Lodge ;—the affiliation of Burns, his election and inauguration as Poet Laureate, and other attendances.

Brother GEORGE MILNE was initiated as far back as 1760,—still an office-bearer of the Lodge, and therefore equally aware of said proceedings.

Brother ALEXANDER FORBES (not recorded), who was "continued as Steward" in 1780, was almost continually in office thereafter, and consequently was also quite aware that Robert Burns was an affiliated member, and had been elected and inaugurated Poet Laureate.

AND

Brother CHARLES MORE, of the Royal Bank, one of the Committee 1802. Initiated 1769. He was Depute-Master when Burns was affiliated, February 1, 1787. His signature appears affixed to the minute of that date, and to the minutes of many of the other meetings which took place while Burns resided in Edinburgh. He also seconded one of the motions, passed 8th June, 1815, relative to the subscription for a Mausoleum to the memory of "*the Lamented Bard*, ROBERT "BURNS, WHO HAD BEEN POET LAUREAT TO THE LODGE." *Vide* minute, dated June 8, 1815.

It is therefore evident that Brother William Campbell, and his early associates in the Lodge, "had many opportunities of giving testimony in favour "of the particulars alluded to" in the minute of 12th November 1845, regarding the Inauguration.

Other matter which relates to this section is reserved for my letter to Past-Master Allan Mackenzie.

Respectfully submitted by

HUGH C. PEACOCK,

*Past-Secretary, and Past-Depute-Master Can. Kil.,
Proxy Master, No. 476.*

Containing further references to Robert Burns, Poet Laureate of Lodge Canongate Kilwinning.

Second reference
in the records
to
ROBERT BURNS
as
POET LAUREATE
18½ years
after his death

Geo. Simson R.W.M
E 1808 April 14
1813 Junior Warden
1814 R.W.M.

Alexʳ Jaffray, Writer.
E 1795 June 24
1797 Secretary
1798 J.W.
1799 S.W.
1801 to 1804 R.W.M.
and again in 1813
Paul Taylor, Secretary
E —— not recorded
1805 June 24 Secre-
tary on to year 1815
1815 to 1816 Treasr.
Thos. Ritchie Steward
not recorded, but
was Steward 1805
and 1806
Jn. Scrymgeour, Tyler
E 1767 December 23

Lodge Meeting

*   *   *

[After a few remarks by the Right Worshipful Master Geo Simson relative to other Business]

It was also stated by the R. W. Master that he had observed a public Subscription had been commenced for the purpose of erecting a Mausoleum to the Memory of ROBERT BURNS *who was a Member and* POET LAUREAT OF THIS LODGE. That a printed Notice had been handed him under the Authority of a Committee of Subscribers appointed to manage the different matters connected with the undertaking pointing out the mode in which it was intended to proceed with the work &c. He then submitted to the meeting the propriety of the Lodge commencing a Subscription in order to contribute towards the erection of that work, being the only manner in which they can testify their respect for the Memory of a *Public Character so immediately connected with them, and who, on many occasions contributed so generally to the harmony of the Masonic Order, and to that of the Lodge Canongate Kilwinning in particular,* which motion was seconded by Worshipful BROTHER JAFFRAY, and, having met with the unanimous approbation of the Brethren, the Secretary was directed to furnish the Steward and Tyler with Subscription Lists in order to carry the views of the Lodge into execution. The Lodge was then duly closed and adjourned to the 17th instant

P. TAYLOR Secy   GEO. SIMSON M.

[*A Copy of each of the Subscription lists referred to will be found on pages* 35, 36].

31

Third Reference

At a Meeting of the General Committee of this Lodge held upon the 8th June 1815, PRESENT

E 1808 April 14
E 1795 June 24
P. & R. 1806 Nov 20
E. 1806 Nov 20
E. 1813 Nov 29
E. 1813 July 30
E not recorded
Sec 1805 to 1815
E. 1769 Feby 8
E 1814 Jany 6
E 1813 Nov 29

R.W.Br Geo. Simson
W.P.M. Alexr Jaffray
D.M. James Harrower
S.M. James Neilson
S.W. Chas Stewart
J.W. Archd. Kennedy
Secretary Paul Taylor
Past D.M. CHARLES MORE
Al. L. Robertson
David Birrell

The Right Worshipful Master   *   *   * stated that he had directed the present meeting to be called for the purpose of taking into consideration whatever the Committee might deem of importance to the Brethren. The R.W. Master congratulated the Meeting on the full attendance of the Members—and stated that while he had to regret that several were unavoidably detained he had full communications with some of them on the subject of the matters which would most likely fall under the notice of the meeting and was prepared to state in particular that on these subjects the following members of the Committee concurred in opinion with him viz.

E 1801 Nov 16
E 1781 Jany 3
E 1799 Nov 17

Brothers John Lawson
James Davidson and
WILLIAM BALLANTYNE

The attention of the Meeting was in the first place requested to the minutes of the General Meeting of the Lodge held on the 9th February last at which it had been unanimously resolved to open a Public Subscription by the Individual Members of the Lodge in aid of the General Subscription by the friends and admirers of *the Lamented Bard* ROBERT BURNS [WHO HAD BEEN POET LAUREAT TO THE LODGE] for the erection of a Mausoleum to his memory. It was

Paul Taylor Secretary
E not recorded
Secy 1805 & on to
1815 continuously

stated by Brother Secretary Taylor that the Subscription List had been presented to and received the Signatures of several of the Brethren, the greater part of whom had paid the amount of their Subscriptions, and those who had not would of course do so when called upon.—That the sum subscribed, as nearly as could be stated with accuracy was about £13 Sterling, but owing to the absence of several of the Brethren and other circumstances the list had not yet been presented to the whole, and there was reason to believe that when it shall have been so the above sum will be considerably increased.

Geo. Simson R.W.M.
E 1808 April 14

It was moved from the chair that, as taking into consideration the state of the funds of the Lodge, the character of its members and the veneration in which all held the memory of Burns no sum below Twenty Guineas could with propriety be offered in aid of such an undertaking—the Committee should authorise the Treasurer to make up from the funds of the Lodge whatever deficiency there shall be after the list has been presented to all the Brethren and that the sum of £21 should be transmitted to the Reverend Thomas Duncan, Secretary to the General Committee of Subscribers for the erection of the Mausoleum, which motion having been seconded by Brother Harrower was unanimously agreed to.

And Brother Jaffray then moved that the R.W. Master should in the meantime write to the Reverend Mr Duncan intimating the intention of the Lodge to transmit the above sum after their Annual Meeting for election on the 24th June when it was necessary that the resolutions of the Committee should be reported to the Lodge, and that the Treasurer should continue his exertions to obtain subscriptions from such of the Brethren as had not yet subscribed,—which motion having been seconded by BROTHER CHARLES MORE, were also unanimously agreed to.

*   *   *   *   *   *

P. TAYLOR Secy   GEO SIMSON M

James Harrower
P & R. 1806 Novr 20
1809 to 1815 DepM.
Alex. Jaffray, Writer
E 1795 June 24

1797 Secretary
1798 J.W.
1799 & 1800 S.W.
Chas More of the
Royal Bank
E 1769 Feb 8

1783 S.W.
1784 to 1786 Dep M
Bro.Chas More signed
the minutes of 1 Feb
and 1 March 1787,
and many others
before and after that
time
Geo. Simson
E 1808 April 14
Paul Taylor
E not recorded
Secy 1805 onwardsto
1815

Fourth Reference

At a General Meeting of the Committee of this Lodge held on Tuesday 11th June 1816

Present

E 1804 Nov 15
1815 to 1818 R.W.M. }
E 1808 April 14 }
1813 JW }
E 1806 Nov 20
E 1814 Jany 6
1815 S.W 1816 & 17 Sub M }
E 1814 Mar. 3., 1815 J.W.
E. not recorded
1805 Sec. on to 1815 }
1815 & 16 Treas. }
E 1795 June 24 1797 Sec 1798 J.W. 1799 & 1800 S.W
E 1769 Feb 8, 1783 S.W, 1784 to 1788 Dep M.

E 1813 Nov 29

E 1813 Nov 29

E 1813 Nov 29

R.W.Br George Burnett Master
W.Br Geo Simson Past Master
W.Br James Neilson Subt M.
W.Br Alexr L. Robertson Senr W.
W.B. William Horn Junr Wardn
W.B. Paul Taylor Treasurer

Br ALEXR JAFFRAY
Br CHAs MORE
Br Chas Stewart
Br Andw Robinson
Br David Birrell Secretary

*   *   *   *

The Committee do further report their opinion that the Treasurer should be enjoined to advance out of the first ready funds in his hands the requisite sum to enable the Right Worshipful Master to remit to the Secretary of the Committee for the erection of a Monument to the Memory of BURNS *the sum of Twenty Guineas voted by the General Meeting in June last year* and to make up the deficiency from the proper funds of the Lodge if the Subscriptions do not amount to that sum

*   *   *   *

Geo. Burnet
E 1804 Nov 15
David Birrell
E 1813 Nov 29

DA BIRRELL Secy   GEO BURNET

FESTIVAL OF ST JOHN
THE BAPTIST

Fifth Reference

CANONGATE KILWINNING LODGE
24th June 1816

*   *   *   *   *

[Brethren who were present and had been nominated to their respective offices].

E 1804 Nov 15	Brother George Burnet	R.W. Master
E 1808 April 14	„	George Simson Past Master
E 1806 Nov 20	„	James Neilson Depute Master
E 1814 Jany 6	„	Alexr L. Robertson Substitute Master
E 1814 March 3	„	William Horn Senior Warden
E 1813 Novr 29	„	Andrew Robinson Junior Warden
E not recorded See 1805 & on to 1815	„	Paul Taylor Treasurer
E 1813 Nov 29	„	David Birrell Secretary
E P & R 1814 March 3	„	Arch Horn Senior Deacon
E 1816 February 1	„	Malcolm McNeil Junior Deacon
		and
Not recorded, but was Steward 1805 & 1806	„	Thomas Ritchie Steward
E 1767 Dec 23	„	John Scrymgeour Tyler

} Pro Tempore

" All which being likewise unanimously approven of these Brethren were " installed in their respective offices with the usual formalities."

The R.W. Master then proposed that the Committee for managing the affairs of the Lodge should consist of the present and Past Office Bearers with the addition of

E 1795 June 24	Brothers ALEXr JAFFRAY
E 1801 Nov 16	John Spottiswood Lawson
P & R 1799 Nov 17	William Ballantine
E 1769 Febr 8 S.W. 1783 Dep M 1784 to 1788	CHAs MORE
P. & R. 1814 Jany 6	Charles Nairne
E.E.R. 1815 Dec 27	J. Lamb
E.E.R 1814 Jany 6	and William Tait

*   *   *   *   *

E

After the election, the Secretary was directed to read *the Minutes of the Committee* of this Lodge of the 11th current, *and the same having been read met with the unanimous approbation of the Brethren, at the same time a motion* "a copy sent to every "brother" *was made that an extract should be printed and a copy sent to every brother belonging to the Lodge within this city,* in a particular manner the clauses 2, 4, 5, & 7—which motion being agreed to, the Secretary was enjoined to have the same printed *and a copy sent to* EVERY MEMBER OF THE LODGE *with all possible dispatch.*

"a copy sent to every "brother"

*   *   *

DA BIRRELL Secy   GEO BURNET Master
WILL. HORN S.W.

Geo. Burnet
E 1804 Nov 15
William Horn
E 1814 Mar 3
David Birrell
E 1813 Nov 29

Sixth Reference
Committee Meeting

E 1804 Nov 15
E 1814 Jany 6
E 1813 Nov 29

General Meeting of the Committee held in the Lodge room on 2nd January 1817.

[Among the members present were]
R.W. Brother George Burnet
W. Brother Alexr L. Robertson
W. Brother David Birrell

The Secretary produced a sealed packet which had been left for him in the course of the day addressed to " Right Worshipful Brother George Burnet, " M. of Canongate Kilwinning Lodge, or the Preses of the Committee for the " time "—which having been opened was found to contain a letter from W. Brother Simson Past Master apologising for his not being able to attend the meeting, and stating that having in consequence of the previous minutes of the Committee and of the Lodge received from the Treasurer the sum of Twenty Guineas which had been voted in aid of the fund for the erection of a Mausoleum to the Memory of ROBERT BURNS late POET LAUREAT OF THE LODGE, he had transmitted that sum to the Reverend Mr Duncan, Dumfries, Treasurer to that fund and had received a letter in return expressed in very proper terms of Gratitude to the Brethren, which letter he now reported to the Committee and requested that if it met their approbation it should be submitted to the Lodge at its first meeting and put up among the archives.

Paul Taylor, Treas.
E not recorded
Sec. 1805 to 1815

The Committee approved of the conduct and suggestion of Brother Simson and directed that the above correspondence should be laid before the monthly meeting of the Lodge on the 8th instant and in the meantime that the Treasurer and Secretary should be authorised to receive such subscriptions as the Brethren should tender—and to apply the same in liquidation of the sum voted or paid from the funds of the Lodge in addition to the Subscriptions of the individual members thereof.

Paul Taylor, Treas.
E Secy. 1805
David Birrell Secy
E 1813 Nov 29

*   *   *   *   *

DA BIRRELL Secy   GEORGE BURNET P.

Geo Burnet
E 1804 Nov 15
David Birrell
E 1813 Nov 29

SUBSCRIPTION LIST, of which the following is a copy was prepared in terms of Minute of 9th February 1815, with the following addition :—

" The present list is therefore directed to be presented to EVERY MEMBER who will please to subscribe his name marking opposite the amount of subscription, and when paid at the time, or to be afterwards paid by him."

NAMES		Amount Subscribed		Paid		NAMES		Amount Subscribed		Paid	
Brother Simson M.	P.T.	„	10	6		10	6	W. L. Neilson	P.T.	„	7	6	„	7	6
E 1808 April 14								E. 3rd Feby 1815							
Brother Jaffray P.M.		„	7	6				Brother Chas More	P.T.	„	5	„	„	5	„
E. 24th June 1795.								E. 8th Feby 1769							
Brother Harrower D.M.	P.T.	„	7	6	„	7	6	Brother Fredk Coventry	P.T.	„	5	„	„	5	„
E. 6th March 1806								E. 9th Feby 1815							
Brother Neilson S.M.	P.T.	„	7	6	„	7	6	Brother Wm Douglas	P.T.	„	7	6	„	7	6
E. 20th Novr 1806								E. 24th June 1801							
Brother Stewart S.W.	P.T.	„	7	6	„	7	6	Brother Dickie		„	7	6			
E 29th Novr 1813								E. 19th Septr 1815							
Brother Kennedy J.W.	P.T.	„	7	6	„	7	6	Brother Dickson		„	5	„			
E. 30th July 1813								E. 29th June 1809							
Brother Taylor Sec & Tr	P.T.	„	7	6	„	7	6	Brother Ballantine	P.T.	„	7	„	„	7	6
Not recorded but Sec. 1805 to 1815								E. 17th Novr 1799							
Brother Tait	P.T.	„	5	„	„	5	„	Br. Maclachlan		„	10	„			
F. 23rd Novr 1802								E. 14th Decr 1814							
Brother Miller	P.T.	„	5	„	„	5	„	Bror Robinson		„	5	„			
E. 2nd March 1786								E. 29th Novr 1813							
Brother Armstrong	P.T.	„	5	„	„	5	„	Bro Darwin		„	5	„			
E. 6th Feby 1803								E. 11th Feby 1806							
Brother Barr	P.T.	„	5	„	„	5	„	Allan Wight	D.B.	„	5	„	„	5	„
E. 29th Novr 1814								E. 6th Jany 1814							
Brother Birrell	P.T.	„	5	„	„	5	„	Bro A. Robertson		„	5	„			
E. 29th Novr 1813								E. 6th Jany 1814							
Brother Adair	P.T.	1	1	„	1	1	„	Bro Abm Armstrong	D.B.	1	1	1	1	1	„
E. 4th Dec. 1788								E. 5th June 1815							
Brother Nairn	P.T.	„	7	6	„	7	6								
E. 3rd March 1803															
Brother Will Horn	P.T.	„	7	6	„	7	6								
E. 3rd March 1814															
Brother Archd Horn	P.T.	„	5	„	„	5	„								
E. 3rd March 1814															
Brother George Boyd	P.T.	1	1	„	1	1	„								
E. 1st Jany 1808															
Brother Brooks	P.T.	„	5	„	„	5	„								
E. 3rd Feby 1815															
Brother Davidson		„	7												
E. 3rd Jany 1781															
Brother John Wilson		„	5												
E. 29th Novr 1813															
Brother Mason	P.T.	„	7	6	„	7	6								
E. 6th Jany 1814															
Brother M onalandj		„	5												

[*List as above completed was submitted to meeting of Committee on 2nd January*, 1817.]

[*Printed Notice referred to in Minute of 9th Feby. 1815*]

SUBSCRIPTION

FOR

A Mausoleum to be erected over the Remains

OF

ROBERT BURNS

In St Michaels Churchyard, Dumfries

We, the Subscribers, agree to pay the sums annexed to our respective names in terms of the Resolutions of a Meeting held at Dumfries on 6th January 1814

Subscriptions received by David Birrell Secy to Canongate
Kilwinning Lodge

	£		
David Nairne		1	1	„
E. 7 March 1816				
J. Chisholm		„	7	6
E. 29th Novr 1813				
Ludovick Grant Paid		„	5	„
E. 7th March 1816				
Sums collected to this date (18th Septem 1816) as per other list by the Treasurer & Secretary		9	11	„

Seventh reference Extract from Brother Simson's letter, dated 2nd January, 1817, to Brother Burnet, referred to in minute of same date :—

. . . . "I beg leave to report to you that having been furnished by your Secretary with the sum of Twenty Guineas, voted by the Lodge as a contribution towards the erection of a Mausoleum to the memory of our late Poet Laureate, Burns, I, in obedience to the instructions of the Committee, remitted that sum to the Rev. Dr. Duncan, Dumfries." . . . .

Eighth reference

COPY OF LETTER FROM DR DUNCAN.

Submitted to Meeting of Committee 2nd Jany., 1817, and Lodge Meeting on 8th January, 1817.

DUMFRIES, *Decr.* 31*st*, 1816.

SIR,—I am commissioned by my brother, who is one of the Secretaries to the Committee for conducting the affairs of the subscribers to Burns' Mausoleum, to acknowledge the very liberal contribution of the Canongate Kilwinning Lodge to their funds ; and in name of the Committee to request that you will communicate to the Lodge the grateful sense which the Committee must entertain of the approbation and confidence of that respectable Brotherhood. This tribute of respect to the memory of your LAUREATE is not only most interesting in itself, but must be highly gratifying to all the admirers of the Bard.

I have this day caused the sum inclosed in your letter (twenty guineas) to be placed to the Treasurer's credit in the Bank of Scotland's office, and send a note of it *to the provincial newspapers,* too late, however, for insertion till next week.

My brother was obliged to go to the country without having it in his power to write this acknowledgment, but requested me to make his apology.—I have the honour to be, Sir, your most obedt. Serv.,   THOMAS T. DUNCAN.

Addressed outside—

GEORGE SIMSON, Esq.,

Writer in Edinburgh.

Ninth reference

Monthly Meeting
Geo. Burnet R.W.M.
E. 1804 Nov 15

The Lodge having been regularly constituted by the Right Worshipful Master he requested the Minute of the Committee of the 2nd of this month to be read which having been done the same met the entire approbation of the Brethren and the Correspondence &c were directed to be put up among the Archives of the Lodge.

*   *   *   *   *

DA BIRRELL Secy

GEO BURNET Master
WILL. HORN Senior Warden

Tenth reference
A. McNeil Advocate
E not recorded on
Committee 1824
SM 1827 RWM 1830
to 1837
W B D D Turnbull
Advocate
E 1833 Nov 21

Minutes of Meeting of Committee of the Lodge Can. Kil. held in the Lodge room 16th January 1835 Brother R.W.M. A McNeil in the chair.

It was proposed by the R.W. Brother M'Neil, Master, and seconded by Worshipful Brother Turnbull Substitute Master that it was expedient that the Honorary office of POET LAUREATE of the Lodge which had been in abeyance since the death of the immortal Brother ROBERT BURNS should be revived, and that James Hogg "the Ettrick Shepherd" on whom his poetic mantle had fallen should be respectfully requested to accept the appointment as the highest tribute to his genius and private worth which the brethren had it in their power to bestow—which motion was unanimously and enthusiastically carried.

John Forbes, Writer.
E P & R 12 Aug 1825

Brother John Forbes in consequence of his being personally acquainted with Mr Hogg was instructed to communicate to him this resolution, and at the same time, in the name of the Master, Office Bearers and Members to invite his attendance at a full meeting of the Lodge on Friday the 6th day of February next at 8'clock evening to have his brow encircled with the laurel

Alexr Mackie Writer
Secretary
E. 1833 June 24

wreath the insignia of his office. The Secretary was directed to provide an entertainment suitable for the occasion, and on purpose to give additional interest to the Meeting to have in readiness the diplomas for the ten Polish Officers lately admitted members to be then formally presented to them.

*   *   *   *   *

E. 1833 June 24

A MACKIE, Secy.

Eleventh reference
A. McNeil Advocate
E not recorded, but
on Committee 1824

1835 *Jany* 24.—Lodge Meeting.

The R.W.M. Master A. McNeil in the Chair.

The Minutes of the General Meeting of the Lodge 27 Decr and Minutes of the Committee of 16th Jany having been read to the Meeting, the same were approved of.

*   *   *   *   *

E. 1833 June 24

A. MACKIE Secy.

Agreeably to above directions to John Forbes on 16 January 1835, he wrote to Brother James Hogg and received the following answer :—

" ALTRIVE LAKE, *January 25, 1835.*

"Dear Forbes.—I am sixty-five years of age this night, I am not a
"Mason, and never have been, having uniformally resisted the entreaties of my
"most influential friends to become one. I am, however, intensely sensible of
"the high honour intended me, which, coming to my hand on the morning of
"my birthday, has, I feel, added a new charm to the old shepherd's life. My
"kindest respects to the Hon. Master and Members of the Lodge, and say that
"I cannot join them, nor be initiated into the mysteries of the Art.

*   *   *   *   *

"JAMES HOGG."

Subsequently, however, Hogg consented to join, and the ceremony was fixed for 7th May 1835. The names of those Members who signed the Minute when he was E. P. & R., are :—

Affd 24 Jany 1834	Jas. Deans, M., P.M. of Emulation Lodge, London, P.G. Sword Bearer Grand Lodge of England.
E March 4 1830	Anthony Traill, W.S., Senr. Warden.
E June 24 1833	A. Mackie, Junr. Warden.
Affd April 30 1835	Jas. Burnes, M.D. (E.I.C.S.), LL.D., F.R.S. (whose Executors presented the Inauguration Picture in the Board Room of Grand Lodge).
E June 24 1824	Adam Wilson, Writer.
Not recorded	Dan. M. Davidson, R.A.
E 21 Nov 1833	John Donald.
E March 25 1835	Wm. Jeffries Dowlin.
Not recorded	Andw. Sievwright.
E Jany 7 1834	Pat. Sandeman, Merchant.
E Feby 5 1824 S W 1827-28	Wm. Pringle (afterwards Poet Laureate).
E July 12 1825	John Forbes, Writer.
Not recorded	C. Neaves (afterwards Lord Neaves).
E March 3 1802	Robert Boyd, W.S.

A. Mackie, Secy.

JAMES HOGG.

Election, 24th June 1835.

Alexr M'Neill, Advocate	.	R.W. Master
Chas M'Dougall, Advocate .	.	Dep. Master
W. B. D. D. Turnbull, Advocate.	.	Sub. Master

Robert Blackwood, Publisher	. Sen' Warden
George Cumming, W.S.	. Jun' Warden
James Deans .	. Secretary
Anthy. Trail, W.S. .	. Treasurer
Daniel M. Davidson .	. Sen' Deacon
John Galt Denniston .	. Jun' Deacon
William Jeffries Dowlin .	. Inner Guard
Revd Hector Holm .	. Chaplain

Revd Hector Holm . . Chaplain
John Miller, Advocate . . 1st Banner Bearer
Timothy Bunton . . . 2nd Banner Bearer
James Hogg, the " Ettrick Shepherd " . . Poet Laureate
Chas Fred^k Gifford . . . . Master of Ceremonies
John Donald ⎫
Patrick Sandeman ⎭ . Stewards
John T. Surenne . . Organist

Committee.

John Wilson, Advocate, " Christopher North," Chairman, E. Feb. 2, 1830.

Alex. L. Robertson, W.S., Past Master — John Leslie, Past S.W.
Alex^r M'Neill, R.W.M. — James Logan, Past S.D.
Chas. M'Dougall, D.M. — Chas Anderson, Past J.D.
W. B. D. D. Turnbull, S.M. — Hector Gavin
Robt Blackwood, S.W. — Thos Knox Beveridge, W.S.
George Cumming, W.S., J.W. — Robt Stewart and ⎫ Tylers.
James Deans, Secy. — Wm Petrie ⎭ (Who were annually re-elected onwards till 1845).
Anthy. Traill, Treasurer

George Ritchie, W.S.

Office Bearers, 24th June 1845.

	Brother A. D. Campbell	.	R.W.M.
	„ W. Mowbray . .	.	D.M.
E May 16 1843	„ James Hunter, of Glencorse	.	S.M.
	„ James Neilson . .	.	S.W.
	„ Jas. Arthur Campbell .	.	J.W.
E June 24 1844	„ Chas Robertson .	.	Secy and Treasurer
E May 22 1844	„ Donald Cameron .	.	S.D.
	„ Wm Scott Henderson .	.	J.D.
	„ Wm Henderson .	.	Inner Guard
	„ Wm Porteous . .	.	1st Banner Bearer
	„ George Moncreiff .	.	2nd „

Brother W. J. Pattison . . . M of Ceremonies
    „   John David Bell   . 1st Steward
    „   George W. Wemyss   . 2d
    „   Robert Stewart   . Tyler

Committee along with the Chief Office-Bearers.

E March 9 1836	Wm Edmonstone Aytoun, Prof. of Literature and Belles Lettres, in the University of Edinburgh, Chairman.
E March 3 1825	Alexr M'Neil . . . . P.M.
E Feby 20 1836	Arch Smith . . . P.M.
E Oct 14 1840	Samuel Somerville . . . P.M.
E June 24 1837	W. J. Pattison
E Feby 28 1844	Edward Fraser, Advocate
Not recorded	Robert Blackwell

Twelfth reference

LODGE CANONGATE KILWINING
ST JOHNS CHAPEL, 12 *Novembr.* 1845

E.P.R 1840 March 26	Present Bro Archd David Campbell R.W.M.
E. 1840 Oct 14	Saml Somerville of Ampherlaw M.D. P.M.
E 1842 Jany 19	William Mowbray D.M.
E 1843 Dec 27	J. A. Campbell J. Warden
E 1844 June 24	Chas Robertson Secry and Treasr
	J. Macdonald
E.P.R. 1837 June 24	W. Jeffries Pattison, 13 Albany St.
E.P.R. 1801 April 2, S.W. 1801 & 1802 E.P.R. 1834 Jany 7. Was one of the Lodge Stewards 1835 when James Hogg was Poet Laureate	Wm Campbell, W.S. 114 Laurieston Place
E 1843, Nov. 15	Patrick Sandeman, Merchant, Greenside Street
Admission not recorded, but he appears on Committee as far back as 1835, and Chairman of Committee 1840	John Gray Henderson, of Abbotsrule, Roxburghshire
Affd Hon. M. 1830 March 4 „ Full M. 1831 Oct. 18	Hector Gavin, Engraver, Croft an Righ
E.P.R. 1828 March 6. SW 1848-9 SM 1850. Sec 1851 to 1867	James Marshall, Solicitor
	Stewart Watson, Portrait Painter
	A. Murray of Edinr Celtic
	James Bell, Visiting Brother of Dunbar Castle Lodge " and various other Brethren "

The Lodge was opened in the first degree by the R.W.M.

The Minutes of the 24th June 20th August and 7th Oct. last read and approved of,—

The R.W.M. having made allusion to Robert Burns as having been a distinguished Member of the Lodge,—

Affd 1830 March 4   Br Jas Marshall stated that he had come to this meeting to reintroduce
E P R 1828 March 6 Br Stewart Watson initiated during winter 1827-8. This Brother, he said, at the

F

commencement of his professional career as an artist, was patronised by Sir Walter Scott whose portrait he painted at Abbotsford, together with other works there extant. He was elected an Associate of the Royal Institution and afterwards went abroad. For some years past he has pursued his professional studies in Rome, and having returned to London, he wrote enquiring among other matters of the condition of Masonry in Edinburgh. In the course of some correspondence that followed, a subject occurred for his brush, the materials of which were chiefly to be derived from the records and traditions of their Lodge and he came now to follow up that purpose. Br Marshall quoted passages from minutes of the Lodge in reference to the attendances of Robert Burns in 1787, and laid on the table a motion "that Br Watson have access to Sketch the " antique and picturesque interior of the Lodge with a view to his painting the " Inauguration of Robert Burns as her Poet Laureate,"—the motion to be disposed of at an after meeting. He felt assured that the subject was worthy of the artist, the artist of the subject ; and the whole would be creditable to the Lodge. The Painting of a Masonic Lodge was a novelty, but the peculiarity of the event chosen was such, that in its execution the mysteries of the Lodge would not in the least degree be trenched upon. Years ago when he, Br Marshall, attended this Lodge he took chief interest in the reminiscences of old men connected with such events, but of these he feared few now survived.

E 1801 April 1
Br William Campbell W.S. said that this motion had taken him by no greater surprise than delight. He had been forty-five years a Mason (and connected with this Lodge) and had had *many opportunities of giving testimony in favour of the particulars alluded to.* He thought the proposition one deserving of every support. He had never been in a Lodge Room with Robert Burns but had travelled in his company, and spent two of the most happy days with him at Auchtertyre Castle the seat of Sir William Murray. He was happy that he had lived to second such an admirable motion.

Br Marshall was requested to furnish the *authenticated particulars* to a subsequent meeting when the motion should be disposed of, meantime it was unanimously entertained.

*　　*　　*　　*　　*

A. D. Campbell, W.S.
E 1840 March 26
James Neilson, S.S.C.
E 1842 June 15
Chas Robertson
E 1844 June 24

CHAS ROBERTSON Secy & Tresr

ARCHD DAVID CAMPBELL R.W.M.
J. NEILSON S.W.

Thirteenth refer-
ence

Present

E P R 1840 March 26   Bro Campbell, R.W.M.
E 1842 Jany 19   „   Mowbray, D.M.
E P R 1837 June 24   „   W. J. Pattison Acting S.W.
E 1842 Dec 27   „   Campbell Jr Wn
E 1844 June 24   „   Robertson Secy & Trer

Bro J. M. Salmon. Sir Wm M. Napier Lodge 695 Donaghadee. W. F Stra-
theam of Kirkwall Kilwinning, W. Ferguson and several other of the Brethren.

The Lodge was opened in the first Degree by the R.W.M.

The Minutes of last meeting were read and approved of.

Affl 1830 Mar 4   Bro Marshall then submitted the motion which was laid on the table at
E P R 1828 March 6   last meeting viz!. "That Bro Watson have access to Sketch the Antique and
" Picturésque Interior of the Lodge with a view to his painting the Inauguration
" of Robert Burns as her Poet Laureate."—the motion was seconded by the
R.W.M. and unanimously carried.

Petitions were presented for admission from John Hunter, Esqr Drum
House and James Graham Smith, Craigends, Stirlingshire, recommended by the
R.W.M. and the Junior Warden—also from John Stewart Esq., 30 Hanover
Street, recommended by the R.W.M. and the Depute Master.

The Ballot having been taken for these gentlemen respectively they
were duly initiated into the first degree by the R.W.M.

The Lodge was then passed to the second degree by the R.W.M. when
Bros James Savage, James Anderson, Wm Ferguson, and Chas. J. Nasmyth
were passed Fellow Crafts.

•   •   •   •   •

CHAS ROBERTSON   ARCH DAVID CAMPBELL R.W.M.
    Secy & Trer   J. NEILSON Sr W

I certify that the *excerpta* at pages 21 and 22, and those at pages 30 to 43
hereof, are true copies.

GEORGE CRAWFORD, R.W.M.

EDINBURGH, *April* 12, 1893.

COPY of CORRESPONDENCE

BETWEEN

Mr J. LINNING WOODMAN, C.S., and Mr STEWART WATSON,
Portrait Painter—the artist who painted the Inauguration Picture—showing
the great care which Brother Watson took in procuring "*authenticated
particulars*" of a subject before painting it.

In the printed copy of correspondence, to which Grand Secretary calls
attention, a letter appears from him under date 18th August 1891, regarding
Robert Burns and his connection with Canongate Kilwinning, in which the
following passage occurs :—

"The beautiful story of his inauguration appears to have been *concocted* in 1845-46,
to supply Mr Stewart Watson (a well-known Edinburgh artist), a member of the Lodge,
with a subject for a beautiful picture.   Mr Stewart Watson also, it may be here remarked,
executed two other similar paintings—that of the Knight Templars and Supreme Royal
Arch Chapter of Scotland in conclave, *both of which*, except as regards the features of the
members portrayed, *are purely imaginative*."

In connection with this quotation, and for the satisfaction of all interested, the
following authentic information is here transcribed :—

No. 1—*Mr Woodman to Mr Watson.*

10th March 1846.

Mr Woodman presents compliments to Mr Watson, and, as instructed by the
Installation Committee, has the pleasure to enclose a ticket of admission, for Mr Watson,
to the ceremonial of to-morrow evening.

No. 2—*Insertion in the Edinburgh Evening Courant, by direction of Mr J. Linning Woodman, Registrar and Secretary, 24th March, 1846.*

"THE ORDER OF THE TEMPLE.—The interesting ceremonial of installing the Grand
Master and Grand Officers of this religious and military order took place in the Music
Hall on the evening of Wednesday, the 11th inst.   The hall was decorated with the
banners of the knights, and stalls were arranged on each side for their reception, &c. &c.
&c.   Stewart Watson, a companion of the Order, who was present, *has been requested to
execute a picture commemorating the imposing ceremonial on the 11th inst.*"

No. 3—*Mr Woodman to Mr Watson.*

17th March 1846

I have written a note to Sir D. Dundas, asking him to call for you, or to drop a note saying at what time he can be with you, so that you may sketch his portrait for the installation picture.—Yours faithfully,

---

No. 4—*Mr Woodman to Mr Watson.*

Can you make it convenient to see the Reverend Mr Boyle, who officiated as consecrating prelate on the 11th inst., next Friday? He generally comes into Edinburgh on the Fridays; and if you can sketch him *here* on that day I shall write him a note on learning from you the *hour* which will be most suitable.—*St Andrew Square,* 18*th March.*

No. 5—*Mr Woodman to Mr Watson.*

20*th March* 1846.

MY DEAR SIR,—I send—1st, the order of procession on the 11th March; 2nd, the names of the parties present, arranged according to rank. I have yet to furnish you with a note of the places in the hall occupied by the different parties during the ceremonial.—Yours faithfully.

No. 6—*Mr Woodman to Mr Watson.*

4*th June* 1846.

I send the Great Roll of the Order of the Temple, Vol. I.; and, accompanying, you have a list of those whose banners, &c., appeared at the installation, the manner in which the same were blazoned, &c.—Yours faithfully.

Note.—All the other portraits were taken successively at periods to suit the individual convenience of members.

Note.—I was enrolled as a member in 1830-31.   S. W.

In the Records of the Order, dated 13th March 1848, it is mentioned that—

"A Letter from Frater Stewart Watson, dated 1st instant, mentioning the near completion of the Historical Picture representing the Installation of the M.E. & R. the Grand Master, on 11th March 1846, having been submitted, the

Chapter-General expressed a hope that arrangements might be made for Engraving a Picture which must prove so interesting and attractive to all Soldiers of the Cross, both at home and abroad. The following is an excerpt from Frater Watson's Letter descriptive of the Painting."

'The point of action selected, and which appeared to me best calculated to
' illustrate this subject, is after the Grand Master has been relieved of the Sword of State
' by the Ex-Regent, Frater Callander, and received the Staff of Office from the
' Preceptor, Frater Whyte-Melville, the officiating Prelate, the Rev. John Boyle B.C.I.,
' having advanced from the Altar, accompanied by the Crucifer and Deacon, is about to
' place the Crown of The Order on the Head of the Grand Master.

' In a few weeks I hope to have the Picture ready for exhibition to the Knights
' and their friends, to whom due notice will be given. Through the kindness of Frater
' W. B. D. D. Turnbull,* I am promised the use of the Rooms of the Antiquarian Society
' for this purpose.'

The foregoing letters and relative quotations illustrate the great care and truthfulness with which Brother Stewart Watson and his friends selected materials for his masterly historical work, " *The Installation of the Duke of Athole as Grand Master of the Order of the Temple,*" which work has ever been universally accepted as a faithful representation of what *actually took place* at the Installation ceremonial of 11th March 1846 :—

Could any photograph have shown forth the impressive scene as truthfully as that painting ?—

Correspondingly, certain minutes of Lodge Canongate Kilwinning already mentioned, and much valuable information contained in the " Winter with Robert Burns," prove that the artist and his friends took equal care in procuring "authenticated particulars" for his other very fine historical work, " *The Inauguration of Robert Burns as Poet Laureate of Lodge Canongate Kilwinning.*"

As to the third of Bro. Stewart Watson's pictures under notice, namely, " *The Supreme Royal Arch Chapter of Scotland in Conclave,*" very little need be said, as it has nothing to do with the question in hand. My sole plea for referring to it is because of Grand Secretary, in his letter of 18th August 1891 above quoted, having made the very strong and unprecedented assertion on the subject

---

* It may be of interest to some readers to know that Frater W. B. D. D. Turnbull, Advocate, above mentioned, was for some time Substitute-Master of Lodge Canongate Kilwinning. The following notice of him occurs in the minute of Committee meeting held 16th January, 1835 :—" It was proposed " by the R. W. Brother M'Neil, Master, and seconded by Worshipful BROTHER TURNBULL, Substitute-" Master, that it was expedient that the Honorary office of POET LAUREATE of the Lodge, which had " been in abeyance since the death of the immortal Brother ROBERT BURNS, should be revived, and that " James Hogg, 'the Ettrick Shepherd,' on whom his poetic mantle had fallen, should be respectfully " requested to accept the appointment, as the highest tribute to his genius and private worth which the " brethren had it in their power to bestow—which motion was unanimously and enthusiastically carried."

of this and the Temple picture—*without any evidence whatever in support of it*—that "*both of which*, except as regards the features of the members portrayed, *are purely imaginative.*"

The proofs are at once obvious and conclusive throughout these pages that the painting of the *Knights Templar* and that of the *Inauguration of Robert Burns as Poet Laureate* are assuredly NOT "purely imaginative." They depict FACTS, and—for all we at present know—it may be the same with the Supreme Chapter picture.

After such distinct evidence of the accuracy of the events represented in these pictures, what ground is there for Grand Secretary's sweeping assertion against them ?

The papers from which the foregoing interesting correspondence and relative quotations are copied were among the effects of the late Mr Stewart Watson when he died. Shortly afterwards [in the year 1870] the said papers were received along with various Canongate Kilwinning Priory, Can. Kil. R.A. Chapter, and other masonic documents, by the late Dr John Middleton, my informant, and by him placed in the repository of the Canongate Kilwinning R.A. Chapter, in the Lodge-room, St. John's Chapel, St. John Street. Dr Middleton was then, and for many years afterwards, First Principal of the Chapter, and the late Companion Stewart Watson had been for a long period one of its most diligent office-bearers.

Respectfully submitted by

HUGH C. PEACOCK,
Past Sec. and Past Dep. Master Can. Kil.
Proxy Master, No. 476.

A WORD

For the late BROTHER STEWART WATSON,

Painter of the Inauguration Picture now in the Board-room of Grand Lodge.

———

Grand Secretary, in his letter concerning Robert Burns, at page 70 of the printed copy of correspondence, says :—"The beautiful story of the Inauguration "appears to have been *concocted* in 1845-46, to supply Mr Stewart Watson (a "well-known Edinburgh artist), a member of the Lodge, with a subject for a "beautiful picture."

Had such an extraordinary assertion been expressed in the lifetime of Brother Stewart Watson it would have been more opportune, because he and many of his friends would have at once answered it ;—had it even been made in the year 1873, when Grand Secretary made "a minute examination of Canongate "Kilwinning's records," and partially discussed the Inauguration question with the Lodge Secretary,—three years after Bro. Watson had passed away,—many of Bro. Watson's intimate friends were still alive, and would have gladly given evidence on the subject. Even *then* there were such witnesses as could have testified to all the "authenticated particulars" referred to in the minute of November 12, 1845, relative to the Inauguration of Robert Burns.

I had the privilege of being acquainted with Brother Stewart Watson. I visited him at his house in Broughton Park Cottage, and, up to *that* time, there never had been any question about the Inauguration picture, or the Inauguration, otherwise I would have taken very good care to get all available information from him regarding both. I am perfectly sure that he would never have allowed any "beautiful story" of the Inauguration to be *concocted* to supply him "with a "subject for a beautiful picture ;"—he had no need to do so, because, independently of the documentary evidence at his hand as Secretary of the Lodge, to which I have made reference, it is proved in the foregoing pages that half a century ago—about the time when the Inauguration picture was contemplated—very much information relative to the Inauguration was available, and was obtained by Brother Stewart Watson from old members and other brethren who had met Robert Burns, and enjoyed his company within the Lodge-room of Canongate Kilwinning.

The late Brothers Sam. Somerville of Ampherlaw, M.D.; Thomas Elder MacRitchie of Craigton and Dunork, W.S.;* David Crawford, S.S.C.; George Cumming, W.S.+ Hector Gavin, and many others *now dead*, would very speedily have refuted any imputation expressed or implied as to the "story" appearing to be "*concocted*," had such imputation been made by Brother Lyon at the time of his correspondence with me in the year 1873.

Many brethren doubtless are aware that the talented artist who painted the Inauguration picture was Brother Stewart Watson, but comparatively few now-a-days know much more about him. It seems, therefore, on this occasion of writing on the subject of his finest and best known historical work—which has afforded unmixed pleasure to many thousands of brethren all over the world—that it is clearly due to the memory of Brother Watson to place on record some further notice of him than is to be found at the present time in any of the books or other chronicles of the Lodge.

Brother "William Stewart Watson, Portrait Painter," is duly recorded as having been entered, passed, and raised in the Canongate Kilwinning on 6th March 1828. Incidentally, it may be mentioned that a picture of him as he appeared "in life's gay morn," hangs on the south wall of Lodge-room, between the organ recess and Junior Warden's chair.

Such a circumstance as that of being a full member of the Lodge so very early in this century as the year 1828 afforded Brother Stewart Watson exceptional opportunities of acquiring at first hand fully authenticated information relative to the Burns period in Canongate Kilwinning. It is amply proved in the foregoing and subsequent pages of this testimony, that in the years 1844 and 1845 there were at least *two* old members alive, and attending meetings of the Lodge—namely, Bro. William Petrie and Bro. William Campbell—who gave *incontrovertible evidence* in favor of the election and inauguration of Robert Burns as Poet Laureate;—and it stands to reason that in the year 1828, among such a numerous brotherhood as there was then, a great many more must have been frequenting the Lodge who entertained Brother Stewart Watson, and other "new links" in the membership, with reminiscences of our first Poet Laureate,—

---

* Bro. Thomas Elder MacRitchie was on Committee in 1873. His membership began in 1818.

+ Bro. George Cumming knew the Lodge well in 1834 and onwards for a long time. He was J.W. 1835 to 1837, while Robert Blackwood, Publisher, his intimate friend, was S.W. Latterly he resided in London, and I had a long and very interesting correspondence with him about old times in the Lodge, in the Chapter, and in the Temple Priory of Canongate Kilwinning.—H.C.P.

"the life of the Lodge,"—as Brother Petrie termed him. Hence was Brother Stewart Watson, above all others, the artist best suited to show forth on canvas the Inauguration of Robert Burns.

In connection with this section of my subject, it will doubtless be of interest to many readers to narrate the following reference to Bro. William Petrie, as another instance—additional to the one given in page 44 *ante*—illustrating Bro. Stewart Watson's extreme conscientiousness in gleaning "authenticated particulars" of a subject before painting it, to wit, that, in November 1845, after the motion relative to the Inauguration Picture had been approved unanimously at the Lodge meetings held on the 12th and 19th of that month, Bro. Watson accompanied the author of the "Winter with Burns" on a visit to Bro. William Petrie, and—quoting from that interesting work—it is said, "William by this time "felt that, in the sad words of Burns,—

> ' *The pale moon is setting beyond the white wave,*
> *And Time is setting with me.*'

" He mentioned that the Grand Lodge had kept on his salary, though he could "never more perform the duties which he had been accustomed to for more than "fifty years. On this Mr Watson remarked that he would remember Robert "Burns? The name operated like electricity; and,—as if a string was touched "long unaccustomed to vibration,—weakness, dulness, and inarticulation were "shaken off like dust in sunshine. and he reiterated,—' Rabbie Burns!—Mind "' Rabbie?—I'll no forget him, puir fallow!—Eh, but he *was* the life o' the "' Lodge!'"

Brother Watson was constant in his attendance at meetings, both of the Lodge and the R.A. Chapter Canongate Kilwinning, till within a short time of his death. He laboured with untiring zeal as Secretary to the Lodge, and in an equally responsible position in the Chapter for many years after accomplishing the magnificent picture of the Inauguration, with which his name will ever be remembered. He died at his residence, Broughton Park Cottage, Edinburgh, on 18th November 1870.

A very acceptable and instructive tribute to his memory at this time will doubtless be an extract from the obituary notice regarding him which appeared in the *Edinburgh Courant* of Thursday, 24th November 1870, as follows :—

" Mr Watson was the son of Captain Andrew Watson. He was born in Edinburgh Castle in 1800, and belonged to a family to whom Scottish art owes much—his uncle, George Watson, having been the first President of the Royal Scottish Academy, and his cousin, Sir John Watson Gordon, the last President.

" Mr Stewart Watson's large picture of the Inauguration of Burns as Poet Laureate of Lodge Canongate Kilwinning, which hangs on the wall of Grand Lodge, is a valuable picture, containing many most excellent portraits of eminent men who took part in that ceremony. His great picture of the Inauguration of the Duke of Athole as Grand Master of the Knights Templar, painted for that Society, is also much admired for truthfulness of portraiture and artistic finish. Among the last pictures which he exhibited in the Academy rooms was, 'The Cossacks of the Don Foraging,' which now adorns the walls of Ayton Castle. It is admitted to be a work of great merit and value. He has left a large collection of fine sketches and copies of Italian frescoes made during his long residence in Italy, which we understand will shortly be offered for public sale. He has also left two large pictures nearly finished—one of which possesses great interest. It is illustrative of the domestic life of Sir Walter Scott, to whom Mr Watson was related, and with whom he was on terms of intimacy.

"In the summer of 1824, Sir Walter Scott invited Mr Watson to spend some time at Abbotsford, and while there he, with the whole Scott family, enjoyed a pic-nic in the Woods of Abbotsford. He sketched a picture of this pic-nic, but never carried it out until near the end of his life.* The portraits are taken from likenesses of the Scott family, painted by him at Abbotsford on the occasion of that visit, and are exquisite likenesses of Sir Walter Scott, Lady Scott, their son Walter, Anne Scott, Mrs Lockhart, and her husband. The originals are in possession of Lady Scott of Abbotsford; and in reference to them he wrote to the artist a letter, which, as it is characteristic of the great novelist, and has never been published, we take the opportunity of giving here:—

"'MY DEAR MR WATSON,—Your packet reached me in perfect safety, and the contents gave me great pleasure, both on account of the strong resemblances of the miniatures and the style of execution. I am particularly pleased

---

* A photograph of this very interesting picture of the Scott family hangs on the north wall of the Lodge-room, within two or three feet of Allan Ramsay's oil painting of William St. Clair of Rosslyn, First M.W. Grand Master Mason of Scotland,—who was initiated, passed, and raised in Can. Kil., 1736.

The following is a reproduction of the printed slip which was issued with each copy of the photograph when published :—

A REMEMBRANCE OF SIR WALTER SCOTT, BART.

PAINTED BY THE LATE STEWART WATSON.

Memorandum made in 1839 as to this Painting by Mr Watson.

"Many years ago I received an invitation to visit Abbotsford, for the purpose of painting miniatures of Sir Walter Scott and his Family. These miniatures are now in the possession of Lady Scott (Widow of Colonel Sir Walter Scott), through whose kindness in placing them at my disposal I have been enabled to paint a picture. I had long thought of representing a scene which took place during my visit. Sir Walter, accompanied by Mr John Lockhart and the other members of his family, also a few friends then residing at Abbotsford, paid a visit to Newark Castle, for the purpose of showing that classic district to Miss Edgeworth. This party forms the subject of my picture."

Note.—The persons represented in the Photograph (beginning at the left) are Mr Archibald Constable, Mr James Hogg (the Ettrick Shepherd), Mr Lockhart, Sir Walter Scott, Miss Ann Scott, Mrs Lockhart, Lady Scott, Miss Edgeworth, Colonel Scott, Miss Scott (niece of Sir Walter), Miss Edgeworth's sister, Mr Charles Scott, and Mr Thomas Shortreede.

with my wife's picture, as her features and expression are not easily hit, and I think you have been very successful. I have no doubt that by continuing to bestow much pains (for that is everything in all difficult arts) you will soon place yourself high in your profession. My wife is greatly obliged by the two screens so beautifully pencilled, and begs me to make her best acknowledgements. I am not less obliged by your attention to my blazonry (*sic*) which is in no sort of hurry. If you look at it in a perfectly idle moment it is quite enough. · *Hogil nam Bo** will, I daresay, cast up among the Macfarlanes in due time.

"'I am, my dear Mr Watson, your obliged humble servant,

"'WALTER SCOTT.

"'ABBOTSFORD, *4th October.*'"†

"'*P.S.*—I will be much obliged to you to look in upon the glass painter now and then.'

"Mr Watson designed the embellishments of the library at Abbotsford, and among his papers are sketches by Sir Walter Scott of the arrangement of the coats armorial of the various families to whom he was related. Mr Watson was an ardent Freemason, and for nearly twenty years acted as secretary to the Lodge Canongate Kilwinning. His ever good temper and gentlemanly manner and disposition gained him the friendship of all who had the opportunity of enjoying his society."

Such was Brother Stewart Watson.

This talented and much esteemed brother,—with so fair a reputation to maintain unsullied,—would never have availed himself of any such "beautiful "story of the Inauguration," as is alleged by Grand Secretary to have been "concocted," in order to supply him [the artist] "with a subject for a beautiful picture!"

Respectfully submitted by

HUGH C. PEACOCK,

Past-Secretary, and Past-Depute-Master Can. Kil.,
Proxy Master, No. 476.

---

* This rendering by Sir Walter Scott of a well-known Highland saying is scarcely correct. A learned friend of mine has very kindly favoured me with the following correct version and explanation thereof:—

"Sir Walter Scott has written much bad Gaelic, and, in the present case, 'Hogil' is his way of "rendering the genitive form of the proper word."

"*Togul na'm Bo* was one of the commonest of phrases, meaning the lifting of the cattle, and this is "the correct form of it. It had, no doubt, reference to the well-known habits of the Highlanders in "raiding the lands of their neighbours." H. C. P.

† 1824.

LETTER

FROM

PAST MASTER WM. N. FRASER of Findrack and Tornaveen

TO

PAST MASTER ALLAN MACKENZIE.

----

41 ALBANY STREET,
EDINBURGH, 12*th April* 1893.

Mr ALLAN MACKENZIE,
 P.M. Lodge Canongate Kilwinning,
  17 St Andrew Square.

MY DEAR SIR AND BROTHER,

Robert Burns.

   Replying to yours of 7th instant, I beg to say that at the time the letter was written to Brother D. Murray Lyon, dated 7th February 1873, I cordially approved of it, and I approve of it now. It had the no less hearty approval of all other members of the Committee of Lodge Canongate Kilwinning, among whom were the R.W. Master and the Past Master, Dr Sam. Somerville of Ampherlaw, Thomas Elder MacRitchie, W.S., of Craigton and Dunork, Past Master Councillor Thomas Drybrough, David Crawford, S.S.C., Past Master Thomas Alex. Hill, and Dr John Middleton, afterwards R.W. Master.

   I have read the printed correspondence and all that has been said against the facts set forth in the Secretary's letter of 7th February 1873, and am surprised at so much being written against said facts to so little purpose. I adhere to the tenor of the communication sent to Brother D. Murray Lyon by the Secretary of Lodge Canongate Kilwinning, in February 1873, as containing substantially the truth relative to Robert Burns and his connection with the Lodge.

   The following is a copy of the document you ask for, extracted from my private diary for 1853, viz. :—

   " On the 1st of March 1787, on the motion of Alexander Fergusson of Craigdarroch, Dumfriesshire, R.W. Master of Canongate Kilwinning Lodge, Brother Robert Burns was elected Poet-Laureate of the Lodge, an office which he held till his death in 1796. When I was R.W. Master of Canongate Kilwinning in 1853 I received corroboration of this well-known fact, from my brother-in-law, Mr James Veitch, Elliock, Dumfriesshire, and he had it direct from his cousin, Cutlar Fergusson, Younger, of Craigdarroch, who was present in the Lodge room on 1st March 1787."—I am, Yours very truly and fraternally,

         WM. N. FRASER,
       Past Master, Lodge Can. Kil. No. 2.

LETTER

FROM

PAST MASTER THOMAS DRYBROUGH

TO

PAST MASTER ALLAN MACKENZIE.

31 ROYAL TERRACE,
EDINBURGH, 21st *August* 1893.

MY DEAR SIR AND BROTHER,

I regret to learn from you that at this late time—a hundred and six years since the Lodge "Can. Kil." was frequented by Robert Burns—the Grand Secretary or anyone else should venture to call in question the time-honoured and universally admitted fact that Burns had been elected and inaugurated Poet Laureate of that Lodge. The letter which the Secretary wrote to Brother D. Murray Lyon, in February 1873, contains the main facts relative to Robert Burns' connection with the "Can. Kil." as they have been handed down to us by the thoroughly trustworthy information transmitted from brother to brother since these old days, and I heartily approve of that letter on reading it again. Half a century ago I became a member of the "Can. Kil.," and was R.W.M. from 1856 to 1860, and had constant association with many old brethren, whose recollection of the Lodge and its eventful history extended back to the early part of this century. All of these brethren were aware, and at various times in my hearing spoke, of Burns having been elected and inaugurated Poet Laureate. Many of them knew of the event from brethren who had actually been present in the Lodge on such occasion, and met Burns. Among the more prominent old members with whom I was intimate were Alex. Lambe Robertson, W.S., who was R.W.M. from 1819 to 1830, and who lived to succeed me and hold the Chair a second time, from 1860 to 1862; Alex. M'Neil, Advocate, was R.W.M. from 1830 to 1838, and who had been connected with the Lodge for many years before that; Professor Aytoun, R.W.M. from 1839 to 1841, and P.M. Dr Sam. Somerville of Ampherlaw; Archd. D. Campbell; Archd. C. Mowbray; also Bros. Alexander Jas. Stewart, Hector Gavin, Jas. Marshall, Solicitor, and Stewart Watson, &c. All these brethren confidently believed in Burns having been Poet Laureate, and had good reason to give for their belief. Why, then, has Grand Secretary waited until all these old members were dead before calling the Inauguration in question? My esteemed friend and Brother, P.M. Wm. N. Fraser of Tornaveen, who held the Chair for years both before and after me, is still alive, and can give his reliable testimony to these, indisputable facts of the Poet Laureateship. It is beyond the time now to call the matter in question.—I am, my Dear Sir and Brother, fraternally and faithfully yours,

THOMAS DRYBROUGH,
Past Master, Lodge Canongate Kilwinning,
Past Junior Grand Deacon, Grand Lodge of Scotland.

Brother ALLAN MACKENZIE,
P.M., Lodge "Can. Kil.,"
17 St Andrew Square.

EXTRACT FROM MINUTE

AND

COPY of CORRESPONDENCE

BETWEEN

The Secretary of Lodge Canongate Kilwinning

AND

BROTHER D. MURRAY LYON, AYR

1873.

Extract from Minute of Quarterly Meeting of Committee of the Lodge Canongate Kilwinning, held in the Lodge-room, Wednesday, January 15, 1873, instructing Secretary to write Bro. D. Murray Lyon.

.   .   .   .   .   .

" Reference was subsequently made to the book announced as being in
" course of publication by Brother D. Murray Lyon of Ayr, in which,—according
" to the report of a visiting brother in this Lodge,—discredit is thrown upon the
" commonly accepted account of the connection which Robert Burns, the Poet,
" had with Canongate Kilwinning during his residence in Edinburgh in 1787.
" The Secretary was desired to write Brother D. Murray Lyon on the subject.
" The meeting then closed.

" H. C. PEACOCK,   J. SCHOPP, R.W.M."
" Secretary.

LETTER from Bro. HUGH C. PEACOCK to Bro. D. MURRAY LYON.

" EDINBURGH, *23rd January*, 1873.

" D. MURRAY LYON, Esq., Ayr.
" Dear Sir and Brother,

" I am directed by the R. W. Master and Office-
Bearers of Lodge 'Canongate Kilwinning,' No. 2, to write you in consequence of
a statement made lately in the Lodge by a visiting brother, to the effect that in

your forthcoming work, entitled 'HISTORY OF THE LODGE OF EDINBURGH
' (*Mary's Chapel*), No. 1, *Embracing an Account of the Rise and Progress of
' Freemasonry in Scotland,*' the connection of Robert Burns, the Poet, with our
Lodge is discredited.

"In these circumstances it is my duty to inform you that there is ample
evidence of the Poet's association with this Lodge as currently reported, and I
shall be glad to be assured by you that the statement referred to is erroneous.

"Yours fraternally,

"H. C. PEACOCK, Secy."

LETTER from Bro. D. MURRAY LYON to Bro. HUGH C. PEACOCK.

"DALHOUSIE COTTAGE, AYR,
"*Jan.* 24 /73

"Dear Sir and Brother,

"Thanks for your note of yesterday's date. The statement to
which you refer is scarcely correct. It is not my object to depreciate any Lodge
in regard to its association with eminent characters. I have, in noticing Burns'
connection with Can. Kil., stated the following FACTS:—1. That B. was "assumed
a member" of the Lodge Feb. 1, 1787; 2. That Feb. 9, 1815, B. is designated
(for the *first* time) POET LAUREATE of the L.; 3. Can. Kil. records contain *no*
evidence of B. being *elected* Po. L., or of his having been *installed* as such—as
represented in the Picture painted by Stewart Watson. But if you can show me
proof that the Picture in question is a representation of *what actually took place,* I
shall only be too glad to avail myself of the evidence. In my remarks on Can.
Kil., I embrace a facsimile of its *original Commission* as a branch of Mo. Kil., and
also give it full credit for the having taken the initiative in the erection of the Gr. L.
of Scotland, and of its being the mother Lodge of St. Clair. My note on B.'s
connection with Can. Kil. will be in the printer's hands in a few days. Communicate at once.

"Yours fraternally,

"D. MURRAY LYON."

LETTER

FROM

Bro. HUGH C. PEACOCK

TO

Bro. D. MURRAY LYON.

[This is the letter which was acknowledged by Brother D. M. Lyon, February 11, 1873, in the terms set forth at page 61, but regarding which he now, in the year 1893, complains to Grand Lodge that the writer "laid a statement "before him embodying alleged facts, which he (Bro. Lyon) unfortunately "accepted as true," and—still relative to this letter—"that the statements "made to him were unfounded."]

"EDINBURGH, *7th February* 1873.

" D. MURRAY LYON, Esq., Ayr.

"DEAR SIR AND BROTHER,

"In reply to your favour of 24th ultimo, I beg to state, on behalf of the R.W.M. and office-bearers of Lodge Canongate Kilwinning, that, although we fully believe, as you profess, that it is not your object 'to depreciate any Lodge in regard to its association with eminent characters,' and we have every faith in your desire to be impartial in your History of the Lodge of Edinburgh (Mary's Chapel), No. 1, yet, the explanation contained in your letter respecting the notice therein of Burns and Canongate Kilwinning, I regret to say, looks very like a confirmation of the report of it, which had reached us ; and, from your mode of stating certain isolated facts, it appears after all that in your intended notice, the connection of ROBERT BURNS with this Lodge, as commonly reported, is discredited.

"If I had that notice before me in full, as you purpose publishing it, I should know better how to reply, and we might be saved some correspondence ; but, with the statements regarding it as are given in your note, I shall nevertheless endeavour to answer you.

"Had any doubt ever been previously thrown on the universally accepted connection of Robert Burns with the Canongate Kilwinning, the nature of your reference to it might be looked for in such a comprehensive work as you propose to publish ; but, when it is considered that only *now*, when few of the living links remain, connecting us with those who had often borne testimony to their personal acquaintance with Burns, and to their having been at meetings of the Lodge, when he was there as its Poet Laureate, the tenor of your notice appears extraordinary.

H

"The work published in 1846, entitled 'A Winter with Robert Burns,' gives a faithful exposition of the picture of Robert Burns' Inauguration as Poet Laureate, and contains much interesting matter relative to the individuals portrayed therein, and the Poet's intimacy with them ; and, when the materials for that work were being collected, there were several members of the Canongate Kilwinning alive, having vivid recollections of the Lodge meetings of 1786-7, from whom much of the information was derived. Such testimony as those then living witnesses of the events of 1786-7, in the Lodge Canongate Kilwinning, is not available to us now, *but what they did testify to was* WIDELY CIRCULATED AND NEVER CONTRADICTED. Their accounts of Burns and his intimate association with the Canongate Kilwinning, of his holding the appointment of Poet Laureate, and of his having been formally elected as such, were never doubted. Such a circumstance, therefore, is strong evidence of the truth of what is narrated in the 'Winter with Robert Burns.'

"It is well known that the author of that work investigated the subject it treats of very thoroughly, and from sources of information which may not now be open to us, especially, as just stated, from his intimate acquaintance with many of the old members ;— and that is shown by his own words and other evidence in the minutes, also, from having had the advantage of much historical information gleaned by a Committee of the Lodge, formed a few years previous to the date of his book, for the express purpose as defined in the minutes, ' of investigating the records of the Lodge, and to frame such an account (of the Lodge) as may seem to them most advisable.' That Committee consisted of Mr H. Jardine, Advocate, R.W.M. (son of Sir H. Jardine, R.W.M. in 1790), the D.M., Mr James Jardine, the Sub M., Prof. William Edmonstoune Aytoun, Mr Alexander L. Robertson, Writer to the Signet, and several others. Further, as one guarantee in favour of the truthful compilation of the work under notice, we have the status and well-known talent of its author ; and as another guarantee, we have the fact, well known to a wide circle of brethren, that the matter contained in it with which we have at present to do, had been certainly *obtained from* or *based upon the minutes* of Lodge Canongate Kilwinning. No one has ever impugned the work in any way, or discredited its narratives ; and, now, after nearly thirty years of its existence, it seems past the time to attempt doing so.

"In 1815 there must have been many among the brethren of a Lodge so strong in numbers who had either been associates of Burns, or well acquainted with those who had been in his company at their meetings ; and in the minute of 9th February of that year the statement incidentally occurs regarding Robert Burns that he *"was a Member and Poet Laureat of this Lodge."* Certainly, if such designation could not then have been truthfully applied, and if the brethren of that time had not perfect faith in it, we are bound to believe that the minutes would not bear any such record. You say that, in your notice of Burns and the Canongate Kilwinning, you have stated certain 'FACTS,' and one of them is 'That Feb. 9, 1815, B is designated (for the *first* time) POET LAUREATE.' I trust to be excused pointing out that such a fact, set forth with any such emphasis, and standing *alone*,—without qualification or further information of any kind relative to it,—is not likely to convey the *real truth* to the reader. It may be the first time the designation occurs in the minutes, but it would be palpably wrong to suppose, therefore, that Burns was only then for the first time termed Poet Laureate, unless the absurdity can be supposed that the men,—of acknowledged worth and status in society,—who took leading part in that meeting, had become for that occasion most unscrupulous and untruthful, and that the men,—of equal position and character,—who formed the meeting of 8th June 1815, when the Poet is again referred to as "*the lamented Bard, Robert Burns (who had been Poet Laureat of this Lodge)*," had likewise become equally dishonorable. The Lodge was a strong one in those days; for a long period its members were exceedingly numerous, and, had either the matter of Burns' Poet Laureateship, or of his formal election to the office of Poet Laureate,—so long and widely known,—been untrue, the contradiction would assuredly have been known also. Brethren who attended those two meetings in 1815 can be shown by the earlier minutes to have been active members of the Lodge for many years prior to the close of last century. In particular, I may mention *Alex. Jaffray* (repeatedly elected R.W.M.), and *Charles More*, who had filled various prominent offices in the Lodge; and here, regarding the latter brother, I may state one fact, which possibly you may have overlooked, namely, that in that minute of 8th June 1815, Brother Charles More seconds a resolution anent the Lodge's subscription towards the general fund then being raised for erecting a mausoleum to the memory of Burns, who is so distinctly at this time, and by so many worthy witnesses, acknowledged as Poet Laureate of Lodge Canongate Kilwinning, and one, therefore, in whom the Canongate Kilwinning had a special interest. *This Charles More,—whose name occurs so prominently in the minute of 8th June 1815,—is the same whose signature as Depute Master is appended to the minute of 1st February 1787, when Burns is affiliated, and to the following minute of 1st March 1787, at which date it is understood the Inauguration took place.* Indeed, Brother Charles More appears, by his signature to the Minutes, to have attended *all* the Meetings during the period of Burns' visits to Edinburgh, 1786-7. The Secretary, Mr Paul Taylor, who wrote those minutes of 1815, had held office for over ten years, and must have been fully conversant with reminiscences of the Poet and his connection with our Lodge, derived from the very men who had enjoyed the Poet's Society.

"It may be reckoned comparatively slender evidence to add to the foregoing, yet it may be remarked as some satisfaction to know, that there are members of the Lodge at the present time who associated for years with those members who had the privilege of Burns' company in the Lodge when he wore the jewel of his office as Poet Laureate; that, further, that jewel was also worn by the Ettrick Shepherd as Poet Laureate of Canongate Kilwinning, and it had the name of Robert Burns engraved upon it when the Poet Laureateship was conferred on him.

"Incidentally, I may state also, regarding the foregoing matter, that in the minute of 16th January 1835, it appears a resolution was carried to the effect 'that it was 'expedient that the honorary office of Poet Laureate of the Lodge, which had been in 'abeyance since the death of the immortal BROTHER ROBERT BURNS, should be revived, 'and that James Hogg, the "Ettrick Shepherd," on whom his poetic mantle had fallen, 'should be respectfully requested to accept the appointment as the highest tribute to his 'genius and worth which the brethren have it in their power to bestow,' which motion it is said 'was unanimously and enthusiastically carried.'

"It is not much to be wondered at that reference to Burns does not occur more often in the minutes;—because, in the first place, the minutes for many years prior to 1789 are few, while we know, from various sources, that meetings of the Lodge were very frequent, and those minutes are invariably brief,—little else but a record of intrants, passings, and raisings,—and generally written in a somewhat clumsy and negligent manner. Their brevity in some instances cannot be excelled,—only a line and a half, or eighteen words,—and this at a time, too, when there is every reason to believe that events worthy of note were frequent in the Canongate Kilwinning ; secondly, at the time that Robert Burns was affiliated to the Lodge, and was elected its Poet Laureate, he was not the distinguished Poet that he afterwards became. Indeed, it was only after his death in 1796 that the man and his works were esteemed at anything like their value, and, only after many years, was his memory regarded with anything like the veneration accorded to it now.

"I have had conversation on this matter with a distinguished member of the Canongate Kilwinning, who has been connected with it for more than five and thirty years, and who stands high in the Craft.* He knew *Brother William Petrie* of our Lodge, who had been *present* at the Inauguration of Burns as Poet Laureate, and has heard from his lips many very interesting reminiscences of the Poet, and of events which had occurred in the Lodge when there in company with him. Further, the member I refer to informed me that he also knew intimately *Brother Wm. Campbell, W.S.*, who was for very many years a member of Canongate Kilwinning, and who had similar recollections of Burns, and I find in the minute of meeting of 12th November 1845, which records matter connected with the project of painting the Inauguration, that *this same Brother Campbell seconds the resolution* 'that Brother Watson have access to sketch the antique and picturesque interior of the Lodge, with a view to his painting the Inauguration of Robert Burns as her Poet Laureate,' and adds, that he had '*had many opportunities of giving testimony in favour of the particulars referred to*;—'that he had travelled in company of Burns,' and spent two of the most happy days with him at Auchtertyre Castle.' It is recorded in this Minute also that Brother James Marshall, who proposed the motion quoted above, concluded his remarks by saying, that 'years ago, when he, Brother Marshall, attended this Lodge, he took a chief interest in the reminiscences of old men connected with such events, but of those, he feared, few survived.' Further on it is said, 'Brother Marshall was requested to furnish the *authenticated particulars* to a subsequent meeting, when the motion should be disposed of, meantime, it was unanimously entertained,'—and, in the minute of next meeting, 19th November 1845, when Brother Marshall brought up his motion as directed, we are told that 'The motion was seconded by the R.W.M. and unanimously carried.'

"But, besides the unimpeachable oral evidence I have just adduced, I should add the instance of another eminent member of Canongate Kilwinning, whom I have the privilege of knowing,† and who has informed me that the late Mr Alexander L.

---

* Past Master Dr Samuel Somerville of Ampherlaw.

† Past Master Wm. N. Fraser of Tornaveen.

Robertson, W.S. (R.W.M. of the Lodge, 1819 to 1830), and Mr Alexander M'Neill, Advocate (R.W.M., 1830 to 1837), whom he knew intimately, had no doubt whatever of the fact of the Inauguration having actually taken place, and they must have associated with, or met many brethren who were present on the occasion.

" Evidence so direct as this cannot be disputed.

" I need add no more now, except that I apologize for delay in replying to your communication, occasioned by very great pressure of business, which certainly has prevented me giving this subject the attention it deserves ; but, should you be kind enough to favour me with a copy or proof of such notice of Burns and the Canongate Kilwinning as you intend publishing, I shall be very glad to write you again with remarks upon it.—Yours, etc.,

" H. C. PEACOCK, *Secy*.

LETTER

FROM

BRO. D. MURRAY LYON

TO

BRO. HUGH C. PEACOCK.

[Being the reply which closed this Correspondence.]

AYR, *Feb.* 11/73.

" MY DEAR SIR AND BROTHER,

I have to thank you for the very full statement you have made anent the Inauguration in name of the R.W.M. and other officers of the Can. Kil. I recognise the satisfactory nature of the evidence you have submitted, and shall have pleasure in giving effect to it in my forthcoming work.

The delay which has occurred on your part prevents my being able to submit a slip of my remarks—the printers being close up to that particular part of my MS. I would take the liberty of saying, that while I shall embody the facts you have put me in possession of, I will not require to *alter* a single sentence of what I had previously written. The *report*, to which you have twice alluded, must certainly have been exaggerated. No one out of Ayr has seen the MS. on the subject as finally prepared for the printer—*i.e.*, before you addressed me on the subject.

Again thanking you.—I am, ever faithfully yours,

D. MURRAY LYON.

H. C. PEACOCK, Esq.,
Edinburgh.

I

OPINION OF A POPULAR HISTORIAN.

"I HAVE given close attention to those pages [History of No. 2, pp. 117 to 126, and Letter quoted in pp. 57 to 61 *ante*] which refer to Burns' inauguration, and it seems to me silly for any one to go behind the evidence therein submitted.

"I have been a student of history all my life, and I only wish that everything which is recorded as *bona fide* historical fact had half as solid a groundwork as the fact of Robert Burns being Poet Laureate of Canongate Kilwinning Lodge."

Communicated by Brother Peter Ross, Author of " A History of Scottish Literature," " Scotland and the Scots," " The Songs of Scotland," etc., etc., also Past Master and Present Treasurer of the Scotia Lodge, No. 634 F. and A.M., New York, 24th October 1892.

THE "APPOINTMENT" AND "INAUGURATION"

OF

ROBERT BURNS.

POET LAUREATE OF LODGE CANONGATE KILWINNING,

Quoted from Brother D. Murray Lyon's "HISTORY OF THE LODGE OF
EDINBURGH (MARY'S CHAPEL), No. 1, Embracing an Account of the
Rise and Progress of Freemasonry in Scotland," pp. 332, 333, and 334.

"Mr Fergusson of Craigdarroch was Master of Canongate Kilwinning at the
date of Burns's appointment to the Laureateship of that Lodge. The Inauguration of
the Poet to this office is the subject of a painting well known to Scottish Freemasons,
executed by a Member of the Lodge, the late Brother Stewart Watson ; it also forms
the subject of a small volume, entitled, ' A Winter with Robert Burns,' * containing
biographical sketches of the Brethren whose portraits appear in the painting. The
minute of the communication held by Canongate Kilwinning in St. John's Chapel, on the
1st of February 1787, contains a record of Burns's assumption as a member of that Lodge,
in the following terms :—"' The Right Worshipful Master having observed that Brother
Burns was at present in the Lodge, who is well known as a great Poetic Writer, and for
a late publication of his works which have been universally commended, and submitted
that he should be assumed a Member of this Lodge, which was unanimously agreed to,
and he was assumed accordingly.' The 1st of March 1787 is mentioned by masonic
writers as the date of the scene which has been portrayed by the artist. But neither the
minute of that date, nor of any other during Burns's lifetime, contains any record whatever of the existence of such an office as Laureate of the Lodge, or of that distinction
being conferred on Burns. The first mention in Canongate Kilwinning minutes of this
office having been held by the Poet is found under date 9th February 1815, when the
Lodge resolved to open a subscription among the members to aid in the erection of a
' mausoleum to the memory of Robert Burns, who was a Member and Poet Laureate of
this Lodge . . . and who had on many occasions contributed so generally to the
harmony of the Masonic Order, and to that of the Lodge Canongate Kilwinning in

* "The author of this work, Bro. James Marshall, was a Solicitor in the Supreme Courts of Scotland, but afterwards emigrated to Australia, and carried on the business of an Attorney in the city of
Melbourne, Victoria, where he died in 1870."

particular.' The Laureateship is again referred to in the minute of 9th June 1815, and also in that of 16th January 1835, which records the restoration, in the person of James Hogg, the 'Ettrick Shepherd,' of the 'honorary office of Poet Laureate of the Lodge, which had been in abeyance since the death of the immortal Brother Robert Burns.'

"Our statement regarding what appears in the minutes on the subject of the Laureateship is founded upon a personal examination of the minute-book. But, while deeming it proper to give the result of that examination, it is equally right that we should state that the commonly received report of the circumstances connected with the Inauguration has never been discredited. The Lodge Canongate Kilwinning is not singular in the omission from its records of facts which have come to be regarded as interesting features in its history. Its minutes at, and for many years prior to, the period of Burns's attendance at its communications are brief to a degree; and this may account for the infrequency of their allusions to Burns, who was not then the distinguished poet he afterwards became. It was only after his death that Robert Burns and his works were esteemed at their proper value, and only after many years that his memory was regarded with anything like the veneration accorded to it now. Commendably proud of its traditionary association with genius, the Lodge has collected and preserved from oral testimony of an unquestionable character the testimony obtained by gentlemen of unimpeachable veracity, from Brethren who were personally known to Burns, who were present at his inauguration, and saw him wear the jewel of his office,—evidence of the event under notice.* In addition to Burns, the Canongate Kilwinning has the honour of being associated with some of the most eminent names in Scottish literature, amongst whom may be mentioned—John Wilson (Christopher North), James Hogg, William Edmonstone Aytoun, D. M. Moir (Delta), J. Gibson Lockhart (the biographer of Scott), Dr Hugh Blair (the eminent preacher and lecturer on Rhetoric and *Belles Lettres*), who were all Members of the Lodge. To these may be added the distinguished name of Henry, Lord Brougham. His Lordship was initiated in the Lodge Fortrose, Stornoway. 'Craigdarroch' was the successful competitor for the relic of the drunken courtier of Anne of Denmark, contended for at Friar's Carse in 1790, as celebrated in Burns's ballad of 'The Whistle.'"

Relative to the foregoing quotation, attention is requested to the following observations :—

1. Brother D. Murray Lyon—with reference to his notice (as above quoted) of "Burns and the Lodge Canongate Kilwinning,"—asserted in his letter, dated 11th February 1873, which is quoted in page 61 *ante*, that he would "not require to *alter* a single sentence of what" he "had previously written." Now, the very opening sentences of the above narration, quoted from his History, contain expressions of a belief in "Burns's appointment to the Laureateship of that Lodge," as well as a belief in "the " Inauguration of the Poet to this office," and for those expressions he is in no respect

---

* "Charles More, who, as Depute Master, signed the minute of Burns's affiliation in 1787, was present in Canongate Kilwinning in June 1815, and seconded the resolution anent the Lodge's subscription towards the Mausoleum."

whatever indebted to the Secretary of Lodge Canongate Kilwinning. Such being the case, it is clearly evident that Brother Murray Lyon had his faith in the Laureateship and Inauguration of Robert Burns well established *before* he received the Canongate Kilwinning Secretary's letter of 7th February 1873. Indeed, it appears by Brother Lyon's pointed assertion, to wit—that he would "not require to *alter* a single sentence " of what" he "had previously written,"—as if he wished the Canongate Kilwinning Secretary to understand that his mind had been already made up on the subject, and that he was glad to receive such satisfactory confirmation in support of his opinion, more particularly, as he added, with emphasis, the comforting assurance—"The *report*, " to which you have twice alluded, must certainly have been exaggerated."

2. Specially deserving of note is the fact that the statement at the very beginning of Bro. Lyon's notice of "Burns and the Lodge Canongate Kilwinning," namely :— "Mr Fergusson of Craigdarroch was Master of Canongate Kilwinning at the date " of Burns's appointment to the Laureateship of that Lodge," does not occur in any form in the letter he received from Canongate Kilwinning Secretary, dated 7th February 1873.

3. It will be very satisfactory if Brother D. Murray Lyon will point out the sentences which he "had previously written," and which he did "not require to *alter*," so that it may at once be seen wherein the Canongate Kilwinning Secretary is blamed for having "misled our eminent historian."

PROCEEDINGS IN GRAND LODGE

DESCRIPTIVE OF

THE PRESENTATION

By the late Brother JAMES BALLANTINE, Grand Bard,* on behalf of the
Family of the late Sir JAMES BURNES, M.D., etc., etc., etc., 2nd
February 1863, of Bro. STEWART WATSON'S Celebrated Painting,
entitled—

THE INAUGURATION OF ROBERT BURNS, POET LAUREATE OF LODGE CANONGATE KILWINNING.

"GRAND LODGE OF SCOTLAND.

" The Quarterly Communication of the Grand Lodge of Scotland was held in
Freemasons' Hall on the 2nd February 1863. His Grace the Duke of Athole occupied
the throne. Bro. Mann, R.W.M., No. 1, acted as Senior Grand Warden, and Bro.
M'Cowan, P.M., No. 3, as Junior Grand Warden. On the platform were Brothers Sir
Alexander P. Gordon Cumming, Junior Grand Deacon ; James Ballantine, Grand Bard ;
John Cunningham, President of the Board of Grand Stewards, etc., etc.

   •   •   •   •   •   •   •   •

" Brother James Ballantine, Grand Bard, presented to the Grand Lodge the
painting of the Inauguration of Robert Burns as Poet Laureate of the Lodge ' Canongate Kilwinning.' Brother Ballantine explained that this painting had been the property
of the late Brother Sir James Burnes, K.H., Physician-General of the Bombay Army,
and that previous to his death it was the wish of Brother Burnes to make this presentation. The Grand Lodge, after expressing their thanks to Brother Ballantine for the
trouble he had taken in the matter, ordered the painting to be hung up in the Grand
Committee room."

---

* Author of the Scottish Novels, " The Gaberlunzie's Wallet " and " The Miller of Deanhaugh,"
also the well-known songs, " Ilka Blade o' Grass keps its ain Drap o' Dew," " Castles in the Air," etc.

COPY OF NOTICE

Published in " Scottish Freemasons' Magazine," 1st July 1863, of the Inaugura-tion Picture having then been placed in the position it now occupies.

" HISTORICO-MASONIC PAINTING.

" INAUGURATION OF ROBERT BURNS
AS POET LAUREATE OF THE LODGE
CANONGATE KILWINNING, EDINBURGH.
1st March 1787.

" It affords us peculiar satisfaction to state, *for the general information of the Craft,* that the above painting, executed by Brother Stewart Watson, Secretary of the Lodge Canongate Kilwinning, has now been permanently hung on the walls of the Grand Committee-room at Freemasons' Hall in this city, where it may be inspected by the immortal bard's admirers. It will be recollected by our readers that this painting was recently presented to the Grand Lodge of Scotland by the family of the late distinguished Brother Dr James Burnes, K.H., Physician-General, Bombay Army."

INSCRIPTION ON THE PICTURE
which Grand Secretary now desires should be " amended:"—

" THE INAUGURATION
OF
ROBERT BURNS
AS POET LAUREATE OF
THE LODGE CANONGATE KILWINNING
EDINBURGH, 1st MARCH 1787.

Presented by JAMES BURNES, K.H., F.R.S., etc.,
To the Grand Lodge of Scotland, 1862."

MINUTES OF TWO MEETINGS OF CANONGATE KILWINNING COMMITTEE, HELD RESPECTIVELY 15TH AND 27TH DECEMBER 1893.

Picture in the Board-room of Grand Lodge of the Inauguration of Robert Burns as Poet Laureate of Lodge Canongate Kilwinning.

Consequent on the action taken by Grand Secretary on 29th December 1892, in pro-posing to Grand Committee that the inscription on the above-named picture should be

" amended " !

a Special Meeting of the Committee of Lodge Canongate Kilwinning was held in

St. John's Chapel, St. John Street, on Friday, 15th December 1893, for the purpose of considering the whole subject, and of hearing read the correspondence between Brothers A. Mackenzie, Hugh C. Peacock, D. Murray Lyon, Wm. N. Fraser, and Thomas Drybrough; and of considering the Evidence submitted to the Committee by Brother H. C. Peacock substantiating the fact of Robert Burns, the first Poet Laureate of this Lodge, having been elected and inaugurated to that office 1st March 1787.

> *Present:*—The Right Worshipful Master presiding; and Brothers James Drummond, P.M.; Allan Mackenzie, P.M. and Treasurer: Robert Bathgate, D.M.; Geo. R. Kerr, S.W.; Wm. Elliot, J.W.; John Fairweather, Secy.: Thomas Cochrane, S.D.; H. C. Peacock, Past D.M.; H. B. Ezard, John Cubie, Robert Boyd, and John Jack.

Printers' proofs and MS. matter were produced, containing most of the facts gleaned by Bro. Hugh C. Peacock relative to this subject, and many of these were read by him to the Committee; but there being insufficient time in this one evening to consider the whole body of evidence submitted, the Committee agreed to adjourn till 27th inst., when the subject should be disposed of. Meantime, it was arranged that printers' proofs of the remaining part of the evidence be furnished to each member of Committee prior to that date, if possible. The meeting then adjourned.

JOHN FAIRWEATHER, Secretary. GEO. CRAWFORD, R.W.M.

Picture in Board-room of Grand Lodge—continued.

At an adjourned Special Meeting of the Committee of Canongate Kilwinning Lodge, held within St. John's Chapel, St. John Street, on Wednesday, 27th December 1893, for the purpose of concluding the business for which the meeting of 15th inst. was called.

> The R.W. Master, Brother Geo. Crawford, again presided; and there were also present Brothers Allan Mackenzie, P.M.; John Fairweather, Secretary; James Drummond, W.S., P.M.; Robert Bathgate, D.M.; Thomas Cochrane, Geo. R. Kerr, Robert Boyd, and H. B. Ezard.

The minute of Committee meeting, held on 15th inst., was read and sustained.

The remainder of the evidence brought forward and undisposed of at last meeting was now dealt with, and the Committee unanimously resolved as follows :—

> "That the cordial thanks of the Lodge are due to Brother Hugh C. Peacock for the valuable mass of information he has so carefully gleaned, and for compiling the well-developed statement of the subject which he has now put on record.
> "That, beginning his labours in 1873, he then discovered and made known points in this question which possibly, but for him, might have remained in obscurity, or, at all events, could not be easily established at this date without his personal testimony; and that much additional proof, throwing a flood of light on matters previously not very clear to the ordinary reader, has since been collected, and certain links have been discovered, by him, which form, with

those already published, a continuous chain of evidence which, it is believed, should satisfy any unbiassed judgment.

"That the Committee are much gratified to observe that Brother Peacock has not hesitated to quote prominently all the strongest and most plausible arguments and assertions advanced by the Historian and the Past Master of Lodge No. 1,—who impugned the statements contained in what is now the famous letter of 7th February 1873,—and he has effectively answered and confuted them."

"That, further, a copy of each minute of the two Committee meetings held respectively on the 15th and the 27th of December 1893 be printed and appended to the Evidence aforesaid, and that three hundred copies—or more, if deemed necessary—of the whole work be printed and published as speedily as possible."

In this connection the Committee remark, as worthy of note, that on 10th December 1892,—only a few days prior to the date of the meeting of Grand Committee, on the 29th of that month, when Grand Secretary submitted that the inscription on the Inauguration Picture should be "amended"—the Right Worshipful Master of Lodge Canongate Kilwinning addressed a letter of invitation to The Right Hon. the Earl of Haddington, then Most Worshipful Grand Master, respectfully soliciting his attendance with a deputation from Grand Lodge, on 27th January 1893, on which date it was proposed that the natal day of Robert Burns and James Hogg should be celebrated.

The R.W. Master's Letter to the M.W. Grand Master.

"St. John's Chapel,
"St. John Street,
"Edinburgh, 10*th Dec.*, 1892.

"The Right Hon. The Earl of Haddington,
"Grand Master Mason of Scotland,
"Tyningham.

"Most Worshipful Grand Sir and Brother,
"The Lodge Canongate Kilwinning cordially invites your Lordship to visit them on as early a date as you may find it convenient. Friday, 27th January 1893, is suggested as a date on which the Lodge celebrates the anniversary of the birthday of Brothers Robert Burns and James Hogg, who were Poets-Laureate.

"The record of visits by each Grand Master ever since the institution of Grand Lodge is continuous, and the members, considering the close connection which some of your Lordship's ancestors had with it—for instance, Lord Binning having been initiated there in December 1768—look forward with pleasure to your visit as a most interesting event.—I am, yours most faithfully and fraternally,

Geo. Crawford, R.W.M."

The above letter was transmitted to Grand Secretary, with the following respectful request that it be forwarded to his Lordship.

The R.W. Master's Letter to Grand Secretary.

"21 St. Andrew Square,
"Edinburgh, 10th Dec. 1892.

"Dear Bro. Murray Lyon,

"Herewith I have the pleasure to hand you letter addressed to the M. W. Grand Master, inviting him to visit No. 2. The date suggested is Friday 27th Jany.; but if this is inconvenient for his Lordship, perhaps the evening of the Grand Lodge Meeting on 2nd February might be substituted.—Yours very fraternally, Geo. Crawford."

The reply received by the Right Worshipful Master was as follows,—and it contains a singular illustration of the futility of attempting to *prove a negative* in respect of the minute dated 1st March 1787:—

Grand Secretary's Reply to the R.W. Master.

"Freemasons' Hall,
"Edinburgh, Dec. 12, 1892.

"Mr Geo. Crawford,
"R.W.M., No. 2.

"My dear Sir,

"I shall forward your invitation to the Grand Master. At the same time it will be my duty to inform his Lordship that Burns' connection with No. 2 lay in his having been assumed a member in 1787 (Feb. 1). 1st March 1787 is the date given as that on which Burns was 'inaugurated' as Poet Laureate of Can. Kil. The minute of the Lodge of that date shews that no such inauguration took place.

"Your Lodge does not require to perpetuate a *myth* in connection with its historical recollections.

"It is sufficient to be able to point to the *fact* that Burns was an affiliated member of No. 2. Masonic fables are at a discount now-a-days.—Ever faithfully,

"D. Murray Lyon,
"Gr. Sec."

The Committee much regret that Grand Secretary should think it his "duty" to so express himself in answer to the respectful request of our R.W. Master, especially when they consider that on 25th January 1884,—the occasion on which the late very worthy Grand Master the Earl of Mar and Kellie honoured the Lodge with a grand visitation,—Grand Secretary then assisted and cordially fraternised with the brethren of our Lodge in celebrating the anniversary of Robert Burns and James Hogg as Poets-Laureate of Canongate Kilwinning.

Further, the Committee find that the assertions and references in Grand Secretary's letter are entirely at variance with his own published statements, which have been widely circulated for years prior to, as well as subsequent, to the "minute examination of Canongate Kilwinning's records," which he claims to have made in 1873, and on which, at this distant date, he professes to found his newly-acquired disbelief in Robert Burns as Poet Laureate of Canongate Kilwinning.

In conclusion, the Committee have to record that no deputation from Grand Lodge attended the anniversary Festival on 27th January 1893.

The meeting then closed.

JOHN FAIRWEATHER,
Secretary.

GEO. CRAWFORD, R.W.M.,
Chairman.

NOTANDA.

COPY of LETTER from Brother LEONARD HORNER to Brother WILLIAM CRAWFORD, R. W. Master of Lodge Kirknewton and Ratho, No. 85 (*vide* Part I., pp. 17, 18, 56 and 57).

"EDINBURGH, *2nd May* 1804.

"R. W. M.,

"I beg leave to present the worthy brethren of the Lodge of Kirknewton and Ratho this testimony of my regard for them. I request you will have the goodness to assure them of my warmest wishes for their prosperity, both as individuals and as Freemasons, and that I shall ever retain a lively sense of the honor they conferred on me by electing me an honorary member of their very respectable Lodge. I shall remember with much pleasure the agreeable hours I spent in their company, which I regret were so few; but so soon as I shall return to Scotland I will take the earliest opportunity to renew my former pleasures amongst them.

"I have the honor to be,

"R. W. M.,

"Your mo. affectionate Bror.,

"LEONARD HORNER."

EXTRACT FROM MINUTE OF THE LODGE KIRKNEWTON AND RATHO, No. 85, *Brother William Crawford, R. W. Master* (*vide* Part I., pp. 17, 18, 56 and 57).

RATHO, 18*th May* 1804.

*   *   *   *   *   *

"The Right Worshipful Master read a letter from Brother Leonard Horner expressing in the warmest terms his affections to the Lodge, and desiring their acceptance of a Bible, which was accordingly presented: the Lodge, highly sensible of the honour conferred upon them by Brother Horner, order the Secretary to return him the thanks of the whole Lodge, and to assure him that the Lodge of Kirknewton and Ratho will long retain his present with grateful remembrance."

*   *   *   *   *   *

The foregoing copy of letter and extract from minute have been supplied to me through the kind courtesy of Brother William Borthwick, R.W. Master of Lodge Kirknewton and Ratho, No. 85, and his friend Brother George Innes, a Past Master of that Lodge.

A Glimpse of Past Times.

THE CANONGATE KILWINNING ANNUAL ELECTION, 24th June 1863.

"The Master, Brother Henry, who was re-elected, is supported by a good staff of office-bearers, among whom may be noticed Dr Winchester, D.M., Ebsworth, S.M., Dr Veale, S.W., Schopp, J.W., STEWART WATSON, *Secretary*, and others. We are sorry, however, to learn that ROBERT STEWART, *the Tyler*,[*] has resigned that post, and although Jamie Baikie† succeeds him, we cannot say we take kindly to the change. Robert is one of the oldest Brethren of the Lodge, and has been Tyler for over thirty years. *He was present with the Canongate Kilwinning at Innerleithen when the Brethren went there to initiate the* ETTRICK SHEPHERD. We are sorry to lose Robert, for a more honest, upright and conscientious man and Mason does not breathe. We trust yet to see him coming among his Brethren of the Canongate Kilwinning, and we hope often to hear him sing one of those droll songs which seem only known to the veteran Tylers of the older Lodges."—Extract from *The Scottish Freemason's Magazine* of 1st July 1863.

REMINISCENCES CONCERNING HECTOR GAVIN AND HIS FRIEND ALEXANDER CUNNINGHAM.

Two links connecting recent times with the eventful year 1787.

A very loyal and useful member of Canongate Kilwinning for very many years was Brother Hector Gavin, engraver, Croft-an-righ. He is frequently mentioned throughout this work; especially I would note the reference in p. 40 of Part II., where he appears as one of the Lodge Committee in 1835, when JAMES HOGG was elected Poet Laureate in succession to ROBERT BURNS, also the reference in page 41 of Part II., where he appears as one of the brethren [among whom were Brother William Campbell, W.S., S.W. 1801 to 1803, and my friend the late Past Master Somerville] at the Lodge meeting of 12th November 1845, who supported the motion for having the picture of the INAUGURATION OF ROBERT BURNS as Poet Laureate painted by Stewart Watson. Brother Gavin claimed to be a very old member of Canongate Kilwinning, and he was acknowledged as such by brethren in 1840, whose recollections of Canongate Kilwinning

---

[*] Associated with William Petrie, Tyler, until 1845.
† James Baikie was Tyler of Lodge Canongate Kilwinning until 24th June 1877.

extended back as far as the year 1814,* although Past Master Somerville used to tell me (1872-3), that when Brother Gavin was an active member, and attended meetings regularly, he was often twitted about the date of his admission not being recorded—although such omission was not an unusual occurrence in the old minute books of Lodge Canongate Kilwinning. The earliest mention of him in the minute books is in 1835, when he with other old members were appointed members of committee. Brother Hector Gavin was a very aged man when I knew him, but he was brisk and conversational, and his faculties seemed unimpaired. He was born 5th October 1784, died 1st March 1874. Early in life Brother Gavin became acquainted with Alexander Cunningham—an affiliate of Canongate Kilwinning from Lodge St. Luke's, 6th October 1779—who was an intimate friend of Robert Burns. Brother Cunningham, originally bred to the legal profession, became a jeweller on the death of his brother; was a nephew of Dr William Robertson, the historian, and was related to the Glencairn family. Brother James Marshall speaks of him thus :—" The instructive and interesting letters to Cunningham by Burns, show that the latter set a high value upon his critical acumen. To him he sent his earliest *proof* of his *Tam o' Shanter*. To him he submitted his songs, down to the last. He admired Cunningham's voice and taste in singing."

The punch bowl of Inveraray marble which belonged to Burns was presented by his brother Gilbert to Alexander Cunningham (figure No. 20 in the picture of the Inauguration), for whom Mr Hector Gavin, then a young man, engraved on its silver rim plate the following stanza :—

> " O ye whom social pleasure charms,
> Whose hearts the tide o' kindness warms,
> Who hold your being on the terms—
>   ' Each aid the others,'
> Come to my bowl, come to my arms,
>   My friends, my BROTHERS."
> —*Burns.*

GRAND LODGE MINUTE *recording Visitation to* LODGE CANONGATE
KILWINNING, *7th December* 1786.

[Copied *verbatim* from Canongate Kilwinning Minute-book, and referred to in p. 13 Part II.]

This is a parallel instance of the "*style-book*" form of record in minute-

---

* Alexander Lambe Robertson, W.S., a very intimate friend of Dr Samuel Somerville, was one of those brethren. He instructed Dr Somerville as to Burns having been elected and inaugurated Poet Laureate. Alex. L. Robertson was initiated 6th January 1814, when Louis Cauvin, Charles More, Baillie Spankie, Lord Torphichen, Baron Norton, and many other brethren who had associated with Robert Burns in Canongate Kilwinning were alive and taking interest in the Lodge. Brother Alex. L. Robertson was elected Junior Warden, 1815 ; Substitute Master, 1816 and 1817 ; R. W. Master, 1819 to 1830 ; Chairman of Committee, 1838 ; R. W. Master again, 1860 to 1862. Such a brother as Alexander Lambe Robertson must have had a great influence in preserving through so long a period among the brethren a conscientious regard for, and a loyal and intelligent faith in, the history, memories, and traditions of the past in Lodge Canongate Kilwinning.

book of Lodge St. Andrew, No. 48, on 12th January 1787, which was quoted and facetiously commented on by Bro. James Marshall at the expense of "the fat pair" (*vide* Part I., pp. 50 and 69).

St John's Chapel *7th Dec^r* 1786.

"This evening the Lodge being constituted by the Right Worshipful Master Thereafter the Most Worshipful Francis Charteris Esqr junior of Amisfield Grand Master Mason of Scotland The Right Honourable Lord Torphichen Dep^t Grand Master The Right Worshipful Thomas Hay Esq. Substitute Grand Master Jas. Home & William McKillop Grand Wardens P T William Mason Esq Grand Secretary and Robert Meikle Grand Clerk preceded by the Lodge of Grand Stewards in their proper clothing were pleased to favour this Lodge with a visit when he was received with that respect suitable to the dignity of his high office and having taken the Chair performed while there the usual and ordinary requisites observed on similar occasions The Lodge was visited by Brethren from the following Lodges viz. Marys Chapel, Canongate & Leith Leith and Canongate, Journeymen Masons, St Lukes Ruglen Royal Arch and the Royal Arch Lodge Edin^r To all whom the proper compliments were paid and due returns made.

"Will Mason G. Secy.   Francis Charteris Junr G.M.

"Ro. Meikle G^d Clk.   Torphichen D.G.M.

Thomas Hay St G.M.

James Home S.G.W. p.t.

Wm MacKillop J.G.W. P.T."

The "Tearful Farewell."

"Adieu! a heart-warm, fond adieu!
Dear brothers of the mystic tie!
*   *   *
One round—I ask it with a tear—
To him, the Bard that's far awa'."

In the admirable little handbook (pp. 23 and 24), intended as a companion to Brother Stewart Watson's painting of the "Inauguration of Robert Burns," Brother James Marshall quotes the clever "versified note" sent by Burns to his friend, Mr John Mackenzie, surgeon, of Mauchline, and introduces a quotation with reference to it, thus:—

"Mr Chambers remarks that, when he was conducted to the lodge-room wherein all this took place, he 'could not view without strange feelings the little stifling cottage room in which a brotherhood, containing such men as Robert Burns and Dugald Stewart, had met to profess the maxims of a boundless philanthropy—the place where the poet of human nature had taken *that tearful farewell of his companions,*' of which, by the bye, '*the minute books contain no notice.*'"

"Burns, it is said [by Allan Cunningham], sung this song in the St James' Lodge of Tarbolton when his chest was on the way to Greenock ;—men are yet living (1834) who had the honour of hearing him :—the concluding verse affected the whole Lodge."

Other instances of omissions from minute books, more extraordinary than the above illustration, are set forth in pp. 48 to 59 of Part I., also in pp. 4 to 19 of Part II.

"LIVING LINKS" IN THE YEAR 1873 WITH PAST TIMES.
(*Vide* footnote, p. 65 of Part I.)

In the year 1873 a "few of the living links"—old Members of Canongate Kilwinning—connecting times past in the Lodge with times then present, because of having long associated "with those who had often borne testimony to their personal acquaintance with Burns,"—were the following :—

Brother Thomas Elder MacRitchie of Craigton and Dunork, W.S. ; E.P. and R. in Lodge
· Canongate Kilwinning, 5th March 1818.
Past Master Samuel Somerville of Ampherlaw, M.D.
Past Master Thomas Drybrough.
Past Master William Nathaniel Fraser of Tornaveen.
Brother George Cumming, W.S., whom I corresponded with for several years, deriving much information from him about old times in Canongate Kilwinning. Brother Cumming had been Junior Warden in 1835, when James Hogg was elected Poet Laureate in succession to Robert Burns.
Brother Henry G. Mapleson, Surgeon, E.P. and R., 7th February 1828. The last meeting of Canongate Kilwinning he attended was in the year 1875. He was born in Edinburgh, 1805, and died there 6th March 1876.
Brother Hector Gavin, Engraver, Croft-an-Righ,—a very old member of Canongate Kilwinning. He was born 5th October 1784, died 1st March 1874. *Vide* further notice of him in *Notanda*, p. 73.

The four brethren at head of this list were members of Committee in 1873, when I was Secretary.
All of the brethren above named learned the fact of Burns having been elected and inaugurated Poet Laureate from the brethren who had associated with him in the year 1787.

SUBSCRIPTION BY THE ROYAL CALEDONIAN HUNT TOWARDS THE SECOND EDITION OF THE POEMS OF ROBERT BURNS, PUBLISHED 1787, REFERRED TO IN FOREGOING PAGES :—

How Authorities Differ!

"Through my Lord's [Lord Glencairn's] influence it is inserted in the records of the Caledonian Hunt, that they universally, one and all, subscribed for the second edition."—*Letter from Robert Burns to Gavin Hamilton, Esq., Mauchline, dated Edinburgh, December 7, 1786.*

"By his [Lord Glencairn's] interest it is passed in the Caledonian Hunt, and entered in their books, that they are to take each a copy of the second edition, for which they are to pay one guinea."—*Letter from Robert Burns to John Ballantyne, Esq., banker, Ayr, dated Edinburgh, December* 13, 1786.

"The subscription was headed by half the noblemen of the North :—the Caledonian Hunt, thro' the interest of Glencairn, took six hundred copies."—*Allan Cunningham's Life of Robert Burns*, vol. I. p. xviii.

"The second edition at last appeared in 1787. It was prefaced by a dedication to the Caledonian Hunt, and followed by a list of subscribers, amounting to 1500 names, and accounting for 2800 copies."—*Gilfillan's Life of Burns*, Div. II. p. xxxviii.

"The price was five shillings. The Caledonian Hunt took one hundred copies at a guinea the copy."—*Ibid.* Div. II. p. xxxix.

What is said on the Subject in Minutes of the Royal Caledonian Hunt, copied from a scarce work, entitled "The Royal Caledonian Hunt," published 1871, *p.* 5.

"The minutes of 10th January 1787 contain the following entry :—' A Motion being made by the Earl of Glencairn, and seconded by Sir John Whitefoord, in favour of Mr. Burns, of Ayrshire, who had dedicated the New Edition of his Poems to the Caledonian Hunt : The meeting were of opinion that, in consideration of his Superior Merit, as well as of the Compliment paid to them, that Mr. Hagart should be directed to Subscribe for one hundred Copys in their name, for which he should pay to Mr Burns *Twenty-five pounds* upon the Publication of his Book.' "

———————

A Reminiscence of the Ettrick Shepherd, by Brother George Cumming, W.S., Junior Warden of Canongate Kilwinning, in 1835 *when* JAMES HOGG *was elected* POET-LAUREATE.

[Postscript from the late Brother Cumming's letter to Brother H. C. Peacock, of 19th February 1879.]

"The Initiation of the Shepherd was quite an event in Scotch masonry.

"He had been for a long time importuned about it, but would not listen to it. Some one had persuaded him that practical jokes of, sometimes, a dangerous kind, were practised on the novice. At length, on *one* condition, the Shepherd consented, viz. :—That the Initiation should be at Peebles, near his house at Mount Benger, so that if he did meet with any harm, he might be near his friends.

"He had still, however, his fears. The great day at length came. But so little did he feel assured that all was at least of a *non*-dangerous kind, that, just as he was being introduced into the Lodge, he said, in a most serious tone :—' Noo, for guidness' sake, mind that I'm a married man ! ! !'

"I need not add that a hilarious evening crowned the Poet's admission.

"G. C."

INTERESTING NOTES *relative to His Grace George Augustus Frederick John Murray, Sixth* DUKE OF ATHOLE, *K.T., etc., etc., and Most Worshipful Grand Master Mason of Scotland, who died on Saturday, the 16th January* 1864.

"*The last meeting of Grand Lodge presided over by His Grace* was the Quarterly Communication, held February 2nd of the past year, at which was presented to the Grand Lodge, on behalf of the late Chevalier JAMES BURNES, Br. Stewart Watson's celebrated picture of the 'INSTALLATION OF THE POET BURNS AS POET-LAUREATE OF THE LODGE CANONGATE KILWINNING.'"

> Extracted from "Masonic Sketch of the late Grand Master, by Br. D. Murray Lyon" in *Scottish Freemasons' Magazine* of 1st March 1864.

"*The last appearance he made in the masonic world*—and how little did we then expect, as he warmly shook the hand which now indites these lines, that death was so near—*was in* the Halls of THE CANONGATE KILWINNING, *where he presided*, the same urbane, kind-hearted, unaffected, and familiar gentleman and Brother, ready to listen to high and low, rich and poor, that has endeared him to us all."

> Extracted from Editorial in *Scottish Freemasons' Magazine* of 1st February 1864.

No one ever ventured at that time—thirty-one years ago—to call in question the truth of Robert Burns having been "appointed" and "inaugurated" Poet-Laureate of Lodge Canongate Kilwinning, as narrated in Brother D. Murray Lyon's ably-written History of Lodge No. 1, pp. 332, 333, and 334.

H. C. P.

HUGH C. PEACOCK
DIED
15TH JUNE 1894

It becomes a painful duty here to record the distressingly sudden death of Brother Hugh C. Peacock—an event which happened on the evening of Friday, 15th June 1894, while on his way to the Annual Statutory Committee Meeting of the Canongate Kilwinning Lodge. It was his intention to report the completion of the foregoing Notanda—indeed, the latter part relating to the death of the Duke of Athole was yet in manuscript. Our late Brother joined the Lodge twenty-two years ago, and down to the moment when his heart ceased to beat there was no one who laboured with greater earnestness for the Lodge, or who had its success more at heart; and it may be safely said that the time has not yet arrived when his services to the Lodge and the Craft can be appraised at their true value.

A. McK.

APPENDIX.

OFFICE-BEARERS AND MEMBERS OF COMMITTEE
OF

LODGE CANONGATE KILWINNING

1784 to 1867.

From 24th June 1784, when BROTHER ALEXANDER FERGUSSON of CRAIGDARROCH was elected R.W. Master, to

WITH SUPPLEMENT, SHOWING MEMBE

Compiled from the Minutes by Brother HUGH

DATE.	RIGHT WORSHIPFUL MASTER.	DEPUTE MASTER.	SUBSTITUTE MASTER.	SENIOR WARDEN.	JUNIOR WARDEN.	TREASURE
1784, June 24	Alex. Fergusson of Craigdarroch.	Charles More.	... ...	Alex. Law, Advocate.	W. Anderson, Writer.	George Spanki
1785, ,, 24	Do.	Do.	... ...	Do.	Do.	Do.
1786, ,, 24	Do.	Do.	... ...	William Dunbar, W.S.	J. Millar, Advocate.	Do.
1787, Mar. 1	... ...	... ...	... ...	... ...	... ...	
1787, June 25	Lord Torphichen.	William Dunbar, W.S.	... ...	J. Millar, Advocate.	Lindsay Carnegie.	George Spanki
1788, June 24	William Dunbar, W.S.	H. Jardine, W.S.	J. Millar, Advocate.	Andrew Forbes.	John Mercer.	Do.
1788, Dec. 12 †	... ...	... ...	... ...	... ...	William Lehré.	
1789, June 24	... ...	H. Jardine, W.S.	J. Millar, Advocate.	Dr James M. Adair.	Dr James Fox Young.	George Spanki
1789, Nov. 3	... ...	... ...	... ...	William Lehré.	Buchanan Hepburn.	
1790, June 24	Henry Jardine, W.S.	Dr Thomas Cochrane.	William Lehré.	Buchanan Hepburn.	Robert Moir.	George Spanki
1791, ,, 24	Do.	Do.	Do.	Do.	Do.	Do.
1791, Nov. 7	... ...	—— Adair.	... ...	... ...	... ...	
1792, June 25	Dr Thomas Cochrane.	Dr W. Farquharson.	Robert Moir.	Dr John Stannel.	Capt. Swindell.	George Spanki
1792, Dec. 27 ‡	Dr William Farquharson.	... ...	—— Adair.	Capt. Swindell.	Robert Wilson.	
1793, June 24	Do.	Robert Moir, W.S.	Capt. Swindell.	Dr Thomas Spens.	Jas. Asplin.	George Spanki
1794, ,, 24	Do.	Do.	Capt. Swindell.	Jas. Asplin.	Chas. Cuningham.	Do.
1795, ,, 24	Robert Moir, W.S.	Dr Thos. Spens.	*No Election.* ..	Chas. Cunningham.	James Dickson.	Do.
1796, ,, 24	Do.	Do	*Do,*	James Dickson.	Robert S. Moncrieff.	Do.
1797, ,, 24	Do.	Chas. Cunningham.	*Do.*	James Dickson.	Robert S. Moncrieff.	Do.
1798, ,, 25	Hugh Smith Mercer, W.S.	*Election postponed.*	*Do.*	Robert S. Moncrieff.	A. Jaffray, Advocate.	Do.
1799, ,, 24	Do.	Robert S. Moncrieff.	*Do.*	A. Jaffray, Advocate.	Geo. Buchanan.	Do.
1799, Nov. 30	... ...	... ...	*Do.*	... ...	... ...	
1800, June 24	Hugh Smith Mercer, W.S.	Robert S. Moncrieff.	*No Election.*	A. Jaffray, Advocate.	Geo. Buchanan.	George Spanki
1801, ,, 24	Alexander Jaffray, Advocate.	Wm. Ballantine, W.S.	John Russel.	Wm. Campbell, W.S.	Joseph Dixon, Writer.	Do.
1802, ,, 24	Do.	Do.	Do.	Do.	Do.	Do.
1803, ,, 24	Do.	Do.	Joseph Dixon, Writer.	James Lang, Writer.	William Douglas.	James Dickson
1804, ,, 24	Robert Moir, W.S. (*Second Time*)	Do.	James Lang, Writer.	W. Lang, Advocate.	J. Lawson, W.S.	Do.
1805, Feb. 7	... ...	... ...	... ...	Do.	... ...	
1805, June 24	... ...	... ...	*Do.*	Do.	Do.	Do.
1806, ,, 24	John Lawson, W.S.	James Lang, W.S.	William W. Brown.	Archibald M'Nab.	Andrew Stevens.	Do.
1807, ,, 24	Do.	Do.	Do.	Do.	Do.	Do.
1808, ,, 24	Do.	Do.	Do.	Do.	Do.	John Mill.
1809, ,, 24	Do.	James Harrower.	Do.	Do.	Do.	Do.
1810, ,, 24	Do.	Do.	Andrew Stevens.	Do.	James M'Donnell.	Do.
1811, ,, 24	Do.	Do.	Do.	Do.	Do.	Do.
1812, ,, 24	Do.	Do.	Do.	Do.	Do.	Do.
1813, ,, 24	A. Jaffray, (*Second Time*).	Do.	John Neilson.	James M'Donell.	George Simson.	Do.
1814, ,, 24	George Simson, Writer.	Do.	James Neilson, Writer.	Charles Stewart.	Archibald Kennedy.	*No Appointmen*
1815, ,, 24	George Burnet, Advocate.	Do.	James Neilson, Writer.	A. L. Robertson, W.S.	William Horn, Writer.	Paul Taylor.
1816, ,, 24	Do.	James Neilson, Writer.	A. L. Robertson, W.S.	William Horn, Writer.	Andrew Robinson.	Do.
1817, ,, 24	Do.	G. Douglas, Advocate.	Do.	Do.	J Hawkins, Advocate.	Archibald Hon
1818, ,, 24	Do.	Do.	William Horn.	J. Hawkins, Advocate.	William Tait.	Do.
1819, ,, 24	Alexander L. Robertson, W.S.	J. Aytoun, Inchdairney.	Do.	C. Lumsden, W.S.	S.F. Mackintosh, W.S.	Do.
1820, ,, 24	Do.	William Horn.	C. Lumsden, W.S.	S. F. Macintosh, W.S.	Donald F. M'Kenzie.	Do.
1821, ,, 25	Do.	C. Lumsden, W.S.	S. F. Macintosh, W.S.	K. Mackenzie, Writer.	Michie Gleig, Writer.	Do.
1822, ,, 24	Do.	Do.	Do.	Do.	Walter Dickson, W.S.	Archibald Mar:
1823, Mar. 6	... ...	... ...	... ...	... ...	Walter Dickson, W.S.	
1823, June 24	Alexander L. Robertson, W.S.	Do.	S. F. Macintosh, W.S.	Walter Dickson, W.S.	John Moffat.	Archibald Mar:
1824, ,, 24	Do.	Do.	Do.	Do.	G. Rutherford.	John Moffat, Sr
1825, ,, 24	Do.	Do.	Do.	Do.	Do.	
1826, Feb. 2	... ...	... ...	... ...	... ...	... ...	
1826, June 24	Alexander L. Robertson, W.S.	David Birrell, Writer.	J. Russell, Advocate.	Walter Dickson, W.S.	G. Rutherford.	David Brown,
1827, ,, 24	Do.	Do.	A. M'Neil, Advocate.	George W. Maxwell.	Robert Henry Liston.	John Brown, W
1827, Nov. 15	... ...	... ...	... ...	James Thomson.	... ...	
1828, June 24	Alexander L. Robertson, W.S.	David Birrell, Writer.	G. Rutherford.	Robert Henry Liston.	George Ritchie, Writer	John Brown, W
1829, ,, 24	Do.	Do.	Do.	George Ritchie, W.S.	A. Morrison.	Do.
1830, ,, 24 §	Alexander M'Neil, Advocate.	Do.	Robt. Kennedy, W.S.	Do.	Do.	Do.
1831, Feb. 11	Do.	Do.	Do.	Do.	Do.	Do.
1831, June 24	Do.	Andrew Dun, W.S.	George Ritchie, W.S.	William Maxwell Gunn	Robert Reid, Writer.	John Forbes, W

* 1785, June 24, Memo. from Minute Book.—"N.B.—There was no meeting on 24th June 1785, but the Offices were continued the same as last yea:
† 1788, December 12, Quotation from Minute of Committee.—"They elected Brother Lehré to be Junior Warden, in place of Brother Mercer, who h
‡ 1792, December 27.—R. W. Master Dr Thomas Cochrane having gone abroad, Brother Dr William Farquharson, Depute Master, was elected R.
§ 1830, June 24.—On a Petition and Complaint of Brother William Weir, Advocate, the Grand Lodge at Quarterly Communication of 1st November
    election has been now set aside."—They met accordingly, as above, on 11th February 1831, and simply re-elected their Offi
OFFICES CREATED during above period—Poet Laureate, 1787; Substitute Master, 1788; Organist, 1800; Chaplain, 1808; Senior and Junior Dea

;T LAUREATE.	CHAPLAIN.	ORGANIST.	MASTER OF CEREMONIES.	CONVENER OR CHAIRMAN OF COMMITTEE.	TYLERS.
... ...	... ...	... ...	... ...	... ...	A. Forbes & Mᶜ Leod.
... ...	... ...	... ...	... ...	... ...	Do.
... ...	... ...	... ...	... ...	... ...	Do.
ⅅBERT BURNS.	... ...	... ...	... ...	... ...	... ...
... ...	... ...	... ...	... ...	... ...	A. Forbes & Mᶜ Leod.
... ...	... ...	... ...	... ...	... ...	Do.
... ...	... ...	... ...	... ...	... ...	... ...
... ...	... ...	... ...	... ...	... ...	—— Mᶜ Leod.
... ...	... ...	... ...	... ...	... ...	A. Forbes & Mᶜ Leod.
... ...	... ...	... ...	... ...	... ...	Do.
... ...	... ...	... ...	... ...	... ...	... ...
... ...	... ...	... ...	... ...	... ...	A. Forbes & Mᶜ Leod.
... ...	... ...	... ...	... ...	... ...	... ...
... ...	... ...	... ...	... ...	... ...	—— Mackay.
... ...	... ...	... ...	... ...	... ...	Do.
... ...	... ...	... ...	... ...	... ...	Alex. Forbes.
... ...	... ...	... ...	... ...	... ...	Do.
... ...	... ...	... ...	... ...	... ...	Do.
... ...	... ...	... ...	... ...	... ...	Do.
... ...	... ...	... ...	... ...	... ...	Do.
... ...	... ...	Robert Purdie.	... ...	... ...	Alex. Forbes.
... ...	... ...	... ...	... ...	... ...	G. Milne & A. Strachan.
... ...	... ...	... ...	... ...	... ...	Do.
... ...	... ...	... ...	... ...	... ...	Alex. Strachan
... ...	... ...	... ...	... ...	... ...	Do.
... ...	... ...	... ...	... ...	... ...	... ...
... ...	... ...	... ...	... ...	... ...	Alex. Strachan
... ...	... ...	... ...	... ...	... ...	George Scrymgeour.
... ...	Francis M'Nab.	... ...	... ...	... ...	John Scrymgeour.
... ...	No Election.	... ...	... ...	... ...	Do.
... ...	... ...	... ...	... ...	... ...	Do.
... ...	... ...	... ...	... ...	... ...	Do.
... ...	... ...	... ...	... ...	... ...	Do.
... ...	... ...	... ...	... ...	... ...	Do.
... ...	... ...	... ...	... ...	... ...	Do.
... ...	... ...	... ...	... ...	... ...	Do.
... ...	... ...	... ...	... ...	... ...	Do.
... ...	... ...	... ...	... ...	... ...	Murray Michieson.
... ...	... ...	... ...	... ...	... ...	Do.
... ...	... ...	... ...	... ...	... ...	Charles Reed.
... ...	... ...	... ...	... ...	... ...	... ...
... ...	... ...	... ...	... ...	... ...	... ...
... ...	... ...	... ...	... ...	... ...	John Macleod.
... ...	... ...	... ...	... ...	... ...	Do.
... ...	William M. Gunn.	... ...	... ...	... ...	... ...
... ...	Rev. D. Ritchie, A.M.	... ...	... ...	... ...	John Macleod.
... ...	Do.	... ...	... ...	... ...	George Halkett.
... ...	... ...	... ...	... ...	... ...	... ...
... ...	Rev. D. Ritchie, A.M.	... ...	... ...	... ...	George Halkett.
... ...	Do.	... ...	... ...	... ...	Do.
... ...	Do.	... ...	... ...	... ...	Do.
... ...	Do.	... ...	... ...	... ...	Do.
... ...	Rev. Thomas Brown.	... ...	... ...	... ...	Do.

W.S., who had the honour of Knighthood conferred on him by George IV., in the year 1825).

t Moir to be Secretary, in place of Brother Lehré.

:-Bearers, with the exception of the R. W. Master, and required the Lodge—" to meet and elect Office-Bearers, in room of those whose

r in London, 1819.

Date	Right Worshipful Master	Depute Master	Substitute Master	Senior Warden	Junior Warden	Treasurer
1832, June 25	Alexander M'Neil, Advocate.	Andrew Dun, W.S.	Wm. Maxwell Gunn.	Robert Reid, Writer.	John Abercromby.	George Scott, W.
1833, ,, 24	Do.	Chas. M'Dougal.	Robert Robertson.	Ladovic Colquhoun.	John Leslie.	Peter Anderson, V
1834, Jan. 18	... ...	... ...	... ...	...	...	...
1834, Mar. 13	... ...	... ...	W. B. D. D. Turnbull.	...	...	...
1834, June 24	Alexander M'Neil, Advocate.	Chas. M'Dougal.	Do.	John Leslie.	John Abercromby.	Francis G. Santer
1835, ,, 24	Do.	Do.	Do.	Robt. Blackwood.	Geo. Cumming, W.S.	Anthony Traill.
1836, Jan. 27	... ...	... ...	... ...	...	...	...
1836, June 24	Alexander M'Neil, Advocate.	Chas. M'Dougal.	James Jardine.	Robt. Blackwood.	Geo. Cumming, W.S.	Anthony Traill.
1836, Nov. 9	... ...	... ...	... ...	...	Chas. E. Allen.	...
1837, June 24	Alexander M'Neil, Advocate.	John Wilson.	James Jardine.	Wm. Jeffries Dowlin.	Henry Hagart.	And. Dunlop, W.
1838, ,, 23	†Henry Jardine, Advocate.	James Jardine, W.S.	Wm. Ed. Aytoun.	Henry Hagart.	James Blair.	Veitch Sinclair.
1839, ,, 24	William Edmonstoune Aytoun.	Do.	Archd. Smith.	J. Blair of Glenfoot.	Alex. Cumine.	Do.
1840, Feb. 12	... ...	... ...	... ...	...	...	...
1840, June 24	William Edmonstoune Aytoun.	Archibald Smith.	J. Blair of Glenfoot.	W. Jeffries Pattison.	Henry Day Cockburn.	Veitch Sinclair.
1841, Mar. 3	... ...	... ...	... ...	...	Arch. D. Campbell.	...
1841, June 24	James Blair of Glenfoot.	Geo. Cumming, W.S	And. Dunlop, W.S.	Arch D. Campbell.	Sam. Somerville, M.D.	Veitch Sinclair.
1842, ,, 24	Archibald Smith, Advocate.	A. D. Campbell.	Sam.Somerville, M.D.	W. Henry Maclean.	H. F. Maclean, W.S.	John Wilson, M.I
1843, Jan. 27	... ...	... ...	... ...	H. F. Maclean, W.S.	Jonathan Bruce.	...
1843, June 24	Sam. Somerville of Ampherlaw.	Archd. D. Campbell.	W. Jeffries Pattison.	Alx. J. Stewart, W.S.	Do.	Wm. Mowbray.
1844, ,, 24	Do.	Do.	William Mowbray.	Do.	James Neilson.	Donald Cameron.
1845, Apr. 15	... ...	... ...	... ...	...	...	Donald Cameron.
1845, June 24	Archibald David Campbell.	William Mowbray.	James Hunter.	James Neilson, S.S.C.	Jas. Arthur Campbell.	Chas. Robertson.
1846, ,, 24	Do.	Do.	James Neilson.	W. J. Henderson.	James Savege.	Do.
1847, ,, 24	Do.	Do.	James Savege.	Chas. Robertson.	George Moncrieff.	Archd. C. Mowb.
1848, ,, 24	Do.	James Savege.	Alex. Penrose Miller.	Stewart Watson.	J. D. B. Hay, Bart.	Do.
1849, ,, 25	Do.	*No Appointment.*	...	...	...	Do.
1849, Dec. 12	... ...	Capt. James Hunter.	... ...	...	...	...
1850, June 24	Archibald Cuthill Mowbray.	Do.	Stewart Watson.	J. D. B. Hay, Bart.	Wm. Fergusson, W.S.	William Watson.
1851, ,, 24	Do.	Do.	J. D. B. Hay, Bart.	Robt. C. Mackenzie.	T. E. O. Horne, W.S.	Stewart Watson.
1852, ,, 24	Do.	Alex. James Stewart.	Sir J. D. Wauchope.	T. E. O. Horne, W.S.	John Ogilvy.	Do.
1853, ,, 24	Wm. Nathaniel Fraser, S.S.C.	Do.	Alx. J. Stewart, W.S.	Wm. Wilkinson.	Wm. Duncan M'Neil.	Stewart Watson.
1853, Aug. 1	... ...	¶ Lord Loughborough.	... ...	...	...	...
1854, June 24	Wm. Nathaniel Fraser, S.S.C.	Do.	Alx. J. Stewart, W.S.	Wm. Duncan M'Neil.	Patrick B. Simpson.	Stewart Watson.
1855, ,, 25	Do.	Alex. Jas. Stewart.	Wm. D. M'Neil.	Patrick B. Simpson.	D. Crawford, S.S.C.	Do.
1856, Jan. 9	... ...	... ...	... ...	H. M. W. M'Vitie.	...	...
1856, June 24	Thomas Drybrough.	D. Crawford, S.S.C.	Andrew Watson of	Do.	D. Woodburn Bowie.	William Hickma.
1857, ,, 24	Do.	H. M. W. M'Vitie.	Torsonce.	Do.	Do.	Do.
1858, ,, 24	Do.	Captain Griffiths.	Dr Hall.	Michael Dowd.	J. Ziervogel.	Do.
1859, ,, 24	Do.	Wm. Hickman.	Robert Stewart, W.S.	Chas. W. M. Muller.	Wm. G. Henry.	J. C. M'Culloch.
1860, ,, 24	Alex. Lambe Robertson, W.S.	Robert Stewart, W.S.	Ch. W. M. Muller.	Wm. G. Henry.	G. H. Ebsworth.	Do.
1861, ,, 24	Do.	Dr Jas. Winchester.	Do.	Thos. Alex. Hill.	H. F. Maclean, W.S.	T. Drybrough, J
1862, ,, 24	William G. Henry, Merchant.	Do.	T. Alex. Hill.	Geo. H. Ebsworth.	Dr Henry R. Beale.	Do.
1863, ,, 24	Do.	Do.	Geo. H. Ebsworth.	Dr Henry R. Beale	Johann Schopp.	Do.
1864, ,, 24	Earl of Strathmore.	Do.	Geo. H. Ebsworth.	Johann Schopp.	H. H. Brown.	Do.
1865, ,, 24	Wm. N. Fraser of Tornaveen.	Geo. H. Ebsworth.	Johann Schopp.	Wm. Moffat Gorrie.	Geo. Melville.	Do.
1866, ,, 24	Do.	Do.	Do.	Do.	Do.	Do.
1867, ,, 24	Conclusion of Brother W. N. Fraser's second term of office as Right Worshipful Master.	... ...	... ...	...	...	...

* 1835, June 24.—William Petrie and Robert Stewart elected Tylers.
† 1838, June 23.—This Annual Meeting was held on June 23rd 1838, as the 24th was a Sunday. During the proceedings, Brother Henry Jardine, R.
‡ 1840, June 24.—Brother Hector Gavin's name appears in the minutes for the first time, on 24th June 1835, at Committee Meeting, as being nominate
§ 1844, June 24.—Robert Stewart and William Petrie elected respectively First and Second Tylers.—Last time Bro. William Petrie elected.   He died :
§ 1845, April 15.—Brother Donald Cameron was appointed interim Secretary and Treasurer, as Brother A. C. Rankine was leaving Edinburgh.
¶ 1853, June 24.—Lord Loughborough—better known by his subsequent title, the Earl of Rosslyn, many years M. W. Grand Master Mason of Scotla
OFFICES CREATED during above period :—Convener or Chairman of Committee, 1835 ; Architect and Superintendent of Works, 1836 ; Master of Cerem
  that Office for several years ; no successor to him was appointed within the period ending June 24, 1867 ; therefore, it has been deemed
NOTE.—Senior and Junior Deacons—who were " created " so recently as 1816—also Banner-Bearers and Stewards, have been excepted from this Cha

Secretary.	Poet Laureate.	Chaplain.	Organist.	Master of Ceremonies.	Convener or Chairman of Committee.	Tylers.
Jas. M'Millan.	... ...	Rev. Thos. Brown.	... ...	... ...	... ...	George Halkett.
Anthony Traill, W.S.	... ...	... ...	... ...	... ...	... ...	Do.
... ...	... ...	... ...	... ...	... ...	... ...	Robert Stewart.
... ...	... ...	... ...	... ...	... ...	... ...	... ...
Alex. Mackie, Writer.	... ...	... ...	... ...	... ...	... ...	Robert Stewart.
James Deans.	James Hogg.	Rev. H. Holme.	John Surenne.	... ...	J. Wilson, Advocate.	*W. Petrie & R. Stewart
... ...	William Hay.	... ...	... ...	... ...	... ...	... ...
James Deans.	Do.	... ...	John Surenne.	And. Dunlop, W.S.	J. Wilson, Advocate.	W. Petrie & R. Stewart
... ...	... ...	... ...	... ...	M. M. de Bartolimi.	... ...	... ...
James Deans.	William Hay.	... ...	John Surenne.	Wm. Ed. Aytoun.	John Leslie.	W. Petrie & R. Stewart
Do.	Do.	... ...	Do.	P. C. Gibson.	Alex. L. Robertson.	Do.
Do.	Do.	... ...	Do.	Do.	Alex. M'Neill.	Do.
Thos. Lewis Gibson.	... ...	... ...	... ...	... ...	... ...	... ...
N. P. C. Lloyd.	William Hay.	Rev. Dr D. Ritchie.	S. W. Strathie.	P. C. Gibson.	‡Hector Gavin.	W. Petrie & R. Stewart
... ...	... ...	... ...	... ...	... ...	... ...	Do.
John Davidson, M.D.	William Hay.	Robt. T. Jeffrey.	... ...	Dr L. H. Thatcher.	Hector Gavin.	W. Petrie & R. Stewart
Do.	Edward W. Lane.	... ...	... ...	George V. Irving.	Do.	R. Stewart & W. Petrie
... ...	... ...	... ...	... ...	... ...	... ...	Do.
Wm. Mowbray.	Edward W. Lane.	Wm. V. T. Drury.	... ...	Col. Kinloch of Kilrie.	Hector Gavin.	... ...
Alex. C. Rankin.	... ...	... ...	... ...	... ...	W. E. Aytoun.	§R. Stewart & W. Petrie
Donald Cameron.	... ...	... ...	... ...	... ...	... ...	Do.
Chas. Robertson.	No Election.	No Election.	... ...	W. J. Pattison.	W. E. Aytoun.	Robert Stewart.
Do.	Francis Nicoll.	... ...	... ...	Wm. Lindesay.	Do.	Do.
Archd. C. Mowbray.	Do.	George Bell.	... ...	W. J. Pattison.	Do.	Do.
Do.	Do.	James Neilson.	... ...	Wm. J. Pattison.	Do.	Do.
Do.	Do.	Do.	... ...	Do.	Do.	... ...
... ...	... ...	... ...	... ...	Do.	Do.	... ...
Robt. C. Mackenzie.	James Marshall.	Rev. Andrew Bonar.	... ...	Do.	Do.	Robert Stewart.
Stewart Watson.	N. J. Mansabuis.	Do.	... ...	Do.	Do.	Do.
Do.	No. Election.	R. W. Bonar.	... ...	Do.	Do.	Do.
Stewart Watson.	Wm. Pringle.	R. W. Bonar.	... ...	Do.	Hector Gavin.	Do.
... ...	... ...	... ...	... ...	... ...	... ...	... ...
Stewart Watson.	Wm. Pringle.	... ...	... ...	No Appointment.	Hector Gavin.	Robert Stewart.
Do.	No Election.	Rev. W. Arnot, D.D.	... ...	Wm. J. Pattison.	Alex. Jas. Stewart.	Do.
... ...	... ...	... ...	... ...	... ...	... ...	... ...
Stewart Watson.	... ...	No Election.	... ...	No Appointment.	Dr S. Somerville.	Robert Stewart.
Do.	... ...	... ...	... ...	... ...	Do.	Do.
Do.	Wm. Pringle.	Rev. —— Horne.	... ...	R. H. Wyndham.	Dr S. Somerville.	Do.
Do.	Anthy. O'Neale Hay.	Rev. A. R. Bonar.	... ...	Do.	Thos. Dryborough.	Do.
Do.	Do.	Do.	... ...	Do.	Do.	Do.
Do.	Do.	Do.	... ...	Do.	Do.	Do.
Do.	Do.	Do.	... ...	Do.	Thos. E. M'Ritchie.	Do.
Do.	Do.	Do.	... ...	Do.	Do.	Do.
Do.	Do.	Do.	... ...	Do.	W. N. Fraser.	James Balkie.
Do.	Do.	Do.	... ...	Do.	Do.	Do.
... ...	... ...	... ...	... ...	... ...	... ...	... ...

elect, was announced as being "the son and grandson of two brethren who had filled that chair."
election on Committee, and he was elected accordingly on following St. John's Day. He was elected Chairman of Committee on 24th June, 1840.
nber 21, 1845.

had been nominated Depute-Master for election this date, but his election postponed waiting acceptance of office. Elected Aug. 1, 1853. Re-elected June 24, 1854.
. 1836. The Office of Architect and Superintendent of Works was " created" with scant ceremony, January 27, 1836, in favour of Brother David Rhind, and he held
cessary to occupy a column throughout the Chart with that information.
cause of want of space, and because Brethren who have held any of those Offices have been usually promoted to other Offices herein recorded.

SUPPLEMENT TO CHART

MEMBERS OF COMMITTEE

OF THE

LODGE CANONGATE KILWINNING,

1784 TO 1867,

Elected Annually on St. John's Day, Midsummer.

~~~~~~~~~~~~

" Present Office-Bearers and immediate Past Office-Bearers, along with—"

1784—Bro. Sir Wm. Forbes of Pitsligo and Bro. David Stewart, Banker.

1785—*Offices were continued the same as last year.* (Note by Bro. Henry Jardine, Secy.)

1786—*No mention of Committee in the Minute of this date. For other omissions during 1786-7-8 (vide Review of Minutes, pages 4 to 11 ante).*

1787—Bro. Dr Nathaniel Spens, and Bro. Thomas Hay, Surgeon.
The Minute of this date has no signature attached to it, another instance of negligence as above, during the Burns' period, (vide pages 4 to 11, ante).

1788—Bro. Thos. Hay, Bro. Alex. Fergusson of Craigdarroch, and Bro. Charles More.

1789— Do., do., do.
1790— Do., do., do.
1791— Do., do., do.

1792—*No names added to list of Office-bearers.*

1793—Bro. Thos. Hay, Bro. Alex. Fergusson of Craigdarroch, Bro. Charles More, and Bro. Wm. Dunbar, W.S.

1794—Bro. Thos. Hay, Bro. Alex. Fergusson of Craigdarroch, Bro. Chas. More, Bro. Wm. Dunbar, and Bro. Henry Jardine, Advocate.

1795— Do., do., do.

1796—Bro. Thos. Hay, Bro. Chas. More, Bro. Wm. Dunbar, and Bro. Henry Jardine.

1797— Do., do., do.

1798—Bro. Thos. Hay, Bro. Chas. More, and Bro Wm. Dunbar.

1799— Do., do., do.
1800— Do., do., do.
1801— Do., do., do.

1802—Bro. Chas. More, Bro. Robert Moir, Bro. Robert Scott Moncrieff of Wellwood and Pitliver, and Bro. Hugh Smyth Mercer.

1803—Bro. Charles More and Bro. Robert Scott Moncrieff.

1804— Do., do., do.
1805—Bro. Charles More.
1806— Do.
1807— Do.
1808— Do.
1809— Do.
1810— Do.

1811—*Committee "as formerly."*
1812— Do.
1813— Do.

1814—Bro. James Davidson, Bro. Wm. Ballantyne, Bro. Charles More, Bro. John Lawson, Bro. David Birrell, and Bro. Andrew Robinson.

1815—Bro. Alexander Jaffray, Bro. John Lawson, Bro. Wm. Ballantyne, Bro. Chas. More, Bro. Charles Nairne, and Bro. Andrew Robinson.

1816—Bro. Alex. Jaffray, P.M., Bro. John S. Lawson, Bro. Wm. Ballantyne, Bro. Chas. More, Bro. Chas. Nairne, Bro. Dr J. Lamb, and Bro. Wm. Tait.

1817—Bro. Alex. Jaffray, Bro. John Lawson, Bro. Chas. Nairne, Bro. Wm. Ballantyne, Bro. Chas. More, Bro. James M'Douell, Bro. James Harrower, and Bro. Nelson Hill. (*Charles More died before next Annual Meeting.*)

1818—Bro. Alex. Jaffray, Bro. James Harrower, Bro. George Douglas, Advocate, Bro. Nelson Hill, Bro. —— Scott, and Bro. Capt. Jas. M'Douell.

1819—Bro. Simson, Bro. Harrower, Bro. Jaffray, Bro. Neilson, Bro. Ewart, and Bro. Law. Bro. David Plenderleath, London, appointed Corresponding Member.

1820—Bro. J. Aytoun of Inchdairnie. Bro. Wm. M'Kenzie of Greenyard, Mark Sprot of Garnkirk, Advocate, Kenneth M'Kenzie yr. of Hilton. Bro. David Plenderleath, London, re-elected Corresponding Member.

1821—Bro. John Anderson, W.S., and Bro. Henry Gordon, Writer.

1822— Do., do., do.

1823—Bro. David Plenderleath and Bro. John Wightman.

1824—Bro. Alex. M'Neill, Advocate, and Bro. George Walter Maxwell of Carruchan.

1825—Do., with Bro. John Russell, Advocate.

1826—Do., with Bro. Ralph Kelloch, Writer.

1827—Do., with Bro. Wm. Pringle, junr, etc.

1828—Do., with Bro. J. M'Millan.

1829— Do., do., do.

1830—Do., with Bro. John E. Elliot, and Bro. John Forbes.

1831—Do., Bro. John Richardson and Bro. Anth. Traill.

1832—Do., Bro. John Leslie, Bro. Arch. Marshall, and Bro. John Forbes

1833—Do., with Bro. Wm. Maxwell Gunn, etc.

1834—Do., with Bro. T. Knox Beveridge, etc.

"In addition to the eight Chief Office-Bearers,—"

835 —Bro. Prof. J. Wilson,* Convener, Bro. Geo. Ritchie, Bro. J. Leslie, Bro. J. Forbes, and Bro. H. Gavin, etc.

1836—Bro. Prof. J. Wilson, Bro. Hector Gavin, Bro. John Forbes, and Bro. Henry Glassford Bell.

1837—Bro. John Leslie, Convener, Bro. Anth. Traill, Bro. Robt. Blackwood, Bro. Geo. Cumming, W.S., Bro. Hector Gavin, and Bro. John Forbes.

1838—Bro. Alex. L. Robertson, W.S., Convener, Bro. Hector Gavin, Bro. A. Traill, Bro. J. Forbes, and Bro. John Wilson.

1839—Do., with Bro. A. M'Neill, Advocate, Convener, and Bro. Arch. Marshall.

1840—Do., with Bro. H. Gavin, Chairman, Bro. A. Marshall, and Bro. Geo. Cumming, W.S.

1841—Bro. H. Gavin, Chairman, and Bro. W. J. Pattison.

1842—Do., with Bro. H. Gavin, Chairman, Bro. Wm. E. Aytoun,† and Bro. J. Leslie.

1843—Do., with Bro. H. Gavin, Chairman, Bro. A. M'Neill, Bro. Wm. E. Aytoun, and Bro. W. B. D. D. Turnbull.

1844—Do., with Bro. Wm. E. Aytoun, Chairman, Bro. A. M'Neill, Bro. W. J. Pattison, and Bro. H. F. M'Lean.

1845—Do., with Bro. Wm. E. Aytoun, Chairman, Bro. A. M'Neill, Bro. Dr Samuel Somerville, Bro. W. J. Pattison, Bro. Edward Fraser, and Bro. R. Blackwell.

1846— Do., do., do.

1847—Do., and Bro. W. B. D. D. Turnbull.

1848—Do., with Bro. Neilson, and Bro. Chas. Robertson.

1849— Do., do., do.

1850— Do., do., do.

1851—Do., with Bro. W. Mowbray.

1852—Do., with Bro. And. Aitken.

1853—Do., with Bro. A. M'Neill, Chairman, Bro. Prof. Aytoun, Bro. Dr S. Somerville, Bro. H. Gavin, Bro. Wm. J. Pattison, Bro. Wm. Hickman, and Bro. A. B. Fleming.

1854—Re-elected—blank page, no election recorded.

1855—Do., with Bro. Prof. Aytoun, Bro. Dr Sam. Somerville, Bro. Anth. Traill, and Bro. Thos. Drybrough.

1856—Do., with Bro. Dr S. Somerville, Chairman.

1857—"As p. List of 15 June, but not recorded."

1858—Do., with Bro. Josiah Livingstone, Bro. Thos. Elder M'Ritchie, and Bro. J. R. Stewart.

1859—Do., with Bro. A. K. Morrison and Bro. J. Pender.

1860— Do., do., do.

1861— Do., do., do.

1862—Do., with Bro. Alex. L. Robertson.

1863—Do., with Bro. Wm. Henry, and Bro. A. O. Hay.

1864— Do., do., do.

1865— Do., do., do.

1866—Do., no additional names.

1867—Conclusion of Bro. W. N. Fraser's second term of office as Right Worshipful Master.

* Christopher North. † Professor of Literature and Belles Lettres.

ERRATA.

Part I., p. 8, line 29, *for* " 14th," *read* " 13th."

   ,,   ,, line 35, *for* " a," *read* " this ancient and."

Part II., p. 3, line 19, *for* " 24th June 1835," *read* " 24th January 1835."

   ,, p. 6, third marginal note, *for* " 1786, December 7," *read*, " 1786, December, 27."

   ,, p. 11, line 3, *for* " extremly," *read* " extremely."

   ,, p. 29, final paragraph :—" Other matter " appears in Part. I., pp. 14 to 19.

   ,, p. 38, marginal note, Tenth Reference, *for* " E not recorded on Committee 1824," *read* " E not recorded, but on Committee 1824."

   ,, p. 41, second marginal note delete.

   ,, p. 48, third par, second line, *for* " house," *read* " home."